MAMMOTH WITHDRAWN

MAMMOTH

JILL BAGUCHINSKY

TURNER PUBLISHING COMPANY

Mammoth
Copyright © 2018 Jill Baguchinsky

Cover Design: Jo Walker
Book Design: Meg Reid
Illustrations:Paige Hall

Library of Congress Cataloging-in-Publication Data
Names: Baguchinsky, Jill, author.
Title: Mammoth / by Jill Baguchinsky.
Description: Nashville, Tennessee : Turner Publishing Company, 2018. |
  Summary: Paleontology geek and plus-size fashion blogger, Natalie Page
  lands an internship working with a celebrated paleontologist, but she
  realizes that in order to stand out in a field dominated by men, she must
  first learn to stand up for herself.
Identifiers: LCCN 2018014597| ISBN 9781684421947 (pbk.)
ISBN 9781684421954 (hardcover)
Subjects: | CYAC: Overweight persons--Fiction. | Self-confidence--Fiction.
Paleontology--Fiction. | Internship programs--Fiction.
Classification: LCC PZ7.B14215 Mam 2018 | DDC [Fic]--dc23
LC record available at https://lccn.loc.gov/2018014597

9781684421947   Paperback
9781684421954   Hardcover
9781684421961   eBook

Printed in the United States of America
17 18 19 20 10 9 8 7 6 5 4 3 2 1

Turner Publishing Company
Nashville, Tennessee
New York, New York
www.turnerpublishing.com

For Dava Butler,
who taught me to dig and let me meet mammoths.
Thanks for the pork chop.

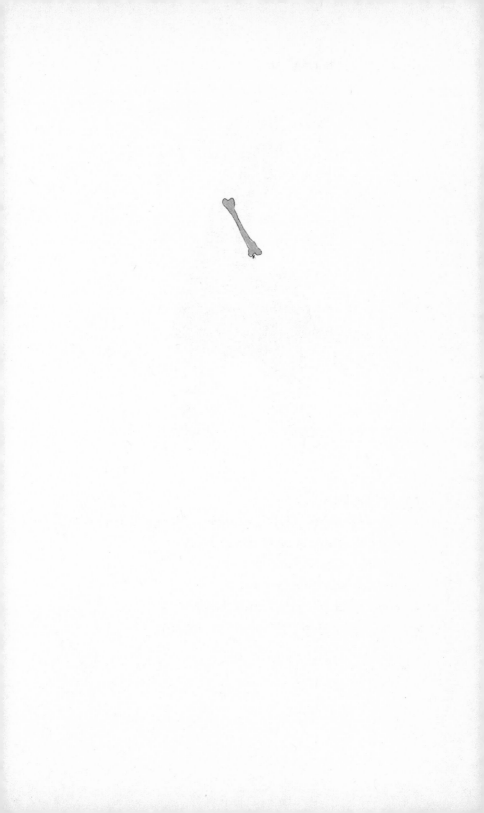

Look of the Day:

- *Navy with bone print shirtwaist dress (designed and made by me!)*
- *Red patent leather belt (Savage Swallow)*
- *Red patent heels (vintage, Escada)*
- *Red headscarf (made by me!)*
- *White cropped cardi (Savage Swallow)*
- *Pinup matte lipstick (Maxwell Cosmetics)*

This is it, my vintage velociraptors. It's not even three in the morning and I'm about to leave for Orlando International Airport. I'll land in Austin around ten fifteen, and I'll be at the Central Texas Mammoth Site by lunchtime.

Am I excited? Oh, I dunno…YEAH, JUST A LITTLE. Get ready to hear alllllll about this internship—you know I'm gonna keep you posted. Live updates from the bone bed!

And yeah, yeah—I owe you a review of the latest Carved in Bone podcast. I'll give it a listen on the plane and get that posted ASAP. (By the way, did you see that new pic of Dr. Carver on his blog? The one from the Argentina dig, where he's holding up that raptor claw? OH MAN.)

I'm going to get my LotD pic posted, and then I'll be on my way. Wish me luck!

It's way too early for a look-of-the-day photo, but my followers will revolt if I don't post one—and my blog just hit sixty thousand subscribers last month, so that's a lot of potential revolting. Phone in hand, I stand in front of my full-length mirror.

I know just how to pose, angling my body to make the most of the size twenty, hourglass figure I've achieved through industrial-strength shapewear under my dress. I jut my neck forward to avoid a double chin, flip my dark hair, put my hand on my hip, and hold my phone in front of my face, which is the most flattering angle I've found for full-body shots. LotD pics are all about showcasing the clothes.

The girl posing boldly on the screen doesn't look anything like what's going on in my head. Even with much of her face obscured, she's a perfect example of what I think of as "being awesome"—confident, easygoing, flawless in her fashionable armor. She's what my followers expect.

While the photo uploads to my blog and mirrors itself on my Instagram and Twitter accounts, my fingers find the black hair band looped around my wrist. They pull back and let go, snapping the elastic against my skin. It's something I do sometimes. I usually don't even notice until the sting sets in.

My silver mammoth necklace hangs on a peg next to my bedroom mirror. Maybe I'll wear it... But no, it's better to keep my look simple today, considering all the traveling I'm about to do.

Then I lug my suitcase downstairs.

I pass my brothers' doors on the way. There's no chance Ryan or Dylan will wake up this early just to say goodbye to their sister, even though I'll be gone for an entire month.

In the front hall, Dad takes the suitcase and goes out front to load the minivan.

Mom's in the kitchen, rubbing her eyes and slurping coffee. "Want some?"

"*Yes.*" I pour myself a mug and knock it back. It's too early to think about complications like milk and sugar, but I regret the black coffee when it hits my uncertain stomach with an acidic splash.

"Did you get some sleep?"

"Eh. A little." I breathe deeply, willing my stomach to settle.

"Excited?"

"Exhausted. And terrified."

She squeezes my hand. "This is going to be an amazing experience, Natalie. We're so proud of you for getting that scholarship."

Dad thunders in. "Almost ready?" His voice is crisp with impatience.

"It's a little early." Mom pours herself more coffee.

"Takes an hour to get to the airport, and Natalie should be there two hours early. We're already running late."

"We'll leave at three thirty. It'll be fine. It doesn't take an hour."

"It does if there's traffic," Dad says.

"Traffic? At three thirty in the morning?"

I snap my hair elastic and think about breakfast, but I doubt my system can handle food, especially when I'm about to get in a car driven by Dad. When he's on edge, his driving is all sharp stops and fast-and-furious turns Vin Diesel would envy.

He mutters something and crashes outside with my backpack.

Mom sighs and empties the rest of the coffee down the sink. "Might as well get going," she says. "You know how your father can be." She takes a couple of protein bars, the ones she eats nonstop when she tries to diet, out of the bread drawer. "Take these in case you get hungry."

"Mom, I'm fine."

But she holds them out. "Just put them in your purse."

"Mom—"

"I don't want to worry about you being hungry. You know I worry."

"I know." She worries and she eats and she feeds; food is her answer to everything. And I'm my mother's daughter.

I put the bars in my red handbag.

"Nat?" Dad calls from the front door.

"I'm almost ready!" I yell before he can get wound up again.

"You have a visitor."

When I step into the hall, I'm tackle-hugged by a cyclone of cherry-print fabric and Sailor Jerry–style tattoos with a waxy red smile.

"Aunt Judy?" I gasp as she squeezes like a python.

"My favorite niece!" She pulls back. "Is this the dress? The one you've been telling me about?"

I step away and spin in a circle, showing off its '50s-inspired shape—perfectly fitted and belted at the waist with a full skirt flaring beneath. Its navy broadcloth has a tiny, white bone print, which is ridiculously appropriate for how I'll be spending the next month. "Finished it last night! What do you think?"

"I think you're a genius, that's what I think."

"I couldn't have done it if you hadn't taught me so much."

"I'm going to miss you this summer," she says.

For the past three summers, I've worked at Aunt Judy's indie clothing company, Savage Swallow. She taught me about sewing and tailoring, and she introduced me to the beauty of well-sourced vintage and the secret magic of proper foundation garments. She rescued me from the pleated jeans and oversized T-shirts I wore in middle school when all the kids called me "Fat Nat" and found endless opportunities to torment me. *Fossilista* started as an offshoot of Aunt Judy's company blog, but its combination of plus-size fashion inspiration and vintage thrifting tips attracted such a large readership that Aunt Judy insisted I relaunch it as something all my own. That was when I added the shameless paleontology geek-outs that soon became part of my trademark.

Above all, Aunt Judy showed me how to forge my armor, physically and emotionally. She taught me how to be awesome.

"Judy?" Mom peers out from the kitchen, her brow furrowed. "What are you doing here?"

Dad's still in the front doorway. He looks bewildered, like he always does when Aunt Judy's around.

"I had to see Natalie off. And I come bearing gifts." Aunt Judy roots around in her purse, as bright red and vintage as mine. "You want a ride to the airport, kiddo? I've got the Mustang."

"We're driving her," Mom says quickly. She crosses her arms. "I told you that last week."

"Cool. I'll hitch a ride with you guys."

"I'm not sure—" Mom starts.

"Aha, here we go." Aunt Judy produces two boxes. I recognize the first, a small, thin brick in glossy black with a Maxwell Cosmetics logo embossed in gold. It's a fresh tube of Pinup, our signature red lipstick. "Just in case," she says, handing it over.

"Thank you! I've been running a little low."

"Can't have that." She hands over the second box. "This just arrived yesterday, which is the real reason I'm here. I wasn't about to let you leave without it. Congrats, Natalie. I'm so proud I could fucking burst, kid."

"Oh! What is it?" I fiddle with the glittery ribbon tied around the red square.

"Remember that friend of mine who makes leather jewelry? I commissioned her to design something special."

The knot finally loosens as I tug at it with my red nails. Inside the box, nestled in crinkled tissue, is a cuff bracelet made from weathered brown leather. A pair of eyelets anchor an antiqued silver plate to the bracelet. The plate is engraved: "Keep digging. —Dr. Thomas Carver."

"My favorite quote! Thank you!" This time, I'm the one giving a python-level hug.

"Thought you'd like it," she laughs. "You talk about that quote enough. Check out the inside."

There are two words stamped into the soft interior suede: "Be awesome."

"Our little philosophy," she says.

It's more than that. It's my way of life, my means of survival. It's the mantra I whisper to myself when I feel less like Awesome Natalie and more like Fat Nat. It's the persona I put on each day, the tight shapers that bind me, the cute dresses, the flawless makeup. It's everything.

"I'll wear it every day when I'm there," I say, fastening it around my right wrist.

"We really need to get going." Dad tries to herd us outside, but he's outdone by yet another female voice. This one hollers my name from the street.

"Charli?" I hurry toward the driveway, where my best friend catches me in a fierce hug.

"Are they driving you nuts yet?" She glances toward the house. "Thought you might need a nonparental lift to the airport."

"God, I wish. Dad's about to lose it. They're pretty insistent on driving, though."

She laughs and runs a hand through her short, messy red hair. "Oh well. At least I get to say goodbye. I don't know what I'm going to do without you for a whole month, lady! Work is going to be a snooze."

"Now or never!" Dad roars, getting into the minivan.

I cringe at his tone. "I'd better not make him wait any longer." But then I see Charli blinking against tears, and I grab her shoulders. "Don't do that! If you start, I'll start, and I'm not about to smudge my eyeliner. It took me ten minutes to get these wings even."

She gives me a wavering smile.

Dad beeps the horn.

"Come along for the ride," I tell Charli. We climb into the back of the minivan with Aunt Judy. Dad guns the engine, and we hurtle down the driveway. Charli's eyes widen as she clicks her seat belt in place.

"Aunt Judy, you remember my friend Charli?"

"How could I forget my favorite redhead?" Aunt Judy reaches over and squeezes Charli's shoulder. "When am I going to get you to come over for a fitting, huh? I've been working on a new flapper-inspired collection that would look amazing on you."

"Too fancy for me," Charli says. She's always been

ultra-casual, and she likes to needle me about being high maintenance. She knew me back before all this started. In middle school, she was Fat Nat's only defender.

"I can see that." Aunt Judy sighs. "Are those pajama pants?"

"Yep." Charli beams down at her striped PJ bottoms.

Aunt Judy laughs. "You wear 'em well, kiddo. I'll give you that." She turns back to me. "I hope you remembered to pack those Chanel flats I loaned you."

"Of course."

Charli looks over her shoulder, eyeing my suitcase. "So just how many pairs of shoes did you pack, lady?"

Before I can tell her to lay off my wardrobe, my phone buzzes with an incoming text. "Oh God," I say when I see the name on the screen.

Charli leans closer, trying to see. "It's not..."

"It is."

She cackles. "Seriously? At a quarter to four in the morning? When's he going to give it up?"

I look at Aunt Judy. "Remember the guy I told you about? Fred Parkmore?"

"The one who asks you out every week?"

"The one who made her life hell in middle school," Charli adds. "I refuse to believe he doesn't realize you're the same Natalie he used to bully."

"I really think he doesn't know." Fred Parkmore's crush proves how thoroughly I reinvented myself the summer before high school.

"He's the teenage version of Roger," I tell Aunt Judy, referencing the lovesick guy who hits on her every time they run into each other downtown. "I handle him the same way too."

Aunt Judy's smile is so bright I can see it in the near darkness. "The old ask-me-again-next-week trick?"

"Yep."

She shakes her head. "It'd probably be kinder to flat-out tell Roger no, but I don't have the heart. I keep hoping he'll take the hint."

"Same here." I glance down at my phone again. *Good luck, gorgeous! How about Tokyo Garden when you're back in town? You like sushi, right?*

I love sushi, but I don't like the idea of sushi with Fred Parkmore at all. Just reading his name and being reminded of the way he always calls me "gorgeous" is enough to throw me back to our first sixth-grade dance, when he dared all the other guys to ask me to dance. He paid those who took him up on it five bucks apiece, but only if they held in their braying laughter long enough to gasp out the invitation. Charli finally stalked over and decked him, getting herself ejected from the dance—but by then, the damage was done. Fred and his mob had found their target in chubby Nat with her bad skin and braces and hair that stuck out in a halo of frizz.

I'd never let him know how he'd affected me, though. Aunt Judy once told me that if I'm not showing confidence, I'm showing weakness. "That's blood in the water to these assholes," she'd said when I explained how Fred and the others treated me. "They'll smell it, and they'll circle like sharks. They devour the weak. Confidence keeps them at bay, and being awesome is the ultimate defense."

I'd balked at that. "But I'm not confident. At all."

"Gotta fake it till you make it, kiddo."

Two years later, I'm still faking it.

Super-busy this summer! I text back. *See you next fall!*

His answer is immediate. *I'm going to keep asking until you say yes, LOL.*

I shudder and put my phone away.

Thanks to the driving skills of Vin Dadsel, we make it to the airport in a record forty-one minutes. Mom asks if I want them to park and come in as far as security with me, but I insist I can handle it on my own. I wouldn't mind Aunt Judy or Charli coming along, but the idea of having an entourage makes me tense up even more. My wrist smarts from the number of times I've snapped my hair elastic.

At the drop-off for my airline, Dad slips me a couple of twenties, hugs me, and tells me to have fun. Mom gets sniffly and kisses my cheek. Charli squeezes me tight and whimpers.

Aunt Judy gives me one last python hug and leaves an air kiss near my cheek to avoid getting lipstick on my skin. "Remember, I want updates! You'll still be blogging while you're gone, right?"

"Yeah, I can post right from my phone."

"Good. Lots of photos!"

I nod. Any response I might have is blocked by the lump rising in my throat.

"Be awesome," she says with another dazzling grin.

I have to get away before I cry. I stiffen my spine, wave goodbye, and march inside, bags in tow. Behind me, the automatic doors slide shut with a pneumatic hiss, sealing me off. My legs want to spin me around and run back before my dad has time to drive off.

No. I can do this. I just have to be awesome. There's a checklist in my head—stomach sucked in, shoulders back, posture perfect, smile pasted in place. I pretend I'm Aunt Judy flouncing through the airport, all confidence and easy sass. *I have every right to be here*, I tell myself. I know exactly what I'm doing.

Ten minutes later, after waiting in the wrong line and being directed to a different desk, I check in and hand over my suitcase.

Security is all but deserted. The guard who checks my ID is a woman. Without even realizing I'm doing it, I give her a quick up-and-down look. *One hundred and sixty.* The number flashes in my head, illuminated like a digital display. Like the numbers on a scale. It's a game I play with myself; I can't meet a woman without guessing her weight. It always makes me feel a little guilty, but working for Aunt Judy and writing about fashion have made me almost too good at estimating things like weight and clothing size. The reaction is so automatic and objective that I can't seem to stop. Besides, when you're as aware of size as I've learned to be, when you're reminded of it every time those great jeans don't fit or some anonymous idiot leaves a rude comment on your blog, you notice aspects of it everywhere.

I slip off my shoes and put my backpack and purse on the

conveyor belt to be x-rayed. My bags make it through fine, but an alarm beeps when I pose, arms raised, in the scanner.

"Ma'am, the bracelet?" the guard at the scanner asks, pointing his blue-gloved hand at my right wrist.

The cuff bracelet from Aunt Judy—it has metal on it. I blush down to my toes. "Oh! Yeah, sorry."

"Ma'am, please step back and remove the bracelet."

"Yeah, of course. Sure." My hands tremble as I fiddle with the bracelet. It takes me two tries to undo the snaps. Another officer has me place the bracelet in a bin so he can run it through the x-ray machine. Despite the early hour, two people wait behind me now, staring as I step into the scanner again.

This time it stays mercifully silent.

"Please step on through, ma'am."

I wish he would stop calling me "ma'am," but at least the alarm doesn't sound again.

Ninety-four minutes before my flight is scheduled to take off, I'm at my gate. Only two other people sit in the waiting area, slouched and dozing in the rows of blue padded seats. A cable news anchor drones about the stock market on a television mounted overhead.

I keep walking until I reach a restroom, where I lock myself in a stall, lean against the door, and exhale. My face still feels hot from when the security scanner went off. Lingering adrenaline coils around my chest. I force myself to breathe the disinfectant-heavy air.

I know this trick well. Restrooms are perfect spots to hide and regroup and decompress in between sessions of being awesome. I do this after lunch in school, after I've held court at the popular table, after I've exhausted myself with chatter and gossip and bright, fake smiles.

When my pulse stops rabbiting and the tension in my shoulders unlocks, I go back to my gate and pull out a book. At the same time, my other hand pulls a protein bar from my backpack. For the next few minutes, I read and chew. The airport dulls and fades around me. My head quiets. The bar doesn't last nearly long enough, though. I'd love to devour the second one as well, but the waiting area is slowly filling up with witnesses, and I'm not fond of people seeing me eat.

Tension creeps back. It's insidious—the muscle tightening, the incessant mental hum gradually increasing in volume, the restlessness twining through my limbs. I snap the elastic against my wrist and check the time. There's still more than half an hour before boarding begins.

Snap. Snap.

I pace up and down the terminal. Still twenty minutes before boarding.

Snapsnapsnap.

I open the blogging app on my phone and check for reactions to this morning's LotD post. The response so far is pretty typical. Eleven reblogs already. Nearly a hundred hearts. Forty-eight comments, forty-seven of which are positive. The last one's from a concern troll who predicts that I'll die of diabetes before I turn thirty. I get my share of trolls—some pick on my size, and others can't handle the fact that I'm a girl geeking out about paleontological finds and science news. I never respond, never give them the thrill of a reaction. In my head, though, that one line of nastiness somehow outweighs all the compliments that surround it. My face grows hot as I delete the comment.

Snapsnapsnap.

By the time we're allowed to board, my wrist is pink and tender.

I have a window seat. I toss my stuff in the overhead bin and sit, grabbing for the halves of the seat belt so I won't have to dig them out from under my butt. I wedge myself into place, my upper arm spilling into the middle seat. When a middle-aged man in a suit sits there, I shift toward the window, surrendering all rights to the armrest between us.

All the armor in the world can't protect me from moments like this.

Be awesome, I tell myself. I can't slip. Not now.

The flight to Austin takes three hours. As soon as elec-tronic devices are allowed, I plug my earbuds into my phone so I can listen to the latest episode of my favorite podcast, *Carved in Bone*. It's hosted by Dr. Thomas F. Carver—or, as I've always thought of him, Thomas Fucking Carver. Dr. Carver is the closest thing the paleontology field has to a legit rock star. He's discovered five new species of dino-saurs and prehistoric mammals so far, the most recent being the *Centesaurus*, a stego relative he uncovered in Utah last year. He has flowing strawberry blond hair he keeps caught back in a messy ponytail, icy-blue eyes, and a square jaw that always seems to have just the right amount of manly scruff. He's ridiculously hot, especially for someone who's almost my dad's age.

For months, I've been hoping that he'll use his podcast to discuss the legal trouble the Central Texas Mammoth Site is facing. I'm not clear on all the details, but from the articles I've read, it sounds like the family of the property's former owner is trying to claim that the first batches of fossils found on the land that would later become the site were unearthed and taken illegally. It seems like nonsense, but I've been worried that the threat of a lawsuit could impact the intern program—plus, issues like this are a big deal in the field, which is why I want to hear Dr. Carver's take.

Instead, though, this episode's about the time Dr. Carver found an *Apatosaurus* skeleton on a remote dig back in the late '90s. "I'd just uncovered a good portion of the skull when the weather report came through on the radio. We were in for a hell of a thunderstorm, and the whole region was under a flash flood watch—in a fucking desert, right? Just my luck. Can't leave the skull unprotected, so we figure out which direction the flood's likely to come from, if there *is* a flood, and we build up a little dam around the skull. We set up the tent over it. I don't care—I'll spend the night out in the rain if I have to. And that's just what the guys and I do. We climb trees and wait out the storm. It turned out to be a fucking deluge, but we survived, and so did the skull."

Thomas Fucking Carver is the shit.

About forty minutes after takeoff, once the seat belt signs are off, the flight attendants squeeze down the center aisle with the drink cart.

"Water, please," I say when the attendant comes by. I'd rather have a Coke, but I can't ask for one without remembering Fred Parkmore and his mob passing by while I used one of the vending machines in the middle school cafeteria. "Like you need all that sugar," he'd said, setting off a bevy of snickers. Diet Coke was worse—"C'mon, Fat Nat. *Diet?* You're not fooling anyone."

"Just water?" the attendant asks. "That's it? You sure?"

I paste on my confident smile. "Yes."

The attendant leans over my seatmates, holding out a plastic cup. When I take it, he says, as confidentially as he can manage over the dragon's-growl of the plane's engines, "Lipstick on your teeth, hon."

I bend my head and furiously scrub at my front teeth with my index finger. It comes away stained with a pale smear of red. A dent in the armor.

I press my forehead to the window as though I can somehow escape through the double-paned plexiglass and fly away. I close my eyes and try to concentrate on the paleo adventures of Thomas Fucking Carver.

When the attendant passes by again with tiny bags of pretzels, he automatically tries to hand me two. *Really?* I refuse them.

We cross a time zone and land a little after eight Austin time. Someone from the college will pick me up around eleven, so once again I'm left with time to kill.

I stop in the restroom and flash my teeth in the mirror, making sure no more lipstick has migrated. I pull out my phone. The text I send Aunt Judy is unapologetic pandering, but I don't care: *Just landed. Remind me that I'm awesome?*

While I wait for her response, I text my parents and Charli, letting them know I'm safely in Texas, and I delete two more troll comments from *Fossilista*. By the time I'm done, my phone is buzzing with a text from Aunt Judy: *Of course you're awesome. We established that years ago, babe. What's up?*

I chew my lip, trying to decide how to answer. *Dunno. Just scared, I guess. Nervous.*

This time her response is immediate. *It's gonna be fantastic. You'll see. I'm a text away if you need me, okay?*

She's right. I know she is. I just have to be awesome.

I spot the sign when I'm halfway down the escalator. The poster board, scrawled with "Mammoth" in thick black marker, waves above the undulating herd at baggage claim. The guy holding it stares over the crowd, his dark eyes sharp and intent.

He's all taut muscle and fierce glare. His deeply tanned skin looks airbrushed.

I have to approach this living mannequin while he's holding a sign demanding large, fat mammals. Wonderful. *Snapsnapsnap.*

For just a second, I hang back. I need one final moment to gather myself. While I wait, two others break from the herd and approach the guy with the sign. Some of my fellow interns, I assume—a strawberry blonde girl (*110, if that*) in denim shorts and brown leather booties, and a tall boy with sandy hair and the most perfect forearms I've ever seen.

After giving my teeth one final swipe with my index finger, I take a deep breath and wheel my suitcase toward the three perfect people. My Pinup smile glues itself to my face. *No weakness. Confidence.* I don't feel it, but I can show it.

Before I can speak up, the guy with the sign spots me and points. "Natalie Page?"

"Yeah." For a second I wonder how he knows. It's not like I included "I'm the fat one" on my application essay. But no, he's just using the process of elimination. I'm his last passenger this morning.

"Great, now we can go." He spins on one heavy boot and marches out toward the short-term parking lot. We fall in line and follow into the heavy Texas heat. The guy with the nice arms comments on the temperature.

"Get used to it," the sign guy says. "The forecast is calling for an especially brutal summer this year."

Even though I'm used to heat and humidity, I still feel like I'm wilting.

"Then again," he goes on, "Texas weather is wild, so who knows? We could end up with monsoons and tornadoes every day."

"I'm more used to hurricanes," I say.

"We get those too. I'm Eli Washington, one of the senior interns," the tall guy tosses over his shoulder at me. "Good flight?"

"It was fine," I say, but he's already turned back around, no longer listening. He leads us to an SUV the same olive color as his cargo shorts. The boy with the forearms takes shotgun. The girl and I climb in back.

"I'm Quinn," the girl says while I'm still buckling my seat belt.

"Natalie," I say, trying not to fumble with the buckle. "Nice to meet you."

"Chase." The boy turns and waves from the passenger seat.

Quinn. Chase. I repeat the names to myself. In my head I picture them written out in neat, looping handwriting by a vintage fountain pen. It's a trick I learned from Aunt Judy, and I've practiced it often while meeting her friends at Metro, the coffee-shop-slash-dive-bar that we cultivated as our usual territory downtown. People like you more when you remember their names.

Quinn crosses one thin leg over the other. I smooth the skirt of my dress and try my best not to glance from her thighs to mine and compare. *You have strong thighs*, Aunt Judy's voice says in my head. She told me this once when I'd whined about my fat legs. *Strong thighs and sturdy legs will carry you far, babe.* But nothing about sitting next to Quinn makes me feel strong.

"Where are you from?" Quinn asks.

"Florida. Near the Atlantic coast. About an hour east of Orlando."

"Oh, I love Florida." Her blue eyes widen. "My parents used to fly us down there all the time, back when my dad was working in Venice. The beaches were gorgeous. It must be amazing to live there."

"It's nice." I hate the beach. Maybe I'd feel differently about running around in a bathing suit if I were built like

Quinn, all legs and bones and insurmountable perk. "What about you?"

"Illinois. Dad's on the board of a museum in Chicago, but we live out in the suburbs." She rolls her eyes at the horror. "So lame, you know?"

"Sure. Chase?" I look toward the boy in front. "What about you?"

Quinn answers for him. "He's from Idaho." She pokes at the back of his seat with the toe of her bootie, right at butt level.

"Iowa," he corrects, turning in his seat again.

"Oh, right." Quinn gives me a *whatever* grin. "Farm boy."

In my head I see Chase tossing heavy bales of hay with a pitchfork, which would explain the forearms.

"He had to change planes at O'Hare," she goes on. "We were on the same flight into Austin, so we got to know each other a little." Again, she pokes at the back of his seat. "He's scared of takeoffs."

He shifts in his seat. "I'm really not."

"Sure. Except he looked like this as soon as we got to the runway." Quinn mimes grabbing onto airplane armrests, squeezing her eyes shut, and baring her teeth in a terrified grimace. He rolls his eyes at her over his shoulder, and she grins.

Aw, crap. She likes him. The realization kicks me in the gut. There's no way I could go up against her and hope to win, not when it comes to a guy who looks like Chase.

Be awesome. Aunt Judy's voice in my head again. She'd

tell me to crumple those thoughts like scrap paper and throw them in the trash. She'd tell me I can get anything—anyone—I want if I have the confidence to go for it.

I sit up a little straighter and catch Chase's gaze in the rearview mirror. His eyes squint a little as he smiles.

I smile back.

"So. You guys." Eli speaks up in a voice sharp enough to make Quinn sit back and stop flirting with Chase. "Welcome to the program, congrats, blah blah blah. Here's how things work. You guys will all report to either me or Mellie, the other senior intern. We're in charge of you, and you do what we say. Got that?"

"Yeah," the three of us say in unison.

"You should know this isn't exactly how either of us wanted to spend the next month. We're paying our dues so that we get more dig time in the fall. Don't expect us to be your best buddies and let you get away with all kinds of shit. Got it?"

"Okay." Chase's tone drops to a subdued mutter.

"Good." Eli turns on the radio, filling the car with bass-heavy music that makes conversation difficult. He's heard enough from his charges for now.

Quinn plays with her phone, occasionally leaning forward to speak to Chase. Over the pounding din of the radio, I can't hear what's said.

Finally we pass a green highway sign directing us to Austin State. The university is affiliated with the Central Texas Mammoth Site, so for the next month, we'll be bunking in its dorms. Eli takes the exit and turns right at a sign that reads AUSTIN STATE UNIVERSITY in huge gold-and-green letters. He parks near a multistory building. "Get your stuff."

We heft our luggage from the SUV. Chase grabs Quinn's suitcase, as well as his own—then he looks at me. "Oh, um, I'll come back down for your stuff next."

"Don't worry about it." I can carry my own bags.

"First floor is guys." Eli says as we lug everything inside. He stops at a door labeled 21-A and hands Chase a key card, then pulls out cards for Quinn and me. "Girls are upstairs in 21-B. Go up and settle in. Welcome meeting's tonight at five." He heads into 21-A, flops on one of the three beds, and puts in earbuds.

Chase leaves his luggage in the room with Eli and comes upstairs with us.

One bed in 21-B is apparently claimed. Several bright-blue crochet pillows are scattered across the comforter. A length of blue yarn is taped to the wall nearby, with photos hanging from miniature plastic clothespins. There's a framed cross-stitch propped on the nightstand—a cartoon owl with "I'll owl-ways love you" embroidered in brown floss.

Bunk beds sit against the wall on the other side of the room. No way am I climbing a ladder into bed each night, so I put my bags on the bottom bunk. "Okay with you?" I ask Quinn, nodding toward the top.

"Sure. Yeah." She's more interested in Chase than in choosing a bed.

The room is small, but a large window on the far wall

lets in plenty of natural light. The floor is industrial gray tile, and the walls are plain white. I'm pleased to find a mirror on the back of the door that'll work for LotD pics. There's no closet, just a recessed area in one wall with a rack for hangers, and a pair of small, rickety dressers. My nicer clothes—the things I brought for when I'm not digging up bones—will wrinkle if I leave them smashed in my suitcase, so I quickly unpack, leaving space on the rack for Quinn.

Then I duck into the bathroom to stash my toiletries. After a quick check of my reflection—makeup intact, hair still fairly neat, teeth lipstick-free—I go back to 21-B.

Quinn pulls clothing from her suitcase while she chatters in Chase's direction. He sits at one of the desks, positioned sideways with one arm hooked over the back of the chair, that forearm in full, glorious view.

Talk! I tell myself, snapping my hair elastic. When Quinn pauses for a breath, I walk in and say, "So I hope the other senior is a little nicer than Eli."

"Right?" Quinn says. "What kind of welcome was that?"

"I wondered for a second if I could get back on the plane and head home." Chase gives me a lopsided grin. "Still better than working on my parents' farm all summer, though."

Again I think of pitchforks and hay bales.

"I don't know about either of you," Chase says, "but I'm starving. Eli said the welcome meeting isn't until five, right? We've got some free time."

I try not to look too interested until Quinn says, "I could eat." Then I nod.

The three of us head out across a green space toward the center of campus. I spot a directory map. Chase studies it and then leads the way toward the cafeteria. Once we find it, Chase orders a double cheeseburger. Quinn gets a slice of pizza. I grab a cranberry walnut salad.

We take over a table in one corner of the lounge and sit down to a late lunch and awkward conversation.

"I'm *so* excited about tomorrow." Quinn drags out her *so* as though we couldn't possibly understand the intensity of her enthusiasm otherwise.

"Me too," I say. At least the internship gives us some ready topics of discussion. We wouldn't be here if we weren't all paleo geeks.

"I mean, I've spent a lot of time on Dad's digs," she goes on, "but that's not the same as something like this. Dad let me help out, but you know…I was always Dr. Carver's daughter. It's not like anyone took me seriously."

I almost choke on a walnut. "Dr. Carver? *The* Dr. Carver?" I almost call him Thomas Fucking Carver, but I catch myself.

"Yeah, that's my dad," she says, as if this doesn't matter.

"Your dad is awesome." I don't care if I sound like a fangirl. I could fangirl Thomas Fucking Carver every day for the rest of my life. "I love his podcast so much! I just listened to the episode where he talked about finding that *Apatosaurus* skull. He's so hard-core."

Quinn shrugs and sips her iced tea.

I can't help it—I press on. "What's he like?"

She raises a brow. "He's really into bones."

"And you've been on digs with him?"

"Yeah."

"Were you there last year when he found the *Centesaurus*?"

"Yep."

"Holy shit. I would have died. I would have died right there and then." I wonder how stupid it would be to ask her to get me her dad's autograph. "Do you think he'll visit while you're here? Maybe come to the site and show us some stuff?"

"Doubt it." Her tone sharpens around the edges. "He's digging in South America this summer. They're filming the dig for his new show. But whatever. Let's talk about something that's not my dad."

New show? I'd read rumors of a reality show, but I didn't know it was already in production. I want to needle her for more information, but the irritated bite in her tone makes me back off for now. "Okay."

"So why are you here?" she asks.

"Same reason we're all here. Paleo's my life."

"Well, yeah, that's why you *want* to be here," she says. "But why are you here? This isn't exactly an easy program to get into. Did your dad make a big contribution to the site like mine did to keep me out of his hair for a month?"

"A contribution? No." I frown. "I filled out an application and wrote an essay."

"Oh, cool. I was just curious. Most of the kids in these internships get picked because their parents pull major strings. That's how these things go. It's a way for the site to do a little fundraising."

"The tuition cost, you mean?" I have no desire at all to admit I'm here on scholarship.

Quinn gives a quick snort. "That's not even a drop in the bucket. No, I'm talking about the generous donations rich parents make so their kids have a better chance of getting a prestigious internship. This shit looks good on college applications."

Chase shifts in his seat and picks at the remains of his burger. He clears his throat. "So anyway, show of hands— who's really here because they were obsessed with *Jurassic Park* when they were a kid?" He raises his hand over his head.

I shake my head. "For me, it was all about this stuffed *Smilodon* I got for my birthday."

Chase laughs. "I had a stuffed *Stegosaurus*. Slept with it every night."

We look at Quinn.

"I had a replica of a *Deinonychus* skull," she says.

I stab the last bit of lettuce in my salad bowl. "I would've given just about anything for that when I was a kid!"

She shrugs. "It wasn't so great. I wasn't allowed to play with it."

There's a girl in 21-B, sitting on the single bed. She leans back against the wall, nested among the crocheted pillows, with a tablet balanced on one thigh. Her short brown hair is pulled into two tiny, messy pigtails with a large swatch of sideswept bangs blanketing her forehead. Despite the day's heat, she wears a thin cream scarf over her blue "Mammoth Site" T-shirt. Rainbow-striped socks peek out from beneath the hems of her khakis.

One hundred forty, I guess.

When I walk in, she hops up and holds out the tablet. "What do you think?"

I recognize the website she's browsing—CraftyKarma. com. Sometimes I use it for sewing ideas, but it features all kinds of do-it-yourself projects. The photo she shows me is of a very realistic *Triceratops* head mounted on a wall like a taxidermy hunting trophy.

"*Papier mache!*" she says before Quinn or I can answer. "Isn't it fantastic? I'm thinking different colors, though. Purple, maybe. And glitter. There has to be glitter, right?"

"Um. Sure." I give her a hesitant nod. Her eyes seem unnaturally large and wide. After seeing the way they gleam when she mentions glitter, I don't want to contradict her.

"Oh! Sorry." She smacks her forehead with the hand not holding the tablet. "I'm Mellie McCormick, one of the senior interns. You guys must be my roomies for the next month!"

Quinn and I introduce ourselves.

Mellie grins. "So awesome to meet you. Anyway, I've been on CraftyKarma for an hour, hearting all these ways to spruce up this room." Her fingers stroke and weave over the tablet screen. "I just cannot deal with plain white walls, know what I mean?"

Her enthusiasm leaves me a little dazed, and I think Quinn feels the same way. We give Mellie matching blank nods. I have to admit, though, there's something instantly likable about Mellie's effervescent chatter. She reminds me of Aunt Judy on one of her caffeine-fueled creative benders.

"I was thinking decals," she goes on, "but maybe we can find something better and cheaper. Banners? Bunting? Garlands? Draped fabric? I don't know. Ugh!" She cringes in an exaggerated way that makes me think of a cartoon character. "Why did I not hit the thrifts when I had time?"

I perk up a little. "Are there any good thrift stores around here?" Clever thrifting is one of Aunt Judy's specialties, and shopping with her taught me a lot about the hunt.

"Austin has *amazing* thrifting." Mellie blinks her owl-eyes at me as though she can't believe my ignorance in the matter.

"Oh, I'd love to go to a few while I'm here!"

Mellie blinks some more. "Hmm. I'm not sure we're allowed to take you kids off campus for anything but approved activities. I'd have to check with Dr. Lauren. I would enjoy having a partner in crime, though, so we'll see. How about you?" She turns her owl-eyes to Quinn. "You up for some thrifting?"

Quinn presses her lips together. "I've never been, um, thrifting."

"What? Oh, honey." Mellie takes Quinn by the shoulders. "You poor, deprived child. Okay, we are definitely going to have to get permission for a thrifting adventure at some point this month."

"Okay?" Quinn's smile is vaguely terrified.

"This is going to be the best month ever," Mellie says. "Now, how are the two of you with crafting?" She scrolls on her tablet again.

Quinn doesn't say anything, so I jump in. "I'm pretty crafty. I'm a really good sewer."

Mellie wiggles. "I knew it! I knew it as soon as I saw your wardrobe." She gestures to the rack where I'd hung my stuff. "I peeked. I hope you don't mind. I couldn't help it. And that dress!" She flaps a hand at what I'm wearing. "That's way too unique to be off the rack."

"Oh! Thanks." I explain about Savage Swallow and what I've learned from working with Aunt Judy.

"That's so amazing! I sew too. And knit. Made these." She points down at her striped socks. "And I crochet and paper craft and upcycle and design my own line of jewelry. And I make mosaics out of broken pottery, and I silkscreen, and paint, and sculpt, and draw, and stencil, and…Well, lots of other stuff too." Her words come faster and faster until I'm lost under a wave of craftiness. "There's just no end to what you can do with a light bulb and a little moss," she says.

"Ah. What?" I give my head a shake. "A light bulb? Like an idea, you mean?" I mime the concept of a light bulb turning on over my head.

"No, silly." She runs to her desk. "I mean a light bulb. See?" She holds up what is indeed a light bulb, minus its cap and filament. Inside is a tiny diorama in which minuscule mammoths march over a bed of primeval moss. "I made this one yesterday."

I notice several more bulbs on the desk, each filled with a little scene and balanced precariously on bottle caps repurposed as stands.

"It's just one more thing I do. My favorite's the zombie one." She grabs another bulb, holding it close to my face so I can see a tiny plastic person, less than an inch tall, running in terror from an equally tiny green ghoul. She holds it out to Quinn.

"I've honestly never seen anything like that," Quinn stammers.

Mellie just grins again. "I know, right?" As she's putting the bulb back on the desk, her phone chimes in her pocket.

"Oh! Time for the welcome meeting. Come on, roomies!" Catching each of us by a hand, she pulls us out of the room. She doesn't let us go until we reach a common area at the end of the hall, where she stops short while Quinn and I stumble to avoid smacking into her. "Sorry," she says. "I'm just so excited to be supervising this year. You have no idea."

Being dragged down the hall like the victim in a paranormal activity movie has given me a pretty clear idea of her excitement level, actually.

I survey the room—two couches, a couple of beanbags and trendy ottomans, a large television. Windows on two walls let in plenty of early evening light.

"Make yourselves at home!" Mellie parks herself on a gray cable-knit ottoman, curling her legs under her.

The beanbags look comfy, but Charli has one in her bedroom and I know how graceful I am when I hoist myself out of it. Picture a hippo lurching up a muddy riverbank. Yeah. I sit on the larger of the two couches instead and cross one leg over the other.

We're still settling when Eli and Chase appear from downstairs, along with another guy and a tall, fifty-something woman with short brown hair and a clipboard (*160 pounds*, and in my head I can hear Aunt Judy *tsking* over the unflattering pleats in the woman's khakis).

When Chase sits between Quinn and me on the couch, my breath catches. The other guy chooses an overstuffed chair.

"Welcome to Texas," the woman says to the four of us. "My name is Dr. Helen Lauren. I'm the assistant director at the Central Texas Mammoth Site. I oversee the intern program, so you'll be reporting to me this month. Dr. Gallagher and I are very excited to have you aboard."

Chase shifts a little beside me, and I lose all ability to concentrate on Dr. Lauren. Did he move closer or is it just my hopeful imagination? If I were to uncross my legs and sit with both feet on the ground, our thighs would touch. The thought sends a buzz down my spine... but then he'd feel my thick thigh against his lean muscle. *Strong thigh*, Aunt Judy would correct me. But it's not strong. Just thick.

No, my legs are staying crossed.

"Let's start with some quick introductions," Dr. Lauren says. She nods at me to go first.

I swallow through a dry throat. "I'm Natalie Page. I'm an incoming junior from Florida. I really want to be a paleontologist, and I'm super excited to be here. I, um, founded a fossil club at my school, and I have a fashion blog called *Fossilista*. It's not just about clothes and stuff, though. I also blog about paleo news a lot." I clamp my mouth shut before my nerves can set off a storm of further babbling.

Chase and Quinn go next. Then it's the other guy's turn: Brendan Mercier. Senior from Las Vegas, where he says his family owns a trio of upscale creole-inspired bistros. "We're originally from N'Awlins," he says. "Mama still makes a mean gumbo."

It's Eli's turn next. Then Mellie. My mental calligraphy grows messier as I note the names of everyone I'll spend the next four weeks with, writing and rewriting each one in my head.

Finally, Dr. Lauren lightly claps a hand against her clipboard. "Now that that's out of the way, let's get down to business." She goes into a speech about various details—schedules, rules, consequences for breaking those rules. We're each given an information packet and a food card for our meals at the cafeteria, and she emphasizes our ten o'clock curfew at least three times.

My stomach grumbles, and I clear my throat to mask the sound.

Dr. Lauren clasps the clipboard to her chest. "I think that's about it for tonight!" she says brightly. "The real orientation starts tomorrow. Any questions?"

Mercifully, everyone is quiet.

"Great. What would you all say to a campus tour and dinner at the cafeteria?" She leads us outside and takes us by various good-to-know locations—laundry facilities, bookstore, administrative offices, student lounge.

In the cafeteria, I settle on a soy cheeseburger on a whole wheat bun and a bag of crackers. At the end of the line, near the cashier, a pile of prepackaged desserts sings like a siren on treacherous rocks. I try not to look, but I'm hungry. And they have snickerdoodles—my favorite. I take two and stare at them on my tray, anxiety blooming in my throat like bile.

I don't have to get them. Chase is behind me in line, though. Putting the cookies back might get more attention than just buying them.

The cashier stares at me, drumming her nails against the register keys. "That it?" she asks, and I realize I've been standing there staring at the cookies on my tray like a weirdo.

"Yeah, that's it." I hand over my food card. She runs it through the register and hands it back, and I take my tray toward the table where the interns and seniors have gathered.

"That's all you're eating?" Mellie asks when I sit beside her. Her tray is heaped with the cafeteria's main dish of the night—lasagna—along with extra garlic bread, a bowl of soup, and a slice of pie.

I hate that question. Sometimes I try to convince myself that I'm paranoid, that no one is actually paying attention to what I'm eating. I get asked something like that, and I know the truth.

"Yeah, I know, I'm a pig," she goes on when I don't answer. "I missed lunch." She pauses for an enormous bite of pasta and meaty sauce and gooey strings of melted cheese. "I'm starved."

"Looks good," I say, nibbling at my soy burger.

"It is." Another shovelful. She has her tablet on the table in front of her, and she's still flipping past idea after idea on CraftyKarma. "Hey, can you draw?"

"I'm decent." I mostly draw fashion sketches.

"Up for a project after dinner?"

I finish off my crackers. "Sure."

"How about you?" she asks Quinn.

"Um, I guess. Sure."

"Perfect! You're our string girl then."

"What the hell's a string girl?" Quinn asks.

Mellie cackles. "You'll see!"

Across the table, I catch Chase glancing at me. He smiles, and my chest seizes up. My left wrist suddenly smarts; I don't remember doing it, but I must have snapped my elastic. Despite the sting, I manage to smile back.

Mellie is sopping up the last of her lasagna grease with her bread. "Hey, want these?" I ask, nudging the cookies toward her. "I'm full."

"Oh. Sure. Yum!" She takes them off my tray, and my shoulders feel lighter.

Later when my stomach growls while Mellie puts us to work in the dorm common room, I regret that decision. From the craft stash she keeps in a storage bin under her bed, she produces a pair of twelve-inch squares of wood about an inch thick. "Natalie, I need you to sketch out a mammoth shape on each of these," she says. "Just an outline. You don't need to go into detail."

When I finish the first one, she takes it back and hammers nails at intervals around the outline. The heads of the nails stick out about half an inch from the wood. The guys are watching a ball game on the common room TV. Mellie's hammering elicits an exaggerated sigh from Eli.

"Shut up," she yells merrily, hammering louder for his benefit.

He narrows his eyes and turns up the volume.

"Your turn!" She hands the board to Quinn and shows her how to wrap yarn around the nails, crisscrossing to fill in the mammoth shape with a stringy spiderweb. "See? String art!"

"Wow," Quinn says. "That's certainly…something."

"These are going to look so great on the walls!" Mellie says. I'm not sure if she's ignoring Quinn's lack of enthusiasm or if she's too lost in her world of string and nails to care.

Quinn spends a few mechanical minutes winding string before she puts the project down. "I'm really not that into crafty stuff," she tells Mellie with an apologetic shrug. She sits on the couch next to Chase. "So who's winning?"

"More for you, I guess!" Mellie hands me Quinn's board.

My stomach grumbles again, and I shift position to quiet it. I'd like to do the same as Quinn, just abandon the project and Mellie and sit with Chase instead.

Thing is, I'm kind of enjoying the string art. Besides, I'm exhausted. My confidence bank is empty. I have no more awesome to give tonight—and going up against Quinn for Chase's attention would take a *lot* of awesome.

I stick with the string.

Look of the Day:
   Green polka-dot swing dress (made by me!)
   Turquoise patent belt (Savage Swallow)
   Turquoise patent peep-toe pumps (vintage, Cara Veronica)
   Fashion Doll pink lipstick (Maxwell Cosmetics)
   Turquoise headband (Savage Swallow)
   Leather cuff bracelet (Kathryn Arbor Designs)

Here we go, fossilistas—first day of the internship! Today's all about site orientation. This is the same place I blogged about a few months back. Remember the post about the stupid lawsuit? I still doubt the family of the original landowner will really be able to claim all the site's fossils, but if they do…Well, I'm lucky to intern here while it still exists.

   More soon! Too excited to type anymore right now, haha.

4

Things I don't include in my *Fossilista* post:

1. How hard it is to grab enough time in a shared bathroom to get my makeup and hair done.

2. How awkward it is when I'm trying to wing my eyeliner just right and Quinn barges in to pee and shower. ("Sorry, I grew up sharing a bathroom with three older sisters," she says as I try to ignore the reflection in the mirror of her undressing next to me. "You lose all sense of shame when you have to fight a crowd like that for bathroom time." Yeah, I guess.)

3. The fact that I can't take a full breath in the shaper I wear underneath my dress.

Dr. Lauren is waiting for us in the Mammoth Site's welcome center, along with an older man with graying hair and a magnificent beard. He welcomes us, introducing himself as Dr. Vincent Gallagher, the site's director. I've read about his career. Dr. Gallagher is one of the field's leading experts in paleontological taphonomy, the study of how organisms decay and fossilize. He's also renowned for his efforts to improve and expand the site.

"This is our main lobby." Dr. Gallagher spreads his arms. Although his voice is tight and nervous, he beams at the opportunity to introduce us to the site. "We just completed a renovation two years ago. We're really proud of how the place came out."

It's pretty impressive. Textured beige floor tiles are interrupted here and there by a line of life-size simulated mammoth footprints, each of which measures close to eighteen inches across. A bronze statue of a baby mammoth stands frozen in mid-march in the middle of the room, and a mural of a mammoth herd stretches up the wall behind the polished wood reception desk. To the right is a small gift shop, set behind a glass divider. I remember the lawsuit. The idea that a site this grand, this permanent could lose its fossils is unimaginable; it'd be like New York City being ordered to hand the Statue of Liberty back to France, or England tearing down Buckingham Palace.

At the reception desk, a girl about our age (the digital display in my mind lights up: *115*) studies us with slightly narrowed eyes. We get a similarly chilly glance from a guy near the back door.

"It's looking great," Quinn says. "You guys were working out of a trailer last time I was here. This is a million times better."

Dr. Gallagher nods at her. "Thank you, Quinn."

Paleontology is a small field; it shouldn't surprise me that Quinn Carver has been here before, or that Dr. Gallagher already knows her. I'm suddenly brimming with the desire to distinguish myself. This is my element—this place, this field, this profession—and I'm determined to mark it as such. Quinn might try to claim Chase, but paleontology is *mine*.

"Didn't you also expand the dig shelter during that renovation?" I blurt out before I can second-guess myself.

Dr. Gallagher smiles again—a broad, proud, Cheshire crescent in a nest of beard. "Yes! Yes, we did. You've done your homework, I see."

"Natalie Page," I say, stepping forward and forcing my right hand out to shake his. I hope he doesn't notice that I'm trembling.

"Of course, Miss Page." His eyes crinkle around the edges. "The...prehistoric hipster. Was that how you put it? Your application essay was very memorable."

To my left, Quinn shifts her weight from one foot to the other. When I glance from the corner of my eye, I swear I catch her glaring.

Dr. Gallagher checks his watch. "I'm due for a breakfast meeting with some of our benefactors, so I'm going to turn this over to Dr. Lauren. I'm leaving you all in good hands. I hope the next month proves to be an enriching experience for all of you." After that, he's gone, rushing out the front door. I get the feeling he's relieved to leave things up to Dr. Lauren.

"Prehistoric hipster?" Chase whispers.

I don't look at him. "My essay was about why I like prehistoric mammals better than dinosaurs even though dinosaurs are more popular."

Dr. Lauren taps her clipboard against the front desk. "All right, let's get started. This is where guests pay for admission. Back behind reception are offices, supplies, and the break room. Martina, one of our summer employees, is working the reception desk today, and Cody's giving tours."

The girl behind the reception desk raises an unenthusiastic hand in something that sort of resembles a brief wave.

We pass through the welcome center and exit through the back door, following Dr. Lauren.

"That building will be our museum," she says, waving her clipboard toward a partially completed structure along the paved path. "It's slated to open next year. Tour groups follow this path down to the dig shelter. I'm going to start you off by sending you on the nine o'clock tour with Cody. Then we'll take a quick walk around a little more of the property while I talk about prospecting."

We pass Cody as we file back into the welcome center. His surly expression has softened into something more welcoming thanks to the presence of half a dozen tourists.

"They're all yours, Cody," Dr. Lauren says. "I'll be back in an hour to show them the rest of the trails. Guys, you'll all be giving tours this summer, so pay attention to how Cody handles this." The four of us join the tour group while Dr. Lauren and the senior interns disappear down the back hallway. I take out my phone so I can snap some photos for my blog.

nursery herd. The remains you see here are of four cows, three calves, and a juvenile bull. Fossils of nine other mammoths are in storage at Austin State. They'll be on display when we open our museum next year.

"We're pretty sure this was a family unit led by the largest cow—that's her over there." Cody uses a laser pointer to indicate an enormous skull peeking out from the hard-packed golden soil. There's a touch of affection in his voice, as though he's discussing a living creature and not a pile of bones. "This group died all at once. From the position of the fossils, we've hypothesized that it was due to a flood, probably about forty thousand years ago."

"Dad!" The little boy pipes up again. "Are those the only dinosaurs?"

"I guess so," his dad answers. "Sorry, buddy. I thought this was more like a museum, with the bones all put back together."

My mouth opens before I can stop it. "Um, excuse me. First of all, they're mammoths, not dinosaurs. Second, you can see fossils in museums anywhere! This is much better—you get to see how it looks when the bones are first uncovered." I wave a hand down toward the bone bed. "I mean, isn't that cool? Don't you want to be down there digging?"

The boy considers this and stares at his dad again. "Do we get to dig down there?"

The man looks at me, the same question in his eyes. Is he kidding?

"It takes a lot of training to excavate without damaging the fossils," Cody cuts in. "I'm afraid we can allow only our employees and interns into the bone bed. However, we do have a training area outside where you can try your hand at digging. I'll show you at the end of the tour."

The boy scuffs his sneaker on the walkway. "I want to see a *T. rex*."

"A full-grown Colombian mammoth weighed as much as two *T. rex* bulls put together," I say before I can catch myself. I realize that I just snapped at a kid, and now everyone's staring.

The boy narrows his eyes and says, "Mammoths are fat," and I no longer feel guilty for snapping at him.

Cody regains control of the tour, explaining more about the bones below. As he talks, several site diggers make their way into the bone bed, their steps slow and deliberate, tools and plastic buckets in their hands. They settle in here and there with picks and brushes, scraping away thin layers of dirt and gravel.

That's where I want to be—hunched over a skull or a tusk or a femur, picking away until my back aches and my legs fall asleep from my uncomfortable position.

On the way back from the dig shelter, Cody goes on about the site's efforts to fund future excavations and museum displays. Near the welcome center, he pauses by what looks like an overgrown sandbox and offers to show the boy how to dig. The boy refuses, pouting behind his dad. Cody shrugs, and we return to the lobby. The tour ends, conveniently, just outside the gift shop. The tourists shuffle in to look at plastic toys and posters and T-shirts, while the interns mill around in the lobby, waiting for Dr. Lauren to return.

"Hey!" Cody hisses the word at me, and he pokes my shoulder with his finger. "Don't do that again." His tone is low but harsh.

I widen my eyes.

"Don't argue with guests. We're supposed to keep them happy. They spend more and donate more if they're happy."

"But I was just—"

"I'm serious. If you act like that when you're giving tours or talking to guests, Dr. Lauren will ream you. Arguing with a kid? Seriously, are you kidding me?"

My wrist smarts as I snap my elastic. "He called them dinosaurs."

"So?"

"So...I didn't like that."

"It doesn't matter."

I square my shoulders. "Oh, sure. It's not like this is an educational site, right? It's not like science or accuracy matter at all."

"As far as you and I are concerned, what matters is keeping the visitors happy. That's how the site keeps itself funded. Well, that and letting a bunch of rich kids play in the dirt because their parents threw some money around."

"I'm not—"

"Look," he mutters, "I'm just trying to help." He retreats behind the reception desk, where Martina rolls her eyes and gives him a wry half grin.

Snapsnapsnap.

Soon Dr. Lauren and the senior interns appear to collect us. "Let's head to the trails out back," Dr. Lauren says. She gives me an up-and-down look. "Natalie, can you handle wooded trails in that outfit? Maybe you should stay up here."

"Sorry, Natalie," Mellie says. "I forgot about the trails. I should've suggested you change this morning."

No way am I skipping any part of today. "I'll be fine."

"Those shoes, though." Dr. Lauren frowns.

"There are some boots in the storage shed," Cody suggests from the reception desk.

"Aha. Yes, that'll work. Thank you, Cody." Dr. Lauren leads everyone outside again, toward a smaller structure behind the main building. She unlocks the shed's door. A moment later, she's presenting me with a pair of decrepit tan work boots several sizes too large. They're so caked in dried mud that I hate to touch them. There's nowhere to sit, so I clumsily put them on while standing. I pull the laces as tight as possible and double knot them, chipping my turquoise nail polish in the process.

The boots look absurd with my dress, and I'm too aware of how they turn my usual gait into awkward clomping. But the path is much easier to navigate this time, and once we bypass the dig shelter and head along a hidden, unpaved side trail, I'm grateful I left my heels behind. My dress is unwieldy enough as our trek becomes increasingly tricky. We continue down an embankment and into the trees, where low branches and thorny vines scratch at my unprotected legs.

"Watch your footing," Dr. Lauren says over her shoulder. "We don't need any sprained ankles."

I'm sweating as I pick my way through the forest floor debris, stepping over fallen branches and avoiding patches of brown muck. Despite the early hour and the tree cover, the steamy heat is settling in quickly. I miss the precise temperature control of the dig shelter.

When I wipe my forehead, my hand comes away with a smear of foundation. My makeup primer is no match for the Texas summer. My shaper is saturated with perspiration. I usually find the hug of it around my torso almost comforting, but right now it's about as cozy as an iron lung. My usual look might be all right for giving tours in the shelter or working in the welcome center, but it's hopeless out here.

But I forget the heat when Dr. Lauren gathers us in a low-lying area. The soil here is damp. Brendan steps in the wrong spot, and his foot sinks into the mud. When he pulls it free, his sneaker is missing. He perches on his other foot while he reaches down to retrieve it. Laughing, Quinn videos the whole thing with her phone.

"We're standing in a riverbed," Dr. Lauren says. "Once the rainy season sets in, this area will be underwater periodically until late fall. The moving water often uncovers new fossils."

I look down, giving the area by my feet a quick visual scan. Bits of rock and rubble pepper the riverbed—could any of them be fossil fragments?

"This is as far as we're going today," Dr. Lauren goes on. "Otherwise we'd need to wear safety vests, in case there are any hunters in the vicinity. It's not hunting season, but that doesn't always stop them."

"Do interns get to prospect?" I ask.

"Sometimes," she says. "A lot depends on the skill you

demonstrate in the bone bed. Prospecting requires a keen eye and superb attention to detail."

The words sound like a wonderful challenge.

"And of course, no one is to be wandering around out here without the supervision of a senior intern. Prospecting is not a solo activity."

Dr. Lauren continues to explain the process, demonstrating how she uses an app on her phone to record and map the precise coordinates of even the smallest discovery. I go back and forth between listening and looking around, eyeballing every fragment, every shard.

Then I spot it—a bit of dirty, off-white bone lodged in the shadow of a fallen trunk, partially mired in the mud. It has to be something! "Dr. Lauren!" I interrupt her in the middle of her lesson on coordinates, and I point to the bone. "Sorry, but what's that?"

She pauses.

Squints.

Steps closer to the bone.

Leans over, inspecting it.

Pokes at it with her pen.

My heart shivers up into my throat. I can't breathe, and I don't care.

"It's a pork chop bone," she says at last, straightening up.

Stifled laughter from Quinn. Brendan snorts. Worst of all, Chase puts a hand to his mouth and coughs in a way that sounds like a choked-back chuckle.

A blush burns across my face, hotter than the Texas sun.

"Good eye, though," Dr. Lauren goes on. "I'm impressed—it takes real talent to spot bone like that. With practice, you'll get better at telling the difference between fossils and newer material."

The praise means nothing. It echoes in my head and fades to silence. All I can think of is the fact that I just got excited about a fucking pork chop.

"How would something like that get down here?" Chase asks.

"When the riverbed fills, the water can carry all kinds of unexpected things down with it. That bone could be from several miles upstream."

It makes sense. It does. Rationally, I know my mistake was honest and minor. The fact that I spotted the bone at all outweighs my identification error. But PORK CHOP PORK CHOP PORK CHOP is all I can focus on. If the river were to flood right now and drag me off like a forgotten pork chop bone, I would be okay with that.

5

I keep waiting for Dr. Lauren to mention the looming law-suit. She never does, though, and I don't feel comfortable bringing it up, at least not yet. Maybe it's a nonissue at this point. I hope so; I don't want anything interrupting my time in Texas.

At the end of the day, she steers us toward the gift shop. "As interns, you're each entitled to two site T-shirts. You're not required to wear them, but they're an easy way to look official."

Stacks of neatly folded blue shirts pile the shelves before us, each screen-printed with the site's logo. Everyone else nabs a couple and heads back to the lobby, but I hesitate. I could grab a unisex XL, guaranteed to fit over my breasts without the fabric straining awkwardly. Unisex sizes are boxy, though. Aunt Judy taught me that early on. Women's sizes have more flattering cuts. Unfortunately, women's

sizes also tend to run small. *Really* small. Do I risk a wom-
en's XXL? I unfold one and hold it up. Maybe. I mean, it
looks tiny, but... Then I notice I'm the last one without
shirts. I grab another XXL, ball both up to hide the size
tags, and rejoin the group.

The cafeteria chatter that evening revolves around
bones—the size of the mammoth specimens in the dig shelter, the discoveries we might make while prospecting, and
most importantly, how long it'll take before we're approved
to dig.

I'm talking with Mellie about how she likes Austin State
when, several seats away, Quinn giggles. She and Chase are
watching a video on her phone. Whatever the video is, it's
making Chase's dimples pop. He's trying not to smile, but
those dimples totally give him away.

"What is it?" Mellie asks. "Funny cat video? Those are
my favorite! Oh, is it the one where the little gray tabby
tries to jump over the fish tank?"

Quinn shakes her head. "Just something I filmed today."
Her eyes dart to me. "In the riverbed."

Eli holds out a hand. "Let me see."

He turns up the volume, and I hear Dr. Lauren's voice.
"It's a pork chop bone."

Eli snorts. "Oh man. I'd forgotten about that."

Brendan's chuckling too. "It never gets old. Natalie,
you're hilarious."

I give him what I hope is a withering grin. My eyes grow
hot, but I'll be damned if I'll let anyone see me tear up. Eli
plays the video again. My chest clenches, and I bring up

CraftyKarma to get Mellie's mouth motoring. Her endless DIY talk soon drowns out the video.

Later, when we're all watching TV in the dorm common room, my stomach is gnawing on itself and I'm regretting eating only a salad. Quinn managed to grab a seat next to Chase on the couch. She keeps laughing just a little too loudly at the sitcom we're watching, and sometimes her foot nudges his.

"Okay if I go for a walk?" I ask Mellie, who's perched on an ottoman, knitting another sock.

She looks up. "Everything all right?"

"Everything's fine. I just need a little air."

"Okay. Be back by curfew."

"Will do."

I stop by the dorm room for my purse. Earlier I'd changed into cuffed jeans and a dolman top with the Savage Swallow logo on the chest. The green dress is drying in the bathroom; I had to wash out half a dozen dirt stains from my time in the riverbed.

The cafeteria is still open, so I grab a slice of pizza, along with a side of breadsticks. I request a to-go container and head into the warm Texas night toward an open-air amphitheater near the center of campus.

The amphitheater is empty, an angled collection of indigo shadows in the moonlight. I choose a bench near the stage and eat in calming silence, texting with Charli and Aunt Judy. When I'm done with my food, I put the box down by my feet and stay in my seat, enjoying the quiet. If I weren't still wearing a perspiration-damp shaper—if I could actually breathe—the moment would be almost tranquil.

"Okay if I join you?"

I jump up and turn. Chase stands behind me, gesturing for me to sit back down.

"Sorry," he says. "Didn't mean to startle you. Wasn't sure you should be wandering around on your own, though."

"I'm fine," I say. I'm female, not helpless. Still, I certainly don't mind when he sits next to me. His proximity makes me shiver, my stomach tensing. Aware of every inch of myself, I lengthen my spine and try to look graceful. *Be awesome.* My foot nudges the to-go box out of sight under the bench.

"Yeah, I know. It's just…I mean, you hear stuff on the news about college campuses. So I thought…You know. This is probably my dad talking. Sorry. He's big on holding doors for women and walking them to their cars and shit. He'd have my ass if he knew I didn't at least check on you." He chuckles awkwardly.

I'm glad it's dark. He can't see the bright, hot pink raging across my cheeks. "Thanks."

"No prob. So anyway…" He trails off.

I force my tongue to unknot. "So your dad's kind of old-fashioned, huh?"

"Not 'kind of.' Completely. I don't think my mom's opened one door for herself since she met him."

I laugh a little. "So he's a gentleman."

"Yeah, a gentleman in overalls and a Budweiser trucker cap." Chase rubs the back of his neck. "I mean, sometimes he literally has a piece of hay hanging out of his mouth. It's like he's a cartoon or something."

"Do you miss him and your mom?"

He shrugs. "I mean, I'm enjoying the break. You know? But...yeah, I guess. A little."

I like hearing about his life, so I keep prodding. "So Iowa, huh?"

"Yeah."

"What's it like?"

"Not too interesting. Lots of farmland. Lots of, you know, corn and stuff. We lead the nation in hog production."

I laugh a little. "Wow, exciting."

"Wait, it gets better. We're also the birthplace of Herbert Hoover and Quaker Oats."

"Must be like living in the middle of Times Square."

"You have no idea." He grins and looks at his sneakers. "I mean, I guess it could be worse."

"Yeah, you could be from a state that's one huge retirement home like me."

"Aw, come on. Florida can't be so bad. You have beaches and palm trees and Disney World and shit like that. And it's warm all year long."

"Warmth is not something I'm grateful for right now." The heavy heat of the day is only just beginning to dissipate into the evening.

"Want to trade? You can help my dad harvest two hundred acres of grain every year and get up at four in the morning to feed the animals."

"Think I'll pass. What kind of animals?"

"Chickens and goats, mostly. And a cow because my mom likes the fresh milk. Oh, and the horses. My sister and I each have one, but I've always had to take care of them because I'm older. Guess who's finally stuck with the job this month, though?" His mouth stretches into a smirk.

"Horses? Okay, now I'm a little more tempted by that trade you offered. How old is your sister?"

"Twelve. Acts like she's six, though."

"Sounds like my brother Dylan," I say with a snort.

"Damn kids." He laughs.

"Seriously." I roughen my voice and mime shaking a cane. "Stay the hell off my lawn!"

"That was a very convincing imitation."

"Hey, you can take the girl out of the giant, statewide retirement community, but..."

"I hear you." He leans back a little, looks at the stars. "So today was pretty amazing, wasn't it?"

"Yeah. I still can't believe I'm here."

"Me neither. Hey..." He glances back at me. "You got the other scholarship, right?"

"You got one too?"

"Yeah. We're the two lucky ones this summer, apparently." His shoulders fall a little, like he's just unclenched. "I'm glad you're the other one."

"How come?"

His sneaker scuffs over the concrete. "I just felt kind of weird yesterday when Quinn was talking about how the whole program is really just a fundraiser and how kids get in because their parents made big donations."

"Yeah. I felt a little strange about that too."

"I felt kind of, I don't know... like an imposter. There's no way my parents could afford to donate a bunch of money just so I could be here. But you're here, and you're on scholarship like me. You obviously deserve to be here, so I guess I do too."

"You think I deserve to be here?" My chest expands a little, pushing against the shaper.

"Are you kidding?" He starts laughing. "I heard you school that kid in the dig shelter."

"Oh God. I shouldn't have done that. That was awful."

"It was amazing. He deserved it. And you did make the first find in the riverbed."

I narrow my eyes. "Uh-huh. Thanks for bringing that up again. Having Quinn get it all on video really wasn't enough humiliation for one day."

"That was kind of...yeah." His smile now is one-sided, sheepish. "But it's still cool. I mean, you spotted a bone. Not a mammoth bone, okay, but you're still ahead of the rest of us."

I wish I could put that same spin on it in my head. To get him off the topic, I ask about his application essay.

"I wrote about the time a *T. rex* nursery got dug up a couple of miles west of my family's farm when I was a kid," he says. "These guys found part of a skull while they were clearing some land, and then a team of paleontologists showed up to excavate the rest. We even had a couple of national news teams in town. North Hogsville, Iowa, was almost famous for about a week," he goes on, chuckling, "and my second-grade class took a field trip to the dig site." He lights up as he describes watching one of the paleontologists work on a section of rib cage. "I already loved dinosaurs, but until that moment I kind of thought of them as fictional. Remember when I said that I used to watch *Jurassic Park* all the time? Dinosaurs were basically movie monsters to me. That day at the dig site was when I really understood that they were real, and that's when I knew I wanted to find more fossils when I grew up."

"I think every one of us paleo geeks has a *Jurassic Park* story."

"Yeah. You grow up watching that, and then you find out that in real life the best dinosaurs in *Jurassic Park* probably all had feathers." Chase's nostrils flare slightly. "I'm still in denial about that."

I laugh. "They keep finding evidence of feathers, though."

"Nope. My childhood rexy was not a giant parrot. Nope. Nuh-uh."

When my phone buzzes in my pocket, I'm tempted to ignore it. But then Chase's goes off as well, so we both check.

"It's from Mellie," he says. "She wants us back at the dorms."

"Same here." I hold up my phone with its identical notification on the screen. "We're late. Guess we'd better head back."

"Let's mosey."

"Mosey? Really?" I say as I stand. "Is that something people say in Iowa?"

He walks close beside me. "It's something awesome people say."

I laugh at his choice of words. I have plenty of practice

when it comes to being awesome, and I've never once said *mosey*. "Oh, yeah. Okay. Whatever."

When we reach the dorms, he holds the door for me. "Thanks," I murmur. He follows me inside, and for just a second, I feel his hand on my back, guiding me in ahead of him. His palm brushes my shirt, just the softest of pressures, and then it's gone—but it leaves tingling electricity in its wake. For a moment, my breath freezes in my throat. When I turn to face him by the stairwell, I hope the trembling glee in my chest isn't visible in my expression.

"I'm glad we got to talk some tonight," he says before I head upstairs.

"Me too." I'm blushing again.

"Cool." He grins. "Good night."

"See you tomorrow." I smile back and let my legs mechanically carry me toward my floor. Thoughts are still flinging themselves in my skull, but now they're moving too rapidly for me to process or even identify them individually. The resulting buzz is overwhelming but strangely pleasant.

Halfway upstairs, I pull out my phone and text Charli. *Um, so there's this guy...* Mellie is waiting for me in the doorway to our room. "Everything okay?"

"Yeah, fine." I wonder if my cheeks are still overly pink. "Just lost track of time talking to Chase." I walk past her and start getting ready for bed. Quinn is already asleep, and the room is dark except for Mellie's desk lamp.

Ten minutes later I'm under the covers, blowing up Charli's phone with texts detailing every moment of the past hour. I'm nowhere near sleep; I feel like I could stay awake for days. One brief touch from Chase and my blood has transformed into pure caffeine. *What does it mean?!* I demand of my best friend.

Her: *LOL—sounds like he likes u.*

Me: *Yeah, but! But!!!*

Her: *But what??*

Me: *But the other girl, the one I told u about!*

Her: *U said he left her behind to follow u. He's puppying!*

Me: *But why?!?!?*

Her: *SIGH. GIRL. Look, I gotta go to bed. Happy for u. Stop freaking out!*

Me: *I'll try. BUT BUT BUT*

Her: *He liiiiiikes u. Night!*

Me: *Night.*

Charli doesn't get it. It's not the thought that he likes me that's hard to believe. I mean, even Fred Parkmore apparently likes me *now*. Well, he likes Awesome Natalie, now that he's forgotten Fat Nat ever existed. But I saw the real him back then, the Fred that wasn't acting on infatuation. What proof do I have that the real Chase is any better?

But still…those forearms, though. That smile. Those dimples.

I press my pillow against my face to stifle my giggles.

Look of the Day:
   Black crops (vintage Ralph Lauren, tailored by me!)
   Black button-front embroidered heart blouse (Savage Swallow)
   Red headband (made by me!)
   Pinup lipstick (Maxwell Cosmetics)
   Black suede ballet flats (vintage Chanel)
   Leather cuff bracelet (Kathryn Arbor Designs)

Hope you enjoyed the dig site pics from yesterday, my fellow fossilistas! Now let me tell you what I learned on my first day: Cute dresses, vintage pumps, and active dig sites just do. Not. Mix. I figured that would be the case, but I thought I could get away with it during orientation. No such luck! I'd post a pic of the boots I had to borrow, but you kids would never trust my style sense again if I did.

I'm playing it safe and keeping it casual for training day at the Austin State University bone lab. Insert your oh-so-hilarious bone-prep innuendo in the comments…

6

The sign near the warehouse-size building reads DR. WARREN ROLAND LAB. I recognize the name from my paleontology books. Dr. Roland was another big deal in the field back in the day. He was in charge of the original dig that eventually became the Mammoth Site, and before that, he founded the paleo program at Austin State.

Dr. Lauren meets us near the front doors. "You're about to view millions of dollars' worth of lab equipment and fossils," she says. "Don't touch a thing unless you're told to."

Inside, we head down a nondescript hallway—industrial carpeting, fluorescent lighting, white walls hung with dig photos. The lab itself is a long, narrow room packed with mismatched tables and desks and cabinets on a scuffed tile floor. Powdery dust scatters over most of the room's surfaces, and the air is bitter with the smell of acetone. The two people working inside wear jeans and sneakers.

"New ducklings!" the woman—*average height, 125*

pounds—crows. Her black racerback tank shows off toned triceps, and she keeps her long blonde curls pulled back in a severe ponytail. Her comment earns a quack from the guy, who wears glasses and a shirt with an eight-bit mushroom graphic I recognize only because Ryan had an old Nintendo system in his room when I was little. The guy's older—not quite Dad's age, probably, but close. He has an impressive beard, and eyebrows to match. When it comes to dudes in the paleontology field and facial hair, I'm starting to notice a pattern.

"Guys, this is Dr. Glass." Dr. Lauren nods toward the man in the Nintendo shirt. "You'll be answering to him when you're on lab duty. Ted, you want to take it from here?" She heads off with her seniors in tow.

Dr. Glass spins in his chair and shoves his glasses farther up the bridge of his nose and stands, grinning awkwardly. He's not nearly as famous as Thomas Carver, but I've come across his name before while reading about digs from the 1990s. When he leads us around the room, pointing out various pieces of equipment, I notice that he walks with a slight limp.

We pause to observe the blonde woman as she works with dental tools, picking patches of dirt and plaster from what looks like a large pelvis bone and then wiping the resulting mess away with a soft brush. An exhaust fan hums over the table, keeping the debris under control.

"Are we going to learn to clean bones like that?" I ask.

Apparently my voice carries above the music in the woman's ear buds, because she bursts into bright laughter.

Dr. Glass shakes his head. "Bone prep requires more training than we can give you in a month. Amy's a grad student, and she just got cleared for advanced prep last semester. You'll mostly be labeling specimens and screen picking sediment from the Mammoth Site."

We file along to see what Dr. Glass has been working on. "Turtle skull," he says. "About sixty thousand years old. Here's how I've been prepping it." He sits down and demonstrates, picking at the skull's crevices with long, narrow spikes like black embroidery needles. I recognize them; I've read about this before.

Quinn beats me to it. "Are those porcupine quills?"

"Very good," Dr. Glass says. "Yes, that's exactly what they are. Quills are great tools for detail work. They're tough and flexible."

"I saw the technique last year when I was working with my dad in Utah," Quinn says.

Amy, the blonde, looks up and pulls out her ear buds. "Oh, hey. You're Tom Carver's daughter, aren't you?"

Quinn nods. "That's me."

"Awesome. We met a couple of years ago in South Dakota."

"The Carlton Park dig? I thought you looked familiar!"

"Yeah, I did an internship there. Your dad's letter of recommendation helped get me into my doctorate program. Tell him Amy Seeker says hey." A faint blush paints Amy's cheeks.

Dr. Glass clears his throat and crosses his arms, drumming the fingers of his right hand on his left bicep.

"I'll pass that on." Quinn edges closer to Amy. "So can I see what you're doing?"

"Yeah, sure. I'm working on this little chunk of matrix that's stuck to this *Dimetrodon* pelvis. It's being stubborn, and I don't want to damage what's underneath." She shifts so Quinn can get a better view. The rest of us crane our necks and try to see.

After we watch Amy's progress for a few minutes, Dr. Glass ushers us down a hall and into bone storage, an area the size of a small warehouse. Rows of industrial metal shelving hold hundreds of plaster jackets, lumpy whitish mounds of various sizes.

Quinn sneezes.

"Plaster dust," Dr. Glass says. "It'll get you every time."

Brendan puts up a hand. "Dr. Glass? Question."

"Go ahead."

"I mean, this is cool and all, but... If there are still bones to dig up out there," Brendan opens his arms wide, "what are you doing in here?"

"That's a good question. I used to dig a long time ago." Dr. Glass takes a breath. "Being out in the field isn't so easy for me anymore. Besides, I prefer it here in the lab. We get bones from dozens of digs here. Some of these specimens will remain in storage for years—we just don't have the time or manpower to prep them right away. We don't even know half of what's in here. We're pretty well organized these days, thanks to computerized records. Back when the lab was getting started, though, bones got stored here all willy-nilly. Tags fell off. A lot of older stuff isn't cataloged yet. It's a *mystery*!" His voice lilts upward and he waves his hands in front of his face like a hokey magician, his generous eyebrows waggling. "Welcome to the wild world of paleontology."

He takes us through the storage area, up and down each aisle, throwing out details about bone storage and transportation as we go. His enthusiasm becomes a constant stream of information. This is turning into a long day, and my eyelids grow increasingly heavy. From the blank stares and little nods of the other interns, I guess they're feeling the same way.

When Dr. Glass has us gather around a skull from the Mammoth Site so he can explain the lab's labeling process, I become aware of someone standing close behind me.

"I have no idea what he's even saying anymore." Chase keeps his voice low. When he follows his words with a brief chuckle, his breath tickles the side of my neck. Electricity zings all the way down to my toes.

"Glad I'm not the only one." I tilt my head so that my hair falls forward, hiding my blush. At least his proximity wakes me up. Suddenly I'm alert and a little giddy, and I can't help smiling.

Our next stop is another storage space, this one crammed with an army of locking metal cabinets. "This is how we store smaller specimens once they've been prepped. Everything in this one is from the Mammoth Site." Dr. Glass swings open a pair of outer doors. Inside is a set of drawers of various sizes. He pulls one out, revealing bits and pieces nestled in open-top boxes, and he lifts out a ridged chunk about the size of his fist. "Any guesses?"

I know those ridges; I saw the same raised pattern yesterday at the site.

"Mammoth tooth!" Quinn and I exclaim at the same time. She and I glance at each other.

Dr. Glass finds this funny. "Nothing like a little friendly fossil competition! Yes, ladies. You're both absolutely right. This is a mammoth molar—from a juvenile's second or third set, most likely." He demonstrates how specimens like the molar fragment are labeled, a task he assures us is slightly less mind numbing than screen picking.

On the way back to the main lab, we cut through another lab area. "Here's where we keep the really gross stuff," Dr. Glass says. "We don't only work with fossils here. Some of our subject matter is a lot...fresher." This room has different equipment—plexiglass tanks, a row of freezers, and several additional refrigerators. "A lot of it's roadkill, stuff like that. Some of us study decay and taphonomy, so this stuff comes in handy."

Thankfully, he limps past the freezers and refrigerators without offering us a peek. There's a handwritten notice taped to the last fridge: "ABSOLUTELY NO FOOD." Considering what goes on in this room, I'm a little horrified such a note is even necessary. Who'd want to put their lunch next to an armadillo road pizza?

"As fun as this part of the lab is," Dr. Glass says, "you won't be spending any time in here."

This relieves me greatly.

Back in the main lab, Dr. Glass marches us past Amy and her *Dimetrodon* pelvis and clears his throat. "Okay, guys, let's head outside."

Amy looks up, her expression suddenly sly and almost

feline. "Oh, is it that time already?" she asks, her tone curling ominously.

"Screen picking isn't that bad," Dr. Glass grumbles.

We head out a back door and through another hallway, and then we're outside again, standing on a wide concrete deck shaded from the sun by a sloped roof. Several troughs stand at waist height. Leaning against them are square wooden frames set with screens of varying gauges.

Dr. Glass instructs Chase to lug a bucket of gravel and dirt to the nearest trough. "Matrix from the Mammoth Site," he says, setting one of the screens in the trough. "All the dirt that's dug up at the site ends up here." A hose provides water to the trough. He turns it on and dumps some of the sediment onto the screen, letting the water flow gently over the frame and wash away the smaller bits of dirt and debris.

"Here's what you're left with after the screen rinse. We call this concentrate." He touches his finger to the screen, where only the larger chunks of bone and rock and gravel remain. "Come on, everyone, step up and give it a try."

Quinn maneuvers herself between Chase and me at the trough. I bite down on my envy as she "accidentally" splashes him. He sloshes his screen to splash her back, creating a wave that runs over the side of the trough and drenches my shoes before I can jump back.

"Sorry!" Chase shrugs sheepishly at me and grins at Quinn. "I'll get you back for that, you know."

"Doubt it." She smiles in a way that wrinkles her nose.

My earlier giddiness sinks as I watch the two of them.

Once everyone has had a chance at the wash station, Dr. Glass takes us back inside and sets us up at a workstation spotlighted by bright lamps. He hands each of us a small bag of concentrate from Florida and shows us how to separate bone fragments from ordinary pebbles.

Quinn sighs. I don't look over, but I can almost feel her eyes rolling.

"Your dad always hated screen picking too," Dr. Glass says, still poking through the pile. "It wasn't glamorous enough for him."

"You've worked with my dad?"

"It's a small field." Dr. Glass sets aside a sliver of bone. "We've all worked together at some point. Okay, guys, see what you can do with the stuff in your bags. Get it all sorted between now and Thursday."

I slip my feet out of my wet shoes and get to work. Screen picking is dull but soothing. Soon I fall into a rhythm, and I don't realize how much time has passed until Eli appears at our table.

"Six o'clock!" he says. "Come on, clean up. You're done for the day. Finish the rest of your picking on your own time and hand it in next time you're in the lab."

We are set free. My dark clothing has gone gray with plaster dust, another reminder that my wardrobe isn't quite syncing up with what I've come here to do.

7

"Cafeteria?" Mellie asks, and we're all in agreement.

As we eat, we chatter and gripe. Quinn is already sick of screen picking. Chase doesn't want to get stuck behind the site's reception desk too often or spend all his time giving tours.

Brendan just grins, leaning back in his chair and popping tater tots in his mouth.

"What?" Chase finally asks him.

"Nothing."

"Come on!"

"Nope." He glances at Mellie and Eli, who are too busy talking to each other to overhear. "Give me a little time and you'll see."

"Dude!"

Brendan just shrugs.

I am tired and calm, and content to steal the occasional

glance at Chase and his glorious arms. When he finishes his meal, he crosses them over his chest. "I just want to know when we get to start in the bone bed. All this gravel-picking and tour-giving is fucking dumb."

Brendan rolls his eyes. "You knew most of this would be grunt work, right?"

Mellie looks away from Eli. "It's not all grunt work. You guys learned about screen picking today."

Brendan raises his brows. "Digging through pebbles all day. Big fucking deal."

"Screen picking is amazing, though," Mellie says. "You never know what you might find. Vertebrae fragments, little bits of tusk, small animal bones... This one time I found all these rib splinters from a prehistoric camel!"

Quinn tilts her head. "And did you make them into earrings and post them on CraftyKarma?"

Mellie's eyes go Disney-princess big. "Oh, I wish! You don't get to keep the stuff you sort."

The fact that Mellie missed Quinn's sarcasm makes me feel a little bad, a little defensive. "That's too bad," I say. "I'm sure you could make some awesome stuff."

"Oh! Well, I did get to keep a lot of shark teeth from my training gravel. Made some fantastic earrings with them. I'll show you a few pairs later!"

"I bet my aunt would love those." I can totally picture Aunt Judy with little shark tooth studs in some of her cartilage piercings.

"Well, I'm with Chase," Quinn says. "You guys can keep your gravel and your camel rib splinters. I'm all about the bone bed." She softens her gaze just enough to turn the words "bone bed" into an innuendo.

If Chase picks up on her meaning, he doesn't show it. "Yeah! I can't wait to get digging."

"Me too," I say, just to pull some of his attention from Quinn. It works—he gives me a wide smile. A little of my giddiness from bone storage returns.

Later, we lounge in the common room with the television on as background noise. I'd like to get a blog post written, but Mellie is determined to get us all to do something together. "Let's play a game. How about two truths and a lie?"

Eli snorts and launches himself off the couch. "G'night," he says on his way downstairs.

"Come on," Mellie calls after him. "Be a buddy!"

The only response she gets is the bang of a dorm door slamming on the first floor.

"Fine then." Mellie pulls a little handmade notebook from her purse. "We'll have fun without him."

Brendan stands. "Actually, I'm pretty tired. I think I might turn in—"

"Winner gets candy!" Mellie says.

Brendan pauses. "What kind of candy?"

An orange package of peanut butter cups follows the notebook out of Mellie's purse.

"That changes everything." Brendan sits back down.

"Yay!" Mellie tears out a sheet of paper for each of us and hands them out, along with every pen or pencil she can fish out of her bag. "Write down two true statements about yourself, and one false one. Then we vote on which one's the lie. Whoever tricks the most people wins."

The peanut butter cups are as good as mine. Bullshitting is one of my specialties; I've been perfecting the art as a way of life for several years.

We take a few minutes to write out our statements. I think hard about mine. I have plenty of unbelievable secrets, secrets no one would ever guess to be true. But how much do I want to give away in front of everyone? In front of *Chase*?

Then we read our lists out loud.

Brendan starts. "I've seen Cher live in concert twice in the past year. I accidentally dropped a whole plate of crawfish on a customer at one of my family's restaurants. I get migraines if I go more than two days without coffee."

Chase: "The pig I raised for 4-H when I was nine won a blue ribbon at the county fair. When I was a kid, I fell off a tractor and had to get six stitches. For the past two years, I've played JV quarterback for the Kennedy High Raptors."

Quinn: "I once dug up a *Triceratops* femur with the help of Spangles, the dog I had as a kid. My childhood nickname was Quinnifer because I wished my parents had named me Jennifer instead. If I go on a roller coaster, I'll be sick for the rest of the day."

Mellie: "I enjoy guerrilla cross-stitch. I graduated at the top of my high school class. I wore Coke-bottle glasses until I was fourteen."

Me: "My favorite hangout back home is a combination coffee-shop-and-bar called Metro. I'm fluent in French."

Deep breath. "In middle school, some jerk filled my locker with Twinkies as a joke." I keep my gaze steady and do my best to keep a blush from blooming as I remember the avalanche of yellow sponge and crinkling plastic and white goo that tumbled out at me the day Fred Parkmore pulled that prank.

I could also have gone with the day Fred got Vic Baldwin, who I'd thought was at least sort of my friend, to challenge me to a contest to see who could fit the most french fries in their mouth. I got to fifty-three before Vic yanked out his phone and snapped a photo of me shoveling them in, my cheeks swollen like a hamster's, fries hanging from my gaping lips. The photo was online by the end of lunch.

No, the Twinkie story is more than enough.

Mellie's lie about her glasses gets her a few points, but Brendan trips up all four of us with his statement about Cher. "Nah, man, I was lying about the migraines. What can I say?" He shrugs. "My ma's a big Cher fan. I keep her company."

"Sure, bro. It's all for your mom." Chase smirks.

Chase's lie—the pig—gets him only one point from Mellie. I've stared at his forearms often enough to notice the small, raised scar near his elbow. I gamble that was where the stitches went, and I'm right.

Quinn gets three guesses for the roller coaster statement, but her lie is the one about Spangles and the *Triceratops* femur. "Like my dad would ever let a dog on one of his digs," she says. "He never even let me have a dog in the first place."

When it's my turn, everyone votes for my Twinkie story. Fred Parkmore isn't entirely useless after all.

"That's awful," Mellie says when I reveal the truth.

I shrug. "Yeah. Well. It was good fodder for this game, at least."

"You and Brendan tied." She holds up the peanut butter cups. "You guys want to split these?"

The Twinkie story has zapped my appetite. "Nah. Brendan can have them."

He grins. "You sure?"

"Yeah."

"Sweet." He devours them.

"So." Chase takes a deck of cards from his back pocket. "Anyone up for a little poker?"

Quinn scoots a little closer, tucks her hair behind her ear. "What are the stakes?"

"Losers finish the winner's screen picking," Chase says, shuffling the cards.

"You guys are supposed to do your own work," Mellie says, but we ignore her and crowd in. Aunt Judy taught me to play so I could whip my brothers' asses. I'd won Dylan's allowance and a portion of Ryan's paycheck more than once.

Chase deals. We bet by adding our bags of gravel to a pile on the coffee table—only in this case the losers are the ones who have to claim the pot at the end of each hand.

Quinn and Brendan drop out early. "I've got enough of this crap to sort," Brendan says, eyeing the gravel in front of him.

Chase is next, folding with two pair and leaving Mellie and me to eye each other over the last hand.

Mellie, of course, has no gravel to contribute. If I can beat her, that'll change. I'm holding a full house—a good hand, but not unbeatable. I try to read her expression while she watches me coolly.

I add the last of my gravel to the pile. Mellie doesn't flinch, doesn't budge.

I stare at her while I reach toward Chase. "Give me your gravel." He does, and I add it to the pile.

Mellie doesn't react.

"Yours too," I tell Brendan.

"You're fucking crazy," he says, eagerly shoving his gravel into the pot.

Still nothing from Mellie. My face is hot. I start to sweat.

"Quinn?" I say.

She adds her gravel.

I stare at Mellie.

Mellie stares at me.

There's nothing left to bet, so I call.

"I fold!" Mellie crows, putting down her cards and gathering the gravel. We stare after her as she scurries off down the hall with all the baggies.

I lay down my cards while Chase holds up Mellie's.

"Straight flush?" Brendan exclaims.

"She could've won the whole thing." Quinn frowns. "She could've walked away with no gravel at all."

"You know how she feels about screen picking," I say. "You heard her at dinner."

"But she didn't even want us to play for the gravel!"

"I guess she saw a chance and took it." I shrug.

Later, when I fall asleep, Mellie is still up, sorting gravel in a state of zen under the glow of the desk lamp.

The next morning, our bags of gravel sit in a row, perfectly sorted and neatly organized. It's like we were visited by screen-picking elves in the night.

Look of the Day:

Cuffed denim capris (Savage Swallow)
Sky-blue V-neck crossover shirt (Trendz, tailored by ME!)
Blue-and-white sneakers (Nike)
White hair scarf (Charmed Life)
Fashion Doll lipstick (Maxwell Cosmetics)
Leather cuff bracelet (Kathryn Arbor Designs)

I can hear your gasps of surprise from here, kids. Yes, your favorite fossilista is wearing sneakers. And not just any trendy tennies either. I'm actually wearing my Nikes. NIKES, you guys. They're cute, but you're right—this is weird and strange and just plain wrong.

My wardrobe for the month needs a little injection of common sense. My look is my life, but OMG, there's no way I can do most of this internship stuff in my usual attire. Do I even need to tell you the story of the black suede Chanel flats that went up against a tidal wave of water at the screen wash station? Talk about a cautionary tale. It was time for a little compromise.

Anyway, you can see from the pics that I'm still awesome. Yes, even in Nikes.

The blue V neck isn't my first choice for today. It's another compromise, one that comes about after I try on one of my new site shirts.

That experiment? Not good. I am encased in cotton-poly jersey. XXL, my ass. An average eight-year-old would have trouble squeezing into this shirt. Off it goes!

Even though I know the situation is hopeless, I drag a shaper tank over my torso and try again. Still no good. The circular Mammoth Site logo stretches oblong over my boobs, and my arms look like they're exploding out of the sleeves, Incredible Hulk–style. The blog entry writing itself in my head is nothing like the one I actually post—but my followers tune in to see what Awesome Natalie is wearing and digging up today, not to read my rants about the inescapable weirdness of women's clothing sizes. I hit a mental delete button.

I suppose I could take the shirts back to Dr. Lauren and ask to exchange them for boxy unisex XLs.

Or…I could get creative. I've performed surgery on ill-fitting T-shirts before. I spin around, studying my reflection in the bathroom mirror with the designer's eye Aunt Judy helped me cultivate. Lack of a sewing machine will make the task trickier, but still…Someone knocks, and I pull off the shirt in a panic, yanking on the blue V neck instead. "Come in!"

It's Quinn. Of course. "Hey, girl!" Just like yesterday, she sits down to pee while I start my makeup. "Last night was hilarious."

"The game?"

"Yeah. I mean, Brendan and Cher? Who knew?" she laughs.

"Looks like Mellie already finished our screen picking," I say, looking away while she wipes.

"Sweet. All that gravel was wrecking my nails."

I glance down at the chipped tips of my own turquoise manicure. "Same here. I need a touch-up."

"Hey, did you bring polish remover? Can I borrow it later?"

"Yeah. Sure."

"Cool, thanks." She punctuates her words with a flush. "Chase's lie was pretty funny too."

"The pig story?"

"Yeah. I can totally picture that being true, can't you?" She closes the shower curtain behind her. "Isn't he a cutie?"

"I guess." I pause in the middle of moisturizing my face. Something about discussing Chase with her has me on guard, and I feel my shoulders bunch up. I can't help thinking of how she's always sidling up beside him, giggling a little too much when he cracks a joke, flipping her hair and grinning and preening.

She peers around the edge of the curtain and gives me an almost elfin smile. "You like him, right?"

The back of my neck prickles. "He seems nice."

"Come on, you know what I mean. I've seen you looking at him. You can tell me. You *like* him."

"Yeah, I do," I say finally, and the admittance freezes my blood in iced-over veins. Why would she ask? Is she actually thinking about backing off?

"Knew it!" She disappears once more behind the curtain.

I finish my primer and foundation. I'm just about done with my eyeliner when she steps out in a towel, finger-combing her hair. We share the mirror. She swirls powder over her face while I trace the curve of my cupid's bow with lip liner.

When I head back to my room, I leave my bottle of polish remover on the bathroom counter for her.

At the site, Brendan and I are assigned to Cody to learn the tour, while Quinn and Chase train in the sandbox with Dr. Lauren. On each lap to and from the shelter, I see the two of them working side by side. Since we're all pretty well supervised, Eli and Mellie get to dig for a few hours. I'm not sure if I envy them or Quinn more.

When no guests show up for the last tour before lunch, Cody seizes the opportunity. He points at me. "Ready to give it a go?"

My stomach tightens, and I hold up my copy of the tour script. "Uh, no. This thing is five pages long. I don't know it yet."

"You can read it if you need to. Come on." He goes to the rear door and waits for me to start. "Anyway, it's not like it's a real tour. It's just Brendan and me."

"Brendan should really go first."

"No way." Brendan gives me an exaggerated bow. "Ladies first."

Sighing, I stand in front of the rear door, just as I've seen Cody do time after time. The tightness of my grip wrinkles the script a little, and I hope my audience of two can't see my hands trembling.

Be awesome. Fake it till you make it. **Be awesome**.

"Welcome to the Central Texas Mammoth Site!" I begin, tensing up and forcing brightness into my tone.

I try to hit all the points of the tour introduction, but it seems like I can't get through more than a sentence or two without Cody interrupting. "Don't forget to ask if anyone needs assistance," or "Remind them about bathroom breaks," or "Slow down and give latecomers time to catch up."

"*Okay.*" I'm bristling, and the weather when we leave the welcome center just irritates me more. There was a small amount of rain overnight, and the heat today is heavy and thick. I'm quickly learning that Texas can go from feeling like a desert to a swamp overnight. Under my shirt, my shaper is already growing damp.

Cody had walked backward down the hill, addressing the tour group the whole way, so I do the same. "Feel that

Texas heat?" I say between careful steps. At least I made the right choice in footwear today. "This area was hot even during the Pleistocene epoch, also known as the Ice Age."

Soon we're nearly to the dig shelter. "Now let's meet the mammoths!" I give the shelter door a grand push and stand aside to hold it open for my tiny tour.

Cody stays outside. "Food and drinks. Gum."

Good lord. Would it kill him to let me go thirty seconds without correction? "Give me a fucking break, Cody."

"Don't let Dr. Lauren hear you talking like that. Especially not where guests might overhear."

Brendan breaks out in a laugh. "Heavens," he says, clutching his chest. "My delicate tourist sensibilities have been ravished!"

I chuckle, but Cody glares at us. "How about we tone down the idiocy and get through this?"

"*Fine*." I shove open the door again. My overheated skin welcomes the rush of cool, dry air from inside.

Cody pulls the door shut. "Food. Drinks. Gum," he says from between clenched teeth.

All I want is air conditioning. "Oh my God. *Fine*. No food in the shelter! No drinks! No nothing! Spit it out! Don't even breathe on the bones, you guys! I'm serious!"

"If anyone finds a wad of gum on a mammoth tusk, I'll know who to blame." He finally lets us inside.

I go on through the spiel, and then I go off script and segue into some paleo facts. "Do you guys know how pale-ontologists tell fossils apart from rocks? There are several methods, but one of the weirder ones is the bone lick test.

It's exactly what it sounds like—you just give the specimen a lick. Bone is drier than rock, and that spongy texture makes it suck in moisture. If your tongue sticks, you've got a fossil!"

Cody quirks an eyebrow at me. I pause, waiting for yet another admonishment, but he stays quiet and gestures for me to go on.

I use the bones of the big bull mammoth to go into detail on how paleontologists determine things like age and cause of death. The more I go on, the less nervous I become. I don't have the script memorized yet, but I *know* this stuff. I know it, and I love talking about it. I go over the digging techniques and tools being used in the bone bed, adding in details I've learned from documentaries and books.

Finally I reach the end of the script. I look at Cody and hold my breath.

He gives me a slow nod. "That...that could have been a lot worse."

"Gee. Thanks."

"I like the extra stuff you added."

Was than an actual compliment? From him? I'm too stunned to speak.

Quinn and Chase are already in the break room, the legs of their jeans marked with dirt. "Mellie went out for Mickey D's," Chase says. "She's getting enough for everyone if you all want some too."

"Works for me," Cody says, flopping into a plastic chair.

Chase has a smudge of Texas clay on his cheek. Quinn brushes it away with her fingers. I get a bottle of water and sit across from Cody. When Mellie shows up with several large McDonald's bags, I claim a burger and a small bag of fries.

"You know your shit," Cody says suddenly.

Me? My gaze shoots from the McDonald's bags to him. "So do you."

"Yeah, but I've been doing this for a while. This is my second year working here."

"Do you go to Austin State?"

"Nah. Reese Ashley High School. I'll be a senior this fall. I'm definitely applying to Austin State, though."

"Oh, for the paleo program?"

"Yep." He runs a hand through his dark hair, pushing it out of his face. "Well, that and the graphic design program. You plan on applying there too?"

"Oh God, yes. It's at the top of my list."

"This internship will give you a boost when you do. Having a job here is good, but getting picked for the internship…" His shoulders hitch in a slight shrug.

Laughter erupts at the other end of the table. I look up in time to see Chase toss a fry at Quinn, who squeals and dives sideways to avoid it. When I glance back at Cody, he's observing the whole thing with a humorless smirk. "Just like last summer," he mutters.

"What is?"

His response is quick and short. "Nothing."

I drop my voice. "No, seriously. What?"

"Just…*that*." He points down the table. "Rich kids get this amazing chance and can't even fucking take it seriously."

"They're just goofing off." I can't believe I'm defending

Chase and Quinn's behavior, but I am. "We're on break, anyway. And we're sure as hell not all rich kids."

"They were carrying on in the sandbox too. You were too busy giving your tour to notice."

"Okay, but what do you care? You get to work here too."

"Yeah. Giving tours. Ringing up mammoth stickers in the gift shop. Hooray." His brows lower. "You guys get to dig. You work in the bone lab. You get to do all kinds of shit that we don't."

"You could have applied for an internship too."

"What makes you think I didn't? My parents aren't rich."

"Neither are mine. Jesus Christ, Cody. I'm only here because I got a scholarship."

He blinks. "Really?"

"Yeah. So lay off the rich-kid rants, okay?"

"I…Fine. Sorry." He tears into his burger, taking a huge bite and staring at the wall while he chews.

I scoot my chair closer to Chase and Quinn. "How's the digging going?"

"Ugh." Quinn's nose wrinkles. "Dr. Lauren is so bossy. I already know how to do this stuff. I've watched my dad do it for years."

"Dr. Lauren's really picky," Chase says, "but I like it so far. Well, except for how bad my back and shoulders are already aching. This afternoon is going to be killer."

"Then you're in luck," Dr. Lauren says. We all jump and turn to find her smirking in the doorway. "Chase and Quinn, you two are training for front desk and gift shop this afternoon." I'm excited until she adds, "Natalie and

Brendan, the weather's getting too iffy for sandbox training. Keep working on the tour with Cody."

Cody taps my shoulder as we go out to collect the next
tour group. "Sorry about earlier," he mutters. "Really."

I nod.

By later that afternoon, he's setting me loose with actual
site guests. He introduces me as a trainee and sticks close
and corrects me as needed.

He doesn't need to correct much.

Brendan has a harder time with the script. Finally, Cody
tells him to give it a few read-throughs in the lobby while
we're on break.

"Buy you a Coke?" Cody asks.

I nod.

In the employee lounge, he gets us each a soda from the
vending machine. I sit at the table. He's about to join me
when he pauses and cocks his head, his brows tilting into
a frown.

"What?" I ask.

He holds up a finger, gesturing for me to wait. He stands
in the break room door, his right hand cupped around his
ear. If I really listen, I can hear a voice—a female voice,
probably Dr. Lauren—but I can't hear what she's saying.

After a moment, he leaves the break room and creeps
down the hall toward Dr. Lauren's office. When he comes
back, he flops into a chair and runs a hand back over his
dark hair. "Thought that had gone away," he muttered.

I try again. "What?"

Footsteps in the hall. He looks over his shoulder, waits

for Dr. Lauren to pass by. She does so without even glancing at us. When she's out of earshot, he speaks, his tone hushed. His voice takes on a touch of gravel when he talks this softly. "Well, there's this lawsuit."

"The one the family of the guy who used to own this land filed?"

"You know about it?"

"Cody, I get email alerts about paleo news. Of course I know about it. They're claiming that every fossil found while their dad owned the land was technically stolen from him." When the first bones were found, Dr. Roland—the same paleontologist whose name is on the Austin State bone lab—supposedly leased the land on behalf of the university, with the agreement that he could keep whatever fossils he unearthed. "How could there not have been a contract?"

"There was, supposedly, but there's no record of it. Fossil recordkeeping was total shit back then."

"That's ridiculous. Dr. Roland wouldn't have stolen fossils."

"I agree. But if the site can't prove otherwise..."

"Do they really think the site would just hand over a bunch of fossils?"

"Yeah, and that's not all they want. They're claiming they lost a lot of potential income from not being able to sell the bones when they were first found, so they're asking for financial damages as well. And since the site is affiliated with the university, and the university has most of the bones, the lawsuit names both. The site could lose its affiliation. That's what Dr. Lauren was talking about on the phone just now."

I can't even fathom how stupid this is. My soda sits forgotten in a puddle of dripping condensation on the table.

"Look," Cody says, leaning closer. "I'm not supposed to know about most of this. I just...overhear stuff."

"Let me know if you overhear more," I say. "Maybe we can find a way to help."

"Don't worry about it. It's not like it's going to affect your internship or anything."

"My internship isn't my main concern." I sit up straighter and harden my gaze.

"No, I know." He glares back, his tone taking a defensive edge. "I didn't mean it like that."

"Give me your phone." I program my number into his contacts. "If you hear anything, text."

"Like this?" He types something onto his screen, and a text pops up on mine. It's nothing but a tiny emoji that glares at me with its tongue out.

"Yeah." I roll my eyes. "Like that."

Gave my first tour today, I text Charli from the common room after dinner. Mellie knits beside me on the couch, her plastic needles clicking together in a soothing rhythm. Her latest sock has grown considerably.

Charli: *Awesome! How'd it goooo?*

Me: *Not too bad! Dude training us is, uh, interesting.*

Her: *Ooooooh, really?*

Me: *Not in that way. UGH.*

Her: *Forget him then. What's up with the cutie?*

Keeping my face carefully blank, I glance across the room. Chase lounges on the other couch, his attention on the ball game on the large television. Quinn sits on the floor, just close enough to let her lean casually against his leg.

Me: *I have competition.*

Her: *The one guy's daughter?*

Me: *Yeah.*

Her: *Then get the hell in there and COMPETE, dork.*

Me: *How??*

Her: *Be your awesome self, of course.*

I can be awesome, or I can be myself. I can't be both.

Look of the Day:

Black-and-white polka dot sleeveless blouse (Savage Swallow)
Black crops (vintage Ralph Lauren, tailored by me!)
Blue-and-white Nikes (yes, again)
Turquoise headband (made by me!)
Pinup lipstick (Maxwell Cosmetics)

I think I'm finally getting the hang of dressing for this internship without looking like a total schlub, my fellow fossilistas. I guess maybe I shouldn't care so much. It's like…I'm here for science, you know? Not a fashion show. But if I can be all serious paleo business while still looking fab, why shouldn't I shoot for that? They say you can't have it all, but I'm coming pretty damn close.

(Yes, though—in response to some of the questions I've been getting lately, I'm pretty sure the Chanel flats are a lost cause. They got drenched. There's no rescuing vintage suede from that kind of abuse.)

It's back to the bone lab today. I think we'll be working with actual Mammoth Site gravel instead of the practice stuff from Florida. Cross your fingers for me—maybe I'll find something amazing amid the endless pebbles.

"If you guys get through all this sediment, there's plenty more in storage," Dr. Glass says.

I survey the series of full buckets lined up for us, and I doubt running out of sediment to wash will be a problem.

"Remember, mind the heat," Dr. Glass goes on. "Frequent water breaks, okay? We don't need anyone passing out. Mellie? Eli? Keep them on task." He leaves us to our gravel.

Underneath my clothes, my shaper constricts and grows sweaty-clammy. I consider sneaking to the bathroom, peeling it off, stuffing it into my purse—but then my real self would bulge and jiggle under the thin blouse, and that won't do. Next to me at the wash station, Quinn is cool and fresh in tan shorts and a ribbed blue tank top. I can't even imagine showing so much of myself, but right now it's almost tempting. She looks so comfortable.

I shove damp bangs off my face and twist my hair into a bun. At least my neck is cooler now. I concentrate on screen washing. And on Chase's forearms as he works across from us. It's very easy to watch his arms while pretending to stare at my screen.

We don't get through even one bucket before Chase puts his thumb over the opening of his hose, creating a spray that pummels Quinn and me. "Told you I'd get you back!"

Quinn shrieks, stepping back and shoving wet hair out of her face.

The front of my shirt is soaked, and my shoes are wet. Again. "What'd I do to you?"

"Collateral damage," he says, laughing. "You stood next to my target."

I aim my hose at Chase. The jet hits him in the chest, drenching his gray T-shirt, splashing down onto his cargo shorts.

He stands straight, arms out at his sides, and tilts his head back with a grin. "Oh God, don't stop," he says when I angle the hose away.

I know what he means—the water is a chilled break from the blanket of humid heat draped over the station—but his words go elsewhere in my mind. My heart pauses then revs up double-quick.

And I spray him again, this time in the face. He sputters and laughs, raising his hands to block the stream and then giving up and turning around to cool his back as well. He grabs his hose and aims it at me. I take shelter behind a post and get a blast of water in my face when I peer around to aim at him. He lets out a triumphant whoop that turns into a sputter when I douse him once more. Quinn joins in, then Brendan, while Mellie pleads with us and Eli yells.

When we finally let up, the other interns and I are laughing too hard to stand straight. I rest my hands on my knees, letting my hair drip onto the concrete.

Eli glares. "Quick fucking around!"

"Come on, guys." Mellie got caught in the cross-spray. She twists the hem of her shirt to wring out the water. "Let's shape up, okay?"

"Oh, man." Chase shakes his hair, flinging water like a wet dog. "Can we go dry off in the sun?"

"No," Eli barks, at the same time that Mellie says, "Just for a few minutes."

"You're too easy on them," Eli says.

"And you're too grouchy for life." Mellie sticks her tongue out at him and waves us away.

"I think they like each other," Quinn says as we step off the platform. I glance back. Eli is grousing at Mellie while Mellie just grins.

There's a field beyond the lab—nothing pretty, just a wide patch of grass that's yellowing in the heat, with a weedy wildflower here and there. Chase flops down on his back. He waves up at us, gleaming drops of water clinging to the fair hair on his gorgeous forearm. "Come on. We'll be dry in no time."

I take my hair down and lie back nearby. After just a few minutes, my front is damp instead of sopping. I'm also roasting, especially under my black pants, but the intensity is almost soothing. It lulls me into a heat stupor. I stretch like a lazy cat and roll over so my back can dry as well. My shaper is still clammy; there's no helping that. But at least the rest of me will be dry soon enough.

When I sit up, I see Quinn lying on her back with her head on Chase's stomach.

She lets out a lazy giggle. "Oh, Natalie. Your hair."

I'm still a little dazed from the sunlight. "What about it?"

"It's just really big. That's all."

"Everything's bigger in Texas," Brendan says.

I run my hands over my hair. Frizz. There goes all the effort I put into blow-drying and straightening it that morning.

If my hair's that much of a mess, what does my face look like? I dig for a comeback, but I have nothing. "I'm going to go grab a water," I mutter, heading back toward the lab. Time for damage control.

My fingers find the elastic on my wrist and *snapsnapsnap*.

Eli has disappeared from the platform. Mellie is still patiently hosing away. "Dry yet?" she asks as I pass by.

"Pretty much."

"Good. Back to work then."

I don't stop. "Need a water first."

"Grab me one too? I'm really parched."

"Sure."

Bottled water is kept in a mini fridge in Dr. Glass's office, which is also where I stash my purse on lab days. I skip the fridge, grab the purse, and head to the bathroom, where I inspect my face in the greenish glow of the fluorescent light over the mirror.

Okay. Whew. It's not as bad as I thought. And I have my arsenal. A cleanser wipe takes care of the mascara smears and I carefully reapply everything from foundation on up.

My hair is hopeless. All I can do is wrap it into a bun again.

By the time I make it back to the wash station, Mellie is already glugging back a bottle of water. "You took too long," she says, her tone short. "Got it myself."

In the afternoon, Dr. Glass sets us up at a table near the storage cabinets with Micron pens and small terra-cotta flowerpots, which he explains are porous like fossils. "You need plenty of practice before you can label specimens," he says. "Watch your handwriting. Keep it small. Keep it neat. Keep it legible." He hands out copies of a page from a paleontology textbook, with one long paragraph circled. "Try to fit the entire paragraph on one pot. That'll keep you busy for a while." He goes to work sorting labeled specimens into drawers, with the senior interns assisting.

The text is dry and dull, something about carbon dating that's too advanced for me to grasp. My mind wanders, and I fumble my pen. It spins from my fingers like a tiny baton and bounces off my shirt, leaving a thin black slash on one white polka dot. I'll have to text Aunt Judy for stain removal tips.

"Damn it," Chase says after a few minutes. He scribbles on his pot then stands to get another.

Quinn's cell phone rings, and she leaves to answer in private. She comes back with a smile on her face that doesn't quite reach her eyes.

"So guys," she says, her tone bright and strained. "Guess what? My dad wants to film some segments for his show here. He'll be at the site tomorrow."

"Wait, *what*?" Chase stares at her. Brendan sits up straighter. Even Eli is impressed enough to raise a brow at the news.

"Holy…I mean…" My thoughts are all crossed wires. "Do we get to meet him?"

"Of course," Quinn says. "He says he wants to feature the internship on an episode."

I shriek and put down my pen before I can drop it again in excitement.

"How long will he be here?" Mellie is so exhilarated she's almost wheezing.

"I don't know yet," Quinn says. "Everything's still being finalized."

Dr. Glass pauses in the middle of opening a drawer. His brows give an almost imperceptible twitch. He says nothing. I wonder about his reaction, but then excitement and endless chatter about our favorite *Carved in Bone* episodes take over the table. We're all happily freaking out about meeting the most famous paleontologist in the world.

Look of the Day:
   Cuffed denim capris (Savage Swallow)
   White linen button-down (Ronnie Hayes, tailored by me!)
   Red tank top (Old Navy)
   Black ballet flats (Steve Madden—borrowed from Mellie)
   Pinup lipstick (Maxwell Cosmetics)
   Red headband (made by ME!)
   Leather cuff bracelet (Kathryn Arbor Designs)

Guys…I just…
I can barely even type right now. You don't know. You don't. You just don't.

   If all goes according to schedule, today I will meet my idol. You know who I'm talking about. Dr. Thomas F. Carver is visiting the site today. I'm not even kidding—I'm about to freak the hell out. BRB, shaking and crying. Okay, not really, but I'm pretty damn close.

   How am I even supposed to handle today? Today is EVERYTHING.

10

When Eli's SUV pulls into the site's parking lot, my lungs forget how to inflate. I force air into them, inhaling until my chest strains against the shaper under my shirts. I'm quivering. *Get ahold of yourself*, I think. *Be calm. Be professional. Be awesome.* I know I look great. I got up an hour early just so I'd have time to get my hair and makeup absolutely perfect. My lips are waxy with a coat of Pinup, and my eyeliner is so precisely winged that even Aunt Judy would be jealous. Even so, my right hand finds the red polka-dot elastic on my left wrist and snaps it until the sting distracts me.

Two cameramen and a boom mic operator stand outside the welcome center, along with several other people I don't recognize—the show's producers, I assume. One cameraman trains his rig on us as we park. The other focuses on a man in jeans, an outdoorsy green shirt, and a well-worn baseball cap.

It's him. Thomas Fucking Carver. Right there, less than a hundred yards away. He's chatting on camera with Dr. Gallagher and Dr. Lauren.

I don't even notice myself getting out of the SUV with everyone else. My feet propel me forward, keeping up with the group, and I can't stop, can't process, can't even think.

Dr. Lauren lines us up and introduces us.

He's right in front of me. He's reaching out his hand and shaking mine. I hope he doesn't see how I'm trembling. Beneath my tank top, the shaper constricts. I'm one of those Victorian women who went around in tightly laced corsets and decorated their homes with fainting couches all over the place, just in case.

"Great to meet you, Natalie," Dr. Carver says, his voice clear as he enunciates for the boom mic. It's hovering over our heads, a hawk on the hunt.

I open my mouth. It's too dry—I can't possibly talk. I can't even form thoughts. Somehow, three words tumble out anyway, no matter how I scramble to catch and contain them. "Thomas. Fucking. Carver."

Dr. Carver's eyes widen.

"Cut!" one of the producers yells.

Someone behind me stifles a snorting giggle, and I know without turning around that it's Quinn.

For the next fifteen minutes, we stand and listen in the welcome center as the producers brief us on the basics of filming—release forms, proper on camera conduct (I earn a pointed glance from one producer at this point), some dos and don'ts of interacting with Dr. Carver. Cody and

Martina try to look professional behind the reception counter, but I catch Cody's eyes darting as he repeatedly glances at Dr. Carver. Although we're in air conditioning now, my torso remains tautly caged, making the room feel ten degrees warmer than it really is. I fan myself with a site map.

"Just because we have special guests, don't think that excuses any of you from your usual responsibilities," Dr. Lauren says. "I want all four of you in the sandbox this morning."

The sandbox. My first day of actual, official dig training, and I have to do it around Dr. Carver. My stomach flips cartwheels, flopping back and forth between euphoria and terror.

The sandbox lies under a striped awning outside the welcome center. It's a large, wood-framed rectangle, full of hard-packed dirt similar to the soil inside the shelter, and it's almost three feet deep. Somewhere in all that dirt, fossil replicas wait to be dug up by interns and trainees (and tourists who've paid an extra fee).

Dr. Lauren assigns us each a square meter. "Chase and Quinn, you guys know how this works, so you go ahead and get started. Natalie and Brendan, each of you grab a bucket of tools and I'll show you how to dig."

I stand on the wooden border and survey the sandbox. The dirt is divided by a string grid that neatly marks off each square meter. The meter Dr. Lauren gave me is near the welcome center's rear door. Any time it opens, I get a quick burst of air conditioning. It might be just enough to keep my face from melting off. Even in the shade, the air is close and sweltering. I set out my tools—trowel, brush, dustpan.

"Get comfortable," Dr. Lauren says. "Don't be afraid of the dirt. It's going to get on you either way."

I sink to my knees, the dirt warm and rough against my bare shins. Mindful of the cameras, I keep my back straight to avoid the extra rolls that even my shaper can't hide.

Brendan's square is next to mine. Dr. Lauren shows us how to scrape at the dirt, using the trowel to remove millimeters at a time. "All the dirt and gravel you remove goes in your bucket," she says, using the dustpan and brush to gather the loose soil. "Watch for anything that might be bone. If you think you've found something, ask me and I'll show you how to proceed." She leaves us to it and walks off toward Quinn.

The work isn't glamorous, but I'm excited anyway. Once I master this, I get to move on to the shelter. To *real* digging. I concentrate so hard that I nearly forget about Dr. Carver until I hear him speaking from the walkway. He's talking to the cameras, offering commentary on dig training and telling stories about his earliest digs. It's the same voice I've heard on over a hundred podcast episodes, only now it's right behind me.

I'm digging at the Central Texas Mammoth Site while Thomas Fucking Carver talks paleontology nearby. If heaven exists, I'm pretty sure this is it.

Then Brendan pauses mid-scrape and leans over, peering at the dirt.

"Find something?" I arch my back, trying to see.

"Um. Don't know. Maybe?" He points at a speck of off-white in the chocolate-brown dirt.

Dr. Lauren returns and bends over, running her finger over the dirt. The white spot breaks up into nothing. "Just a discoloration in the soil," she says. "Good eye, though. The more you do this, the easier it'll get to tell the difference."

At least it wasn't me and a pork chop this time.

Scrape, brush, scrape, brush. Sweat and heat make the shaper hug me closer. It's getting harder to fill my lungs, and my vision shimmers around the edges. My head starts to float. I can't keep this up.

"Dr. Lauren? Water break?" She nods and waves me inside. I head for the restroom, where I undress and peel the shaper from my overheated skin. Instant bliss!

Not too bad, I think at my reflection after I'm dressed again—minus the shaper, which I stow in a supply closet to pick up later. Without it, my hourglass figure has a few extra hours. I'll have to suck in and keep my posture as perfect as possible to make up for it.

In the lobby, Cody stands near the rear door, watching through the glass. "How's it going?"

"It's amazing."

"I see the incredible Dr. Carver has you enthralled."

I frown.

He points at my face. "You're blushing."

"It's hot out there, okay?"

"Whatever you say." He smirks and turns back to watch the dig training.

"Hey, your next tour doesn't start for half an hour, right?"

"About that, yeah. Why?"

"Come out and dig with us a little."

He gives me a short laugh. "Yeah, Dr. Lauren would love that."

"I'm sure she wouldn't mind. Want me to ask?"

He steps back from the door and waves away the question. "I appreciate the thought, but I'm not one of you. I'd better stick to the job they pay me to do."

I want to press the matter, but he's already ambling away toward a shelf in the gift shop that needs straightening.

Getting rid of the shaper makes a huge difference in the sandbox. I can actually feel the hint of a breeze through my thin shirts, and I can breathe while I hunch over my square meter of dirt.

A few minutes later, I uncover a speck of my own. Another discoloration? I give it a gentle poke with my fingertip, and it stays intact. A pebble? A bit of debris?

I take a deep breath and call Dr. Lauren over.

She kneels beside me and inspects the speck, nudging it ever so softly with the bristles of my brush. "This could be something," she says. "Very good, Natalie."

I beam.

"Now you want to start a pedestal," she explains. "Keep digging very gently. Uncover a bit more and start leaving a small buffer of soil around the speck. You'll be able to tell soon enough if you're dealing with something large or small. If it's small, you'll eventually be able to bag and label it for the lab. If it's large, it may need a jacket. Keep going and see what you find."

I'm aware of movement around me. The cameramen and producers are closing in to watch my progress. I don't dare look up, but I catch a glimpse of a familiar green shirt to my right. Dr. Carver.

My throat closes. My hands clench and freeze, binding my trowel in a sweaty death grip. The tiny white spot stares at me—a trial, a challenge.

I force myself to unfreeze, and I move my trowel toward the spot. I'm shaking. If I can't be precise, I risk damaging the specimen. I pull back a little. Breathe. Go in again.

The trowel falls from my clammy fingers. It thumps to the dirt, inches from the speck.

"Shit!" I whisper. I clamp my jaw shut and wonder if the boom mic picked that up.

"Nice and easy," a rough voice says softly as I pick up the trowel. I look up—and Dr. Carver gives me an encouraging nod. He smiles, and a hundred tiny crinkles edge his eyes.

Oh my God, did that just happen?

This time I'm calmer, less shaky. I remove dirt, just a tiny bit at a time, from around the spot, scraping and brushing with intense care. Soon I can tell that the spot is the tip of something larger. I do my best to pedestal as Dr. Lauren instructed, but this thing is so big that no matter how deep I go, it just goes deeper. Soon my bucket is full of matrix, and I'm still uncovering more bone. It's long, thin, cylindrical, curved.

What I originally uncovered was the tip of a tusk... well, a replica of a tusk. But still.

Dr. Carver crouches beside me, offering advice. I know this is all for the cameras, but I hardly realize they're rolling anymore. It's just me and Dr. Carver and a gigantic tusk.

When Cody comes by with a tour group, he stops for a minute so the guests can observe. Suddenly I have an even bigger audience. I peek up and toss him a wide grin. He gives me a thumbs-up.

Several meters away, Quinn watches me. She's not even digging; her tools are laid out beside her bucket. She sits with crossed legs and stares as her father helps me learn to dig. Her face is unreadable.

Dr. Carver pulls out his phone and has one of his producers take a photo of him posing with me and the partially visible tusk. "For my website," he says. "Nice bracelet, by the way."

The sudden redness in my cheeks isn't from the heat.

11

That evening, Quinn's on her laptop in our dorm room. "Hey," she says. "Your pic's on my dad's site."

"Let me see!" I sit next to her and lean in toward the screen. I'm still slightly dazed from the events of the day. The butterflies that had finally gone to sleep in my stomach don't need much encouragement to wake up and flutter again.

There I am in his latest blog entry, guiding my trowel along the edge of the pedestal while Dr. Carver points at the exposed tusk tip. Our faces are in profile—he's talking to me. My face is blotchy, I'm sweating, and my arm looks enormous.

But it's a photo of me working with Thomas Fucking Carver.

"Holy shit, I need to reblog that." I want to text the link to Charli and Aunt Judy and Mom and everyone I know,

but then I remember the blankness on Quinn's face earlier, when Dr. Carver was watching me dig. She practiced
digging until lunchtime and never found a thing, and then
her dad's producers decided they had enough footage for
the day, and they packed it in. "Hey, Quinn? My nails are
a mess from digging, so I'm going to redo them. Want me
to do yours too?"

Her brows shoot up so fast they nearly launch off her
face. "Sure. Cool."

From the bathroom, I fetch my remover, a few cotton
balls, and the little bag of polishes I brought with me.
"Choose," I say, handing her the bag and then going to
work on my nails with the remover.

"You have some cute colors," she says, lining them up on
the desk near Mellie's light bulbs.

"Thanks. My favorites are the textured ones, but I'm
afraid they'd get really nasty while I'm digging."

"Ew, yeah." She chooses a translucent blue jelly full of
tiny black-and-white polka dots.

"Nice. Love that one." For myself, I choose a rosy pink
with gold shimmer. I go back and forth between my nails
and hers. File, base coat, two coats of polish, quick-dry
topcoat.

At first, she's quiet while I concentrate on neat application. Then, as I swipe a second coat of blue jelly onto her
pinky nail, she says, "Dad says he'll be back to film at the
lab sometime next week."

My heart and stomach start flip-flopping again. It's like
they've taken up ballroom dancing in my torso. I try not to
let it show. "Oh. Cool."

She holds her phone up for me to see. The screen displays a text from Dr. Carver. *The one with the leather bracelet is Natalie, right? Might do a screen picking scene with her.*

Quinn scrolls down a little so I can see his next message as well. *And for Christ's sake, Q, start trying harder in the sandbox.*

I look from the phone to her.

When her eyes meet mine, her gaze hardens. "I just thought you should see that."

"I'm...sorry. I don't know what to say. Maybe he was just trying to encourage you?"

"It's just that I know he's your idol and everything," she says, "but he can kind of be a jerk. That's not something you get a sense of from interviews or his podcast. I figured you should know."

"I'm sorry," I say again.

She shrugs. "I'm used to it."

"All done," I say, screwing the cap on the topcoat. "They'll be mostly dry in a minute or two."

"Thanks." She flaps her hands a few times to help the drying along, and she smiles. "Hey, if you want to borrow my laptop to update your blog, go ahead. Easier than using your phone."

"Oh...Yeah, it would be. Thank you."

"Sure. Just leave it on my bed when you're done. I'm going to head out to the common room."

Half an hour later, I shut the laptop lid. I go to thank Quinn again and find her on one of the common room couches with Chase, practically in his lap while they watch a sitcom. She has her phone in one hand, and she stretches out her other arm and strokes the shoulder of his T-shirt with the fingernails I painted for her. He grins and casually slings his arm around her.

My throat constricts, and I go back to the dorm room.

His arm settled so easily around her...I don't want to keep thinking about that. I text Charli the photo of me and Dr. Carver. *LOOK LOOK LOOK LOOK LOOK!!!!!*

Her: *Wait, is that the podcast dude?*

Me: *Um, YEAH. Thomas Fucking Carver.*

Her: *WTF HOW???*

I fill her in, and she fusses and squeals on my behalf, although I know she doesn't quite understand the excitement of meeting yet another paleontologist. She changes the subject: *Soooo what's going on w/ the cutie??*

I remember Chase's arm around Quinn's shoulders. *Nothing's going on with him. Nothing.*

Her: *Wait, what happened?*

Me: *What happened is that I can't compete w/ Carver's daughter.*

Her: *She's still after ur cutie?*

Me: *She keeps flinging herself at him.*

Her: *So fight back. U gotta make some moves here too. Show him how goddamn awesome u are, idiot.*

But that's not me. That's the armor I wear. I try explaining this, but she tells me to stop whining, and I clench my jaw as my temper flares.

Me: *Shut the fuck up. U don't get it.*

Her: *I guess I don't. I can't deal w/ u when ur like this. Stop being so fucking rough on yourself.*

Me: *Whatever.*

Her: *Just GO FIGHT FOR HIM!!! JESUS.*

I toss my phone facedown on the bed.

Fight for him.

This isn't about someone like Fred Parkmore. This is someone I actually like. What if I do go out there? What if I go out and fight and Chase chooses Quinn?

Or what if he doesn't?

I've never come at a situation from this angle before. It's easier when I'm keeping myself shielded. When I'm not interested, there's no risk.

I close my eyes. Breathe. Check my face and hair in the bathroom mirror. I'll just ask if he wants to take a walk around campus. I'll tell him I want to talk to him about... well, about something. Doesn't matter what. He'll come with me. He'll choose me.

I will be awesome... even if inside I'm all acid and brittle nerves.

I just need a final shot of confidence. I open Quinn's laptop to look at her dad's blog again. I reread the entry, stare at the photo of him and me. I glance at the comments. There are over a hundred of them already, but the boldface used on number sixty-seven catches my eye.

Who's the fat ass?

Ice pierces my chest. It's just a blog comment. A stupid, anonymous comment. Something some jealous asshat said on the internet, no different from the troll comments I get on *Fossilista*. It means nothing. It's just one tiny pinprick... but it pierces my armor.

When I stay holed up in the dorm room instead of joining the group in the common room, Mellie notices. "Everything okay?" she asks, poking her head in.

I'm hunched over my sketchbook, my site shirts puddled beside me on the bed with my travel sewing kit. "Yeah. Just doing a little DIY."

"Oh, can I see?"

She's already looming over me, so I lean sideways to give her a better view. "Cute! I especially like this one." She points to one of my sketches, a scoop neck design with cute contrast stripes running vertically down the sides.

"Me too. But I'd need more jersey for the side panels, and I'm about a thousand miles away from my fabric stash."

"Hmm. Hold on." Mellie digs through a drawer and pulls out a lighter-blue T-shirt. "Could you use this?" When I won't reach out, she tosses it beside me on the bed. "Take it. Consider it my contribution to the world of fashion."

"Are you sure?"

Already on her way out, she waves. "Can't wait to see the final product!"

I spread a site shirt out on the bed and take some measurements, calculating where and how much to cut. I do the same with Mellie's, sacrificing it for contrasting side panels to make the site shirt larger and bolder. Sewing the panels in by hand takes forever, but the end result is a shirt that skims my curves without being too boxy or too tight. I cut away the original collar to leave a raw-edged scoop neck.

The second shirt's redesign is simpler. I design it to be worn over a tank top, with vents cut into the sides and woven together in a peek-a-boo pattern that loosens the fit. Matching vents on the sleeves let me resize those as well.

Then I try on and tinker, over and over. Finally, I'm satisfied with both.

I've forged new armor.

Look of the Day:
> Cuffed jeans (Savage Sparrow)
> Central Texas Mammoth Site T-shirt (altered by me!)
> Blue-and-white Nikes
> Black-and-white polka-dot headband (made by me!)
> Pinup lipstick (Maxwell Cosmetics)

Something big is going down, my vintage velociraptors. There's a surprise being cooked up for us interns today, and all we've been told is that we should wear something we won't mind getting messy. That leaves out the dress I was planning to wear. Your favorite fossilista is playing it casual. Can't skip that Pinup, though!

I'll post again later to spill the surprise! All I know is that the big reveal doesn't involve Dr. Carver—he's already on his way back to South America. Still can't believe I actually got to train with him on Friday!! And you saw that link I posted last night, right? I've been blogging about him for years, but I never thought I'd see him blog about me. I don't know how many more surprises I can even handle this week…

12.

The perky voice I use for my *Fossilista* posts is getting harder to conjure. How am I supposed to crow about Dr. Carver's blog when thinking about it just reminds me of that stupid *fat ass* comment? There's a rant building in my head, a bold statement about how the size of my ass has nothing to do with what I can learn working side by side with someone like Dr. Carver...

But that's not the kind of thing I post. My blog is all cute clothes and paleo-squeals. Those are the topics my followers tune in for, and that's what I have to give them. The few times I've made more serious posts, I've gotten more trolls than usual and comments telling me to stick to fashion, and I always lose at least a dozen subscribers. If my readership knew what I really think sometimes, or how I really feel... That'd be about as brilliant as reminding Fred Parkmore that I'm really Fat Nat.

My reflection looks a hell of a lot cuter than I feel. I study myself, turning this way and that, cringing at the bulge of back fat under the altered T-shirt that had seemed to fit so perfectly just last night. Maybe just a light shaper...I hurry to my suitcase to get one.

Five minutes later, Quinn and I step into the dorm hallway at the same time.

"Your shirt," she says.

"Oh." I glance down. "Yeah. Does it look okay?"

"I like it." She speaks haltingly, as if she's surprised. "You did that yourself?"

"Yeah."

"Nice. Maybe, I don't know...you could show me how to do that to one of mine. Or something."

"I could do that. Sure."

We all meet in the parking lot and pile into Eli's car. Chase and Mellie are raving over my appearance in Dr. Carver's blog. Brendan brings up the blog on his phone so we can all have another look. I smile and try to seem enthusiastic, but I don't want to see the post again. I know that stupid comment is there, and I really don't want anyone else noticing it.

The exit Eli takes has a sign pointing the way to the West Park Zoo. Dr. Lauren is waiting for us in the empty parking lot. "Morning, interns! Since we can't introduce you to actual living mammoths, we've arranged some time with their cousins."

"Wait, you mean elephants?" Brendan says.

Dr. Lauren's nod melts away a layer of the gloom in my head. I'm perking up whether I want to or not. We all glance at each other, and I see the same excitement mirrored in everyone else—except Quinn, whose smile is thin and unsure.

I fall into step beside her. "You okay?"

"I'm fine," she says through her teeth, the clenched smile staying in place.

We follow Dr. Lauren past the admission windows to a side entrance, where a small woman (*122*, the digital display in my brain guesses) in a tan uniform unlocks the door and waves us in. Dr. Lauren introduces her as Dr. Paver, the head zookeeper.

Dr. Paver's smile is hospitable, but her tone when she welcomes us is direct and no-nonsense, and her stride is quick and sharp. We nearly have to jog to keep up with her as she leads us along the path toward the elephant enclosure.

"Austin State's zoology department is affiliated with our zoo, so if any of you decide you want to work with living animals instead of long-dead ones, you might just end up spending a lot of time mucking out the enclosures here." She throws a quick smirk at Dr. Lauren. "One benefit of paleontology, right? Even the shit's long since turned to stone."

There's an earthy heaviness in the morning air that proves Dr. Paver's point. "I suddenly feel like I'm home again," Chase mumbles under his breath. "Smells like a barn."

"We're more of a sanctuary than a zoo," Dr. Paver goes on. "Our animals are all rescues. They've been through a lot, so we do whatever it takes to accommodate them and keep them happy."

The elephant enclosure—two acres of dusty ground
with scrubby vegetation and a watering hole—is empty.
She takes us past it, into a large structure. "I'm going to
need all of you to listen to me and do exactly what I say
while we're in the barn. Our elephants are good girls, but
they can still hurt you if they're in a mood and you get too
close—and believe me, if that happens, you're not getting
any sympathy from me."

"Not gonna be a problem," Quinn mutters.

We head single file down a narrow hall permeated by
a concentrated version of the same earthy smell. I end up
between Quinn and Chase. We turn a corner, and in front
of us are two enormous barred stalls. Inside each is a full-
grown elephant. They swing their trunks casually and blink
their honey-colored eyes, watching us with interest.

"These are our girls," Dr. Paver says, smiling. "This one
is Georgia, and that's Olivia farther down."

At the sound of her name, Olivia reaches her trunk
through the bars like she's waving at us.

Dr. Paver has us stand against the wall opposite the
stalls, keeping us out of reach of trunks and tusks. I've seen
elephants before, of course, but never so close. I can see
the tough texture of Georgia's whorled gray skin, the thick
lashes around her amber eyes. She moves slowly, calmly,
shifting her weight with surprising grace as she steps closer
to the bars.

"She's gorgeous," I say softly, staring up at the elephant
while she stares right back.

Beside me, Quinn presses her back against the wall.

"They're really big. Bigger than I remember."

"You've been up close to them before?"

"Not quite this close," Quinn says. "But close enough. I was in Kenya once, visiting my dad on a dig—" She stops short as Georgia's trunk reaches for us.

"She can't reach us back here," I say. "What happened in Kenya?"

"You don't remember the podcast he did about taking his family on safari? The way he laughed about his daughter getting spooked when an elephant charged the Jeep?"

I do remember, now that she's mentioned it.

At the other end of the barn, Olivia trumpets. "We're getting to you!" Dr. Paver calls down. Olivia answers by sticking out her tongue and blowing a raspberry through the bars. We all chuckle.

"Yeah," Dr. Paver says, "it's hilarious the first time you hear it. Not so funny the thousandth time."

Apparently inspired by the laughter, Olivia makes the noise again.

Dr. Paver ignores her and demonstrates the elephants' morning routine. She has Georgia hook one enormous foot over a horizontal bar on the stall door. Her sole is nearly as big around as a hubcap. "Pedicure time," Dr. Paver says. "Who wants to help?"

"Quinn?" Dr. Lauren says.

I see Quinn's eyes widen, and I step forward to let her off the hook. "I'll do it."

Dr. Paver has me rinse the elephant's foot with a hose and then waves me over for a closer look. I stroke my hand over Georgia's sole. The skin is thick, not rough, but not terribly smooth either. It has a grain like heavy leather. My fingers trace the ridges of her broad toenails.

I'm petting an elephant. She's enormous and amazing, and I'm touching her foot, and she's letting me.

Georgia's trunk snakes through the bars toward me. Instantly, Dr. Paver bangs on a bar and barks a firm "*No*" while waving me back with her other hand.

Georgia huffs, as if to say, "You see what I put up with here?" She flaps her ears, raises her trunk, and blows a heavy puff of air at Chase and me. The hot and musky air forces Chase's hair back and ruffles my bangs.

We laugh. "That was awesome," Chase says.

Dr. Paver is less impressed. "Just be glad it was a dry blow," she tells us before turning back to Georgia. "If that's how you're going to be, we'll just move on to your neighbor."

We head to the other end of the barn, where Olivia starts up with the raspberry noises again, her bright eyes watching keenly for our reaction. When several of us laugh, she shakes her head with delight and trumpets again. The noise echoes sharply in the barn. Quinn leaps sideways around me and grabs Chase's arm.

"Okay, come up two at a time," Dr. Paver tells us. She points to Chase and Quinn. "You first."

Quinn steps forward, lets go of Chase, and darts to the wall. "Someone else can go."

I step up beside Chase. At Dr. Paver's command, the elephant stretches out her trunk, keeping it low and still so we can touch its cobbled skin. Wiry hairs tickle my palms.

Dr. Paver hands us each a pellet. "Want to give her a treat?"

Holding my breath, I offer up the pellet on my flattened palm. Olivia snuffles along my hand. The tip of her trunk is damp and cold as she searches. When she finds the treat, she neatly suctions it, pops it into her mouth, and shakes her ears. Butterfly wings take flight in my stomach.

Then she moves on to Chase, taking his pellet as well.

This day has become perfect. I'm standing next to my crush as we feed an elephant. A fucking *elephant*.

Chase grabs my shoulder. "Did you feel that?" he asks. "It was so cold! I didn't think the end of her trunk would be cold like that. And the way she sucked up the treat! Did you feel that? It tickled!"

Giddy, I grin as we get back in line. "Yes! She just grabbed it! It was amazing!"

He laughs. "And the way she was looking at us! I mean, did you see—"

"Yes!" There's something unreal and magical about right now. It keeps me from forming complex sentences or thinking about anything other than the cool tickle of Olivia's trunk against my palm.

Without even thinking about it, I step forward and hug Chase. "It was amazing! Wasn't it amazing?"

He hugs me back, and that's amazing as well. His arms are around me. My face is right up against his T-shirt collar. I wonder what he smells like; I can't pick up anything but elephant in the barn.

Over his shoulder, I catch Quinn glancing at us as she leans against the wall. Whatever's going on in her expression, I can't register it, can't translate it, and I don't care. For once I just. Don't. Care.

Chase is beaming down at me when I pull away. "Best day ever!"

"Oh, yeah," I say, and it's not just because of the elephants.

Once everyone's had a turn, Dr. Paver says it's time for the girls to head outside. Georgia trumpets again as we file out past her stall. When we don't stop and pay attention, she sticks her trunk in her water trough, aims, and puffs once more. Again, Chase and I are her targets—and suddenly I understand what Dr. Paver meant earlier by "dry blow." This one isn't dry at all. The spray splatters us, and it's not just water—there's a generous amount of elephant snot mixed in. It lands in my hair, on my shirt. It gleams on my arms and soaks into my jeans.

I freeze. So does Chase. We stare at each other...And he starts laughing. And so do I.

We burst into uncontrollable laughter, the kind that shakes your chest and strains your ribs and clenches your torso, and you're so damn happy that you don't care that you can't breathe. We laugh until we're gasping and wheezing, and then we look at the stuff dripping off of each other and we start all over again.

And it's wonderful.

Dr. Paver rolls her eyes and hands us a stack of paper towels from the barn's hand-washing station.

Outside, I'm still catching my breath while we watch Georgia and Olivia lumber into their enclosure.

Chase rubs at his hair with a handful of paper towels. "Did I get it all?"

"No, hold on. There's still some left." I reach up to towel off a thick glop of goo that's stuck to the side of his head. "There. Now you're presentable. You're going to need a shower, though."

"So are you," he chuckles, wiping some stray snot off my shoulder. The gesture sends a very enjoyable shiver up my spine. Despite the fact that I'm smeared with rapidly drying elephant mucus, I can't remember the last time I felt this happy. Or this...pretty.

I feel like myself, like I don't have to try so hard. I feel *good*. And Chase is still grinning at me.

After our session with the elephants, we're allowed to wander the zoo for a few hours. When it's time to head back to campus, Eli eyes the two of us suspiciously. "You guys sure that's all dry?"

"It's dry," Chase says.

"And crusty," I add, which makes him start laughing again.

Eli's mouth thins into a straight line as we pile into his SUV. "Don't get that crap on my seats."

"They're fine, grumpypants," Mellie says. She turns to us. "Get cleaned up when we get back, okay? Special dinner tonight."

"Don't call me grumpypants," Eli mutters, merging onto the highway.

Mellie snorts and pokes him on the shoulder.

"You were so right about them," I whisper to Quinn.

Instead of answering, she scoots a few inches away.

Dinner turns out to be pizza at the site. Folding chairs are scattered through the welcome center, and delivery pizza boxes line the reception counter. We pile slices on paper plates, choose drinks from a cooler full of soda cans and water bottles, and find seats while Dr. Lauren flips through papers on her clipboard and chats quietly with Dr. Gallagher.

When everyone is settled, Dr. Lauren says, "You've all survived the first week of your internship. Congratulations!"

I smile around a bite of melty cheese. The day has left me cheerful and content. I'm freshly showered and free of elephant snot, and I'm back in my navy bone dress at last. I feel so ridiculously *decent* that I can't stop grinning.

Chase sits nearby. His hair is still damp from his shower, and he smells like soap.

Dr. Lauren goes on. "I always like to gather everyone together and check in at this point. You'll have some additional privileges and responsibilities starting tomorrow." She consults the clipboard. "You've all been approved to give tours. Special recognition goes to Natalie—I'm told you've shown exemplary skill when it comes to educating our guests."

I don't care that my cheeks are pinking or that I don't even like giving tours all that much. I'll have to thank Cody for giving Dr. Lauren a good report.

Dr. Lauren discusses a few other new responsibilities before saying, "And now for the job you're all really here for—digging in the bone bed. Chase, Natalie, and Brendan have been cleared. Starting tomorrow, you'll be put to work in the bone bed for at least half of each day you're scheduled here at the site."

I squeak a little when she says my name.

Chase shifts so that his knee taps against mine. "Congrats!" he mouths.

"Same to you!" I murmur back.

His smile crinkles the skin near his eyes.

On Chase's other side, Quinn's face is blank. Her fingers tug at her paper napkin, tearing off ragged scraps.

And for Christ's sake, Q, start trying harder in the sandbox.

I don't envy her having to explain tonight's news to her father.

13

That evening, we're watching a zombie show in the common room when Mellie speaks up. "So guys? Can Eli and I trust y'all to your own devices for a few hours?"

"Depends," Brendan says. "Why?"

From a chair in the corner, Eli scowls. "I don't like this."

Mellie shushes him. "There's a special showing at the Drafthouse that we really want to see."

"That *you* want to see," Eli mutters.

"Take us with you." Brendan leans back with a negotiator's grin.

"It's an anniversary showing of *Dirty Dancing*." Mellie's tone grows bubbly. "The best romantic classic ever!"

"Never mind," Brendan says.

"So..." Mellie raises her brows at us.

I shrug. "Sure, go."

"I still think this is a shitty idea," Eli says.

Mellie jumps up and tugs on his hand, pulling him off the chair. "Come on. Nobody puts Eli in a corner!"

Eli grunts.

After they leave, we watch another fifteen minutes of zombies. Brendan tilts his head in Chase's direction. "Hey, man. That thing I told you about?"

Chase nods, and they stand.

On their way out, Brendan points to Quinn and me. "Amphitheater. Twenty minutes."

When they're gone, I glance at Quinn. She shrugs.

My phone vibrates with an incoming text: *So I'm losing my tour assistant, right?* It's followed by an emoji with glaring eyes and an outstretched tongue. Cody.

I text back a trio of question marks.

Him: *You got approved for digging, didn't you? Dr. L was supposed to announce all that tonight.*

Me: *Yeah, but I'll still be giving tours too.*

Him: *Not as often, though. You'll be too busy in the shelter.*

Me: *Well, yeah.*

Him: *Congrats.* With that tongue emoji again. Apparently it's his favorite.

Me: *Wish you could dig too.*

Him: *Yeah…Hey, it's cool. The perks of being an intern, right?*

Me: *Speaking of that, something's up tonight. Dunno what—Brendan planned it. Wanna join?*

I don't expect him to accept, but after a moment, he answers with *Okay. Be there soon.*

A few minutes later, Quinn and I head out. On our way down the path I spot Cody jogging toward us from the parking lot. I wave him over.

At first, the familiar shadows make the amphitheater look deserted, layers of indigo and rising moonlight painting the benches and pillars with strange, lonely gloom.

Then I spot a couple of odd shapes near the rear of the stage. One shape raises an arm and waves.

The shapes turn out to be Chase and Brendan sitting cross-legged with several twelve-packs of beer between them.

"Dig in, guys!" Brendan says, raising a can. "Hey, it's…you," he adds when he focuses on Cody.

"Sure is," Cody says coolly.

I hesitate. I've had a couple of beers at parties before, but I don't want to do anything to risk my internship.

But everyone else takes a can.

"Don't be a fucking nerd," Brendan says when he sees me empty-handed. "Don't be *that* asshole. Come on, Pork Chop."

My stomach knots. "Fuck you, Brendan." If I don't join in, I'm a target. I step up and take a can. Just one should be fine. I know I can handle that much without getting messed up.

After all, it's not like I'm a lightweight.

We end up sitting in a crooked circle on the stage.

"Just how I wanted to spend my Sunday night." Cody mutters this in my direction, his drawl thick with sarcasm. He smirks and clinks his beer can against mine.

"Yeah, sorry," I whisper.

"It's okay." He winks. "Hey, I saw you on Dr. Carver's blog."

I keep my voice low. "Ugh. Don't bring that up."

"Why not? I figured you'd be over the moon about it."

"Yeah, well... The internet is full of assholes, okay?" I drink my beer so I don't have to elaborate.

"Seriously needed this tonight." Quinn swigs deeply. "Where'd you get it?"

Brendan gives her a leering grin. "Remember that one fridge at the lab? The one that says ABSOLUTELY NO FOOD?"

I wrinkle my nose. "Ew. I figured it was full of roadkill."

"That's what everybody thinks, apparently." Brendan shrugs. "Which makes it the perfect spot for some of the lab techs to hide their beer stash. I spotted one of them restocking it, and I found a side door into the lab that doesn't lock right. Just had to wait for the right time to raid it."

"Won't someone notice it's missing?" Quinn asks.

Brendan snorts dismissively. "Most of the techs are just college kids. They're not supposed to have this shit on campus in the first place. If they get us in trouble, they get in trouble too." He lies back, supporting himself on his elbows, and stares beyond the amphitheater roof at the dark sky. "Besides, they'd have to admit to drinking this cheap-ass beer."

I sip, and the beer paints the back of my throat with bitterness—but it's cold, and the flavor is light, and I am thirsty and nervous. The can empties far too quickly.

Chase, lounging beside me, hands me another. He leans closer, closer, until his nose nudges into my hair. He sniffs. "You smell good."

"Um, thanks." Warmth blooms in my chest, and I swig my second beer to cool it. He scoots closer, his forearm brushing mine, and I try not to tremble at the proximity. It's not like I haven't been, um, sniffed before. Fred Parkmore tried it once at lunch. That hadn't felt like this, though.

This...this makes my head swim and my core quiver.

I keep drinking, moving on to a third can. The more beer I swallow, the more at ease I feel. The interlocked tension in my chest and stomach loosens.

Quinn knocks back another, pulls out her phone, and opens a music app. The sound is thin and empty through the phone's tiny speakers, but it's audible, and that's all she needs to jump up and gyrate to the beat. "Love this song," she slurs, strutting catlike across the stage. She shrugs her cropped cardigan off her shoulders, revealing her lace-edged tank top.

"Oh, jeez, here we go." Still nursing his first beer, Cody rolls his eyes.

Chase chuckles at the show before giving me an unfocused smile.

"Hey, Natalie—" he begins, but then someone's hand grabs mine, yanking me to my feet.

Quinn. "Hey, girl!" she says, her voice loose, her eyes sleepy. "Let's dance. Come on. I don't want to be the only one."

I nearly pull away, but the song she's playing is really catchy. I start to sway, haltingly at first.

"Let loose, bitch!" Quinn says, her tone upbeat and lively.

I finish off my beer, let the can fall to the concrete, and move my hips more seductively as the alcohol wraps its confident tendrils around my brain. Is Chase watching? I bet he's watching. I hope he's watching. I am beautiful, I am sexy, I am irresistible.

Quinn laughs and throws an arm around my shoulders. "So, um, I think Chase likes you!" she purrs near my ear, her tone low and secretive. "I mean, who would've thought, huh? You like him, and he likes you…"

My jaw clenches. "Quinn, shut up."

"And my dad likes you too. I mean, not in the same way, know what I mean? Because that'd be weird, right?" Laughing, she catches my hand again and runs a finger over my leather cuff. "He calls you the one with the bracelet."

"I know. You showed me the text."

"Yeah. He always likes his fangirls." She giggles some more and stumbles into me. "He likes a fangirl who can dig even more! Since, you know, his own daughter can't."

"Quinn, no. He shouldn't have said what he did. That was awful of him." I pause for a moment, marveling at the fact that my tongue doesn't quite seem to fit in my mouth anymore. "I can help you with the digging thing."

She stares at me, not really focusing. "Wait, what? Really?"

"Yeah, why not? I'll help you practice." Another beer suddenly seems like a brilliant idea. As I lean to grab one from the case, I spot Cody raising his brows at me. "What?" I ask him.

"You sure that's smart?"

"Shut up. You're drinking too."

"I've had one. I'm done." He shakes the empty can. "Eventually I have to drive home."

"Well, I don't."

He shrugs and looks away.

Quinn grabs another beer too and swigs down half of it. "We could go *right now*!"

"What?"

She grabs at my hands, sloshing my beer can. "Let's go to the site. Now! All of us! We can dig!"

Laughter to my right. Cody.

Quinn narrows her eyes. "What?"

"Site's three miles away. How are you going to get there?"

"You could drive us, Mister One-Beer," I say, just to needle him.

"Hell, no." He laughs again.

"Then we'll walk," Quinn says, wavering on her feet.

"Dude, yeah!" Chase jumps up beside us. "Let's walk. We'll walk to the site and dig up mammoths! We can do this!"

"Aw, fuck." Brendan lies back on the concrete stage. "I ain't walking no three miles in the dark. I'm staying here with my little friends Pabst, Blue, and Ribbon." He hugs the mostly empty twelve-packs to his side.

Quinn tries to pull me down the amphitheater steps, but I resist. "Guys, I don't think this is a good idea."

"Why?" Quinn gives me another tug.

Beer makes my objections hard to articulate. "Because we're not supposed…We can't…We might…"

"Come on, Natalie." Chase puts an arm around my waist and leads me down the stairs. "Come with us." His voice, soft near my ear, eases itself into my brain. Suddenly I can't remember the arguments I was trying to make.

"Natalie?" A voice behind me. I turn and see Cody watching me, one side of his mouth quirked crookedly.

"What?"

He gestures at the three of us. "Seriously?"

"You should come too," I tell him.

He shakes his head. "That's still a no from me. Even if you idiots make it that far—which you won't—the dig shelter will be locked."

"So we'll pick the lock," Quinn says with a sleepy grin. "I mean, they do it all the time on TV. Can't be so hard."

"Good luck with that." Cody turns to leave. He glances over his shoulder and focuses on me. "Be careful."

I stick my tongue out as he saunters off.

"We really doing this?" I ask as Chase starts off across the grass with us in tow.

"Why not?" he asks.

"We could get in trouble."

"We won't get in trouble!" he says, chuckling. "Dude, we'll find a new mammoth or something, and everyone'll be too impressed to be mad."

I gulp the last of my beer to make his theory seem sounder. "Do you even know how to get there?"

"We'll figure it out," Chase says. "The site's off…that road, you know? That road."

"Ember Road?" I ask.

"Yeah! See? You know."

"But how do we get to Ember Road?"

Chase snorts. "I don't know. We'll figure it out. We'll know the way when we see it. Come on!"

Quinn stops. "Wait."

We turn and look at her.

She sits down in the grass, her eyes glassy. "You guys, I think I'm going to puke."

I take a few steps back, just in case.

"Go on without me," she says, her voice arching with drama.

I don't want to leave her here. "We should take her back to the dorm—"

"She'll be okay," Chase says. "Brendan's right over there."

I can hear snoring from the amphitheater.

Quinn gets to her knees then says, "Nope," and sits back down.

"Come on," Chase says, tugging on my arm.

I shove him away. "No, wait. We can't leave her."

"Fine." Chase's tone shortens, but he hooks his hands under Quinn's arms and lifts her onto her feet. Together, we help her stagger back toward the dorm. When she nearly crumples again, Chase scoops her up and carries her the rest of the way. Even though he's drunk, his steps are sure and easy. It's like she's weightless.

We get her upstairs, and I half drag her into our room.

"Bathroom," she mutters, so that's where she and I head. She kneels next to the toilet and rests her head on the seat.

"What can I do?" I've dealt with a tipsy Charli at parties a time or two, but she's never been this bad.

"God, just go," she says, glaring. "Let me puke in peace."

"Are you sure?"

She turns her face away. "Chase is waiting for you."

My head floats like it's full of helium while Chase and I head outside. I let him pull me toward the parking lot and the main campus entrance.

The entrance road is quiet, the shadow of its asphalt interrupted at intervals by the pooled yellow light of the school's decorative streetlamps. Giggling, I cling to Chase's arm. We're each leaning on the other, just a bit, and our walk is an uneven ramble—a stumble to the left, a stagger to the right.

"We are going to dig up so many bones." The beer softens his tone into something almost velvety. He punctuates the remark with a carbonated laugh.

I shove down the doubt blooming in the pit of my stomach. *It's going to be okay. We're not going to get caught. Don't be lame. Not now. Fake it. Be the kind of girl who can get a guy like Chase. Be awesome.*

"Hey, Natalie," he says when I don't answer.

"What?"

Another chuckle. "Hey, Natalie!"

"*What?*"

"I like you." His voice is slurred and loose, but what he says still sends a shiver down my spine.

"I like you too." The words nearly trip up my tongue. Saying them out loud leaves me uneasy, unguarded, although the beer gentles my discomfort. I've never been this honest with a guy. Keeping my walls up around boys like Fred Parkmore is easy, but now I want to strip those barriers away.

He slings an arm around my shoulders. "You're really hot. And you…you know your stuff. You know *so much stuff*! I mean, I hear you giving tours sometimes, and you're…you're just…" He laughs lightly and shakes his head. "Sorry. Can't think straight."

I giggle too. My head is full of bubbles. "I know what you mean."

He leans in, his voice an exaggerated whisper. "*I think it's the beer.*"

"Probably," I snicker. And that's part of it, yes—but only part. The night, his proximity, the easy weight of his arm around me—it's all intoxicating.

We reach the turnoff onto the main road, and we go right. This street is darker, its streetlights dimmer and farther between. The half-full moon overhead is just enough to outline the roadside trees. The shadows we walk through are thick.

It's easier to be brave in the dark. It's easier to act on instinct. I stop and face him, my hands on his shoulders. I can't really see his face in the dark, but I can make out certain things—brow, cheekbone, jaw.

"You okay?" he asks. His breath is a warm hush over my face.

Instead of answering, I kiss him.

Everything stops—there's no campus nearby, no road beneath us, no moon peeking through the branches overhead. There's just Chase's mouth against mine, hot and wet.

I haven't kissed anyone since last fall, when I went to the homecoming dance with Lance Miller and he got worked up during the last song of the night and tried to swallow half my face and feel me up at the same time. This isn't like that. This is... better.

. . . It is, right? It's better?

Yes. Wet, but better. Chase could use a few lessons in keeping more of his spit to himself, but oh well. This is what I want, right? To hide in the dark, pressed against Chase with those glorious forearms locking me in place? To make out shamelessly with my crush? To lose myself in the demanding exploration of his lips?

His tongue laps a long line up my neck. That's, um... weird.

But I like it. I do, right? I do.

I think.

He holds me closer, kisses me again. My heart slams in my chest, a trapped tiger battling the walls of its cage. It's almost enough to make me forget once and for all that this is a boneheaded plan.

Almost.

"Chase?" I say once the kiss breaks.

"Yeah?" he says, but then his lips are back on mine.

"Should we be doing this?" I pull away.

He steps closer again. "What do you mean?"

When he tries to duck in for another kiss, I put a hand on his chest. "Going to the site."

"You don't want to go?"

I'm not sure what I want. I wish my head would stop this

swimmy thing it's doing. "I just...Maybe we should head back to campus."

"We could do that." He catches the hand I've been using to push him away, and he uses it to pull me closer.

"Chase—"

He silences me with another kiss, his teeth catching my lower lip in a way that makes me gasp.

"Damn it, Chase," I say when I can get a breath.

"So we'll go back." He touches his cheek to my hair.

But when I try to walk, he holds me in place and tries to keep making out. Now I'm kind of annoyed, and a little panicked. I want to kiss him again, but I also want to tell him to fuck off. I want him to listen instead of placating me with words that don't match his actions.

Finally, we turn back toward campus. "Hey, know what?" he says after a minute.

"What?"

"Quinn's probably passed out in her bed by now."

"Probably. So?"

"So...I mean, she wouldn't know if you and I go back to your room for a while."

"What?"

"It'd almost be like we had the room to ourselves."

"God, you're such a...such a *guy*." I'm more annoyed than ever, but my stomach flips at the implication of his words.

That's what every guy wants. Charli's voice in my head. *Why should this one be any different?*

Because he wants it with me.

Charli would roll her eyes at that. What was it she texted the night we argued? *U gotta make some moves here too.*

Do I?

Should I?

He pulls me out of the yellow light, back into the darkness. Kisses me again.

I kiss him back, my thoughts racing and wavering at the same time. When his palm brushes my breast, I reach up and block his hand with mine. *Too much, this is too much.* I push him away. "Yeah, no."

"Aw, come on, Natalie." He steps toward me, and I ready myself to push away another advance. Before that's necessary, headlights come around the corner, heading toward campus. One second, we're in shadow. The next, we're blinded.

"Shit," Chase mutters as the car stops and two people get out.

Could we run? I look toward the trees. If we really took off...

"Natalie? Chase? What the hell?"

I raise a hand, trying to shield my eyes from the blazing headlights. "Mellie?"

She stomps toward us in vintage cowboy boots. "What's going on?"

Eli follows, jaw working, nostrils flaring. "What the fuck are you doing out here?"

Chase stifles a choked giggle.

Mellie's eyes get even bigger and rounder than usual. "Are you guys drunk?"

I swallow, trying to calm the tremor building in my throat. "How was your date?"

At this, Chase breaks into full-on braying laughter. He can't stop even when he falls onto his butt on the side of the road.

"The end sucked," Mellie says thinly. "Come on. In the car."

I've never heard her voice get harsh before. It's enough to sober me up the rest of the way. I get in Eli's SUV and buckle up.

"Shotgun," Mellie hisses when Chase tries to slip in beside me. He gets in next to Eli, and Mellie sits next to me.

The ride back to campus is short and silent. Eli grips the wheel so hard I half expect his fingers to crack and crumble away, one by one.

"You guys are in a shitload of trouble," he says once he parks. "Out."

My stomach ices over. "What's going to happen?"

"I wouldn't be surprised if you're both thrown out of the program."

I'm not sure if it's the alcohol or Eli's prediction that sends a lurch of bile into my throat. I manage to make it upstairs and into the bathroom before I throw up.

The next morning, my mouth is lined with cotton, and a bongo player has taken up residence in my skull. Quinn is in the bathroom when I stumble in. Freshly showered and wrapped in her towel, she leans toward the mirror as she puts on mascara. "Almost done in here."

I grunt in response.

"What happened last night?"

"Chase and I got caught." I lean against the wall and rub my eyes.

"What?"

I fill her in. "How the hell are you even upright?"

"I drank a shitload of water once I stopped puking. And I took these." She digs a container of ibuprofen from her makeup case. The pills rattle together as she tosses me the bottle. "Here. Two of these. And water. Tons of water."

"Okay. Thanks."

"So...what happened before that? Did you make it to the site?"

"No. We just..." I don't want to tell her the truth, not when I know she likes Chase. Besides, I feel a little weird about the whole thing. I kissed my crush—shouldn't I be giddy about that? Instead, I keep remembering how Chase just kept persisting, even after I wasn't really into it anymore. Even after I said no. I wonder how much farther he would have tried to go if Eli's SUV hadn't shown up when it did. "Mellie and Eli caught us before we got a mile down the road."

I stay in the shower as long as I dare, letting the water beat against my head and wash away a bit of the fog. I don't get out until Mellie pounds on the door and yells at me to get moving.

I struggle to pull myself together. No winged eyeliner today. My puffy eyes can't even handle contact lenses, so I wear my cat's-eye glasses. I settle for lip balm instead of my usual bright lipstick. Even that barely seems worth the effort when I'm this tired. I can't even be bothered to put on my usual armor; I dress in boot-cut jeans, sneakers, and a Savage Swallow logo tee. Good enough. I'm too nervous to care. And it's not like I'll be covering this debacle on *Fossilista*, so I don't have to worry about my look of the day.

At the site, all of us—interns and seniors—file into the break room at Dr. Lauren's command. On my way to a seat, I grab a water bottle from the mini fridge.

Dr. Lauren stands at the head of the table, arms crossed, lips pressed into a thin frown. "Anyone want to tell me what went on last night?"

We all glance at each other.

"Where'd you get the beer?" Dr. Lauren prods.

"Fridge in the roadkill room at the lab," Brendan mutters. I'm guessing he got caught red-handed at the amphitheater.

"The bone lab? You found beer in the *bone lab*?"

"The techs hide it there." Chase slides low in his chair.

"I'll make sure to bring that up with Dr. Glass. Were all four of you in on this?"

Quinn could feign innocence; she was already passed out when the rest of us were discovered. Before she can make any claims, though, Brendan says, "Yeah."

She narrows her eyes.

Dr. Lauren sighs. "This is ridiculous. If I were smart, I'd expel all four of you from the program. It's what this stunt deserves."

Oh God. I put down the water bottle and snap my hair elastic hard against my wrist. *Oh God, oh God.*

"The logistics of sending you all home early would be a huge pain in my ass, though, so I'm giving you one more chance."

The words barely make sense in my head, but as they sink in, I start shaking. This does nothing for the dull thudding in my head.

"Quinn and Brendan, you two are on probation for the rest of the week. No more screwups, got it?" Then Dr. Lauren focuses on Chase and me. "And you two...Mind explaining why Mellie and Eli found you off campus, stumbling around in the road?"

"They were trying to walk to the site," Brendan says, his voice low and sullen.

"Dude!" Chase hisses.

"What the hell were you going to do if you got here?"

My shoulders sink, but I speak up. "I don't know, really. It was a stupid idea that made sense at the time."

Dr. Lauren rubs her left temple. "I don't even know what to think about any of this. Chase and Natalie, you two are on probation for the rest of the program.

"I'll be keeping my eye on all of you," she goes on. "I expect your best behavior. No, I demand it. Don't give me a reason to go through the hassle of expelling you."

Then she focuses on Mellie and Eli. "I expected more from you two as well. You left these guys unsupervised. That's not going to happen again—not if you want your course credits for this month."

Eli scowls at Mellie.

"I expect better," Dr. Lauren says, "from all of you."

When she finally lets us go, Brendan spots Cody waiting for his first tour of the day in the lobby. "Hey! He was there too."

Cody frowns.

"Brendan!" I whisper.

"He was! He was drinking too."

Dr. Lauren groans and motions for Cody to follow her back to the break room. "The rest of you wait here for a minute," she tells us.

Once she's out of earshot, I turn on Brendan. "Why the hell did you do that?"

"If I'm in trouble, so is everyone else."

My hands clench into fists. "You're such a douchebag."

"Whatever." He stalks off and flops onto a seat near the gift shop.

When Dr. Lauren lets him go, Cody rushes by us to his tour without even looking at us. I wonder how much trouble he's in. It's my fault for texting him and inviting him over. At least he hasn't been fired...as far as I know.

None of us are allowed to dig all morning. I end up running the register in the gift shop. Quinn is at the front desk since Martina is off today. Dr. Lauren puts Chase to work filing papers in her office, and she sends Brendan out to collect trash and tidy up the grounds.

Although I'm still dragging, the ibuprofen is finally kicking in. Remembering Quinn's suggestion, I keep guzzling water. I'm at the water fountain near the restrooms, refilling my bottle for the fifth or sixth time, when Cody wanders over after finishing a tour. "How much trouble did you get in?" I ask, stepping aside in case he wants a drink.

But he just squints at me.

I stare back, my expression blank. "Hello?"

"What?"

I try again, enunciating each word. "Are you in trouble?"

He shrugs. "A little. Not really. It's fine."

"You didn't get fired?"

He waves away my concern. "Nah. She said not to let it happen again. That's all."

"Really? She was so mad at us."

"Yeah, well, I guess she knows who instigated the whole thing. Told her I was just trying to socialize with the interns and I didn't know what you guys had planned. Which was true."

"Sorry I invited you."

He shrugs and stares at me again.

"*What?*"

"Did you do something different today?" he asks finally.

"Something different? With what?"

"With...I don't know. With this." He waves a hand at my face. "Maybe it's the glasses. Or your makeup or something. You look different."

He's so weird. I roll my eyes. "Yeah, I guess. I didn't feel too great this morning—"

"I bet."

"Shut up. I didn't feel well, so I just kind of rushed through things."

"Oh. Well, I like it better."

"Excuse me?"

"You look more like a person this way."

I square my shoulders and frown. "What's that even supposed to mean?"

He shrugs. "Just that I like it better. You look nice. Softer. That's all. You feeling okay now?"

"Yeah. Getting there." I swig water as an excuse not to say more.

"Cool." He turns and spots his next tour forming. "Gotta go."

"Yeah. Okay." *Finally.*

The gift shop is still empty, so I duck into the restroom. Guzzling water all morning makes a girl have to pee.

While I wash my hands, I stare at myself in the mirror. Except for first thing in the morning and before bed, I'm so used to seeing my usual makeup that my reflection without it seems odd. Unfinished. I do look different, I suppose. I do look...softer.

My head turns *softer* into *vulnerable. Unprotected.*

Fat.

I remember a day in the seventh grade when I felt especially gross. I had my period, so I was bloated and broken out. I'd snapped my glasses in half the day before, and Dad had temporarily mended the frames with duct tape. At lunch that day, someone smacked my tray out of my hands, leaving me with a lasagna stain on my T-shirt.

"God, Nat, you look *gorgeous*," Fred Parkmore had drawled when I walked into fifth period.

"So beautiful I can't even bear to look at you," another boy said.

Fred had cried out and covered his eyes. "I looked at it! I looked at it, and now I'm blind!"

I shudder and snap my elastic. There's makeup in my purse in the break room. I'll grab it and fix my face as soon as I have a chance.

You look nice. God, what a douche.

15

"**Ready to be a** full-fledged excavator?" Dr. Lauren asks after lunch.

I stop short on my way back to the gift shop. "Really?"

"Yes. You're still in trouble—don't doubt that for a second. But you're also here for a reason, and you're too talented for me to punish you by keeping you out of the bed. Can I trust you to be on your best behavior for the rest of the program?"

"Yes! I swear it!" Water and ibuprofen have worked their magic, and I'm feeling pretty good. Even if I weren't, no hangover is keeping me out of the bone bed. I'd be here even if I had the plague, flesh-eating bacteria, and raging appendicitis.

She gathers Chase and Brendan as well and walks us into the bed. "Watch your step," she reminds us, but I already choose my footfalls carefully, steering clear of exposed bone as we pass by the half-buried mammoths.

Near the west end of the shelter, we reach several square meters of earth, each individually marked off and labeled with an index card with a name on it. I look for mine, and there it is—a square of dirt with a card that says *Natalie*.

This is it. My spot. My territory. My very own corner of the bone bed.

"Remember everything you learned last week," Dr. Lauren says. "Go slowly. If you think you find something, even if you're not sure, call someone over. You're dealing with real fossils now. Let's try to cause as little damage as possible, okay?"

As I put down my bucket of tools, I nod. "Definitely."

Chase's square meter borders mine. Before he gets to work, he stretches, exposing a thin stripe of flat belly.

I try not to stare. I try, and I fail. I'm remembering the heat of his lips against my mouth, the press of his arms, the way his touch and his voice made me waver in so many ways. I just wish he hadn't been so pushy.

"Is your head pounding like mine is?" he asks, settling in.

"Yeah, a little." My voice sounds tight and reedy, but he doesn't seem to notice.

After a few minutes, he twists his neck to peer into my square meter. "Find anything yet?"

"Nah." I empty my dustpan into my bucket. I'm not sure that I'm really in the mood for talking. When I look at him, my brain gets all foggy. He's so cute and I'm so attracted to him, but then I think about his hands moving in where I didn't really want them, and the way I had to shove him away. I feel like that's what we should talk about, and I'm not quite ready.

Either way, a tour will come through shortly and there are other diggers nearby, so this isn't the time to press for a discussion.

Besides, I have more important things to think about this afternoon. Like digging.

Starting in one corner of my square meter, I kneel and use the side of my trowel to move about a millimeter-thick layer of soil at a time. Scrape. Scrape. Scrape. Brush. Dump the loosened matrix in my bucket and repeat. Just like in the sandbox. Only now there's a chance I'll find something real instead of just a replica.

Two hours later, my back aches and my feet are asleep from being sat on, and I don't care a bit. I've barely even made a dent in my area, which means I'm doing it right. Four times I've called over Dr. Lauren or one of the more experienced diggers to show them a bit of gravel or a discolored spot in the soil. So far none of my discoveries have been legit, but it's early yet. I'm only just getting started.

I hear Chase call for Dr. Lauren. I look up to see if he's found something, but he's just asking for permission to take a break. She nods. "Take a walk. Natalie, you want to go too?"

I'm about to refuse, but Chase cocks his head, inviting me along. So I go.

Pins and needles erupt in my feet, and I almost stumble on my way out the shelter door. "Careful," Chase says, grabbing my arm to keep me upright.

"Thanks. Guess I was kneeling for too long."

He chuckles a little. "I know the feeling. My calves are cramping and my thighs are killing me from all that squatting."

"Ouch. That's not good." I test my own thighs, tensing, stretching. They're a little tight, but they seem all right. (*Strong thighs*, Aunt Judy's voice insists in my head.)

"Nope. It isn't."

We go quiet after that, as we wander one of the paths near the shelter. I search for words to break the awkward silence, but my mind blanks.

Then Chase does it for me. "Hey, Natalie?"

"Yeah?"

"I just...I'm sorry about last night. I don't remember everything, I don't think. But I'm pretty sure the walk was my idea."

My heart jumps a little. "It was Quinn's, actually, but you were kind of enthusiastic about it."

"Damn it. Was I being an asshole out there? You can tell me if I was."

"Actually, yeah. You were."

"I was afraid of that. I mean...I think I kissed you. Did I? I remember that."

I nod. "To be fair, I kind of kissed you first."

"Oh." He hesitates and gives me a little grin. "Okay."

"But you came on really strong after that. Everything just got kind of...stupid, I guess. From now on, if I say no about anything..."

"I'll listen. I will. I promise." He nods. "Natalie, just so you know...I really do like you."

"I like you too." The words escape me in a hush.

We quiet down again after that, but it no longer feels awkward. As we walk, he catches my hand, holding it loosely in his.

Before we get back to work, I suggest we go by the welcome center for water. On our way up the path, we pass Cody heading up a tour group. When he sees us, he throws us a slightly puckered look.

"Did you notice that?" I ask Chase once we've passed the group.

"What?"

"Nothing. It was nothing."

From the sandbox, Quinn watches us approach. "Hey," she says, focusing on our clasped hands.

I remember some hazy notion of a promise. "Hey, I said I'd help you learn this stuff, didn't I?" Leaving Chase on the path, I step into her square meter and hunker down beside her. "Show me your technique."

She's too tense—I see that right away. It makes her heavy-handed. And she hurries the process, which means she's liable to damage anything she finds before she knows she's found it.

I hold out my hand for the trowel. "Can I?" When she hands it over, I demonstrate. "See? Try to scrape a little more lightly. Go a little slower."

She tries, and at first she seems to get it.

"Natalie?" Chase says. "We should probably grab those waters and get back to work."

The tension returns to Quinn's arms, and she takes out a chunk of dirt. "Damn it!"

"In a minute," I tell Chase.

"No, go," Quinn says. "I need to be by myself so I can concentrate." Her hair falls forward, hiding her face.

I shrug and follow Chase into the welcome center.

So are we talking again, or are u still giving me the silent treatment?

The sight of Charli's name on the text notification makes me bunch my shoulders.

Chase glances over. "You okay?" He's sitting beside me, his arm draped over the back of the couch behind me. At any moment, it might casually inch down to rest on my shoulders instead. His fingers already touch one shoulder, the subtlest of grazes. Wait for it...Wait for it...Maybe I should reach up and tug on his hand. Give him a little encouragement. My hand twitches, but instead of touching him, I snap my hair elastic a few times.

"Yeah. I'm fine."

That's good enough for him. His attention returns to the action movie on the common room TV.

"Yeah!" Brendan punches the air as a stolen car explodes on the large screen. Quinn perches on an oversize ottoman, typing on her laptop.

I haven't heard from Charli since we bickered.

Me: *I thought u were the one giving me the silent treatment.*
Her: *I guess I just...needed a few days, u know?*
Me: *Same here.*
Her: *Things going all right out there?*

Me: *Yeah. Got approved for digging. I started today.*

Usually I would have followed up a statement like that with about a thousand exclamation points and a hugely grinning emoji, but I'm not quite feeling back to that level with Charli. Not yet.

Her: *That's awesome! Congrats!*

Me: *Thanx.*

Her: *Any other ... new developments? With that Chase dude?*

Keeping the movement slow and subtle, I shift away from Chase just enough to prevent him from glancing at my phone and seeing his name.

Me: *Um. Yeah.*

Her: *WHAT? Spill!! Wait, Imma call u!*

My phone starts shivering with the insistent vibration of an incoming call. "Be back in a minute," I mumble to Chase. When I stand, Quinn glances up from her laptop, her mouth a taut line. I head down the hall to my room.

"Tell me what's going on!" Charli squeals as soon as I answer, before I can even say hello.

"I think...I think we may be a thing!" I fill her in on everything—the morning with the elephants, our tipsy ramble, the walk at the site, the hand-holding, the things that were said.

"He totally likes you," she confirms when I'm done. "He's into you, and you're awesome, and that daddy's girl can shove it."

"Quinn? Yeah, you should've seen the look she just gave me."

"She's jelly."

"I think maybe she's finally laying off a little. I haven't seen her hang on him all day."

"Finally figured out she can't compete with you, huh? Good."

"Eh…" I drop my voice a little. "It's just weird, you know? Sometimes she's actually nice. I turn around and suddenly she's batting her lashes and flipping her hair and practically stripping down to get Chase's attention."

"So don't turn around. Don't give her that chance."

"I don't get it. I even tried to help her with digging today—"

"Why does she need help with that?"

I snicker a little. "She sucks at it."

"Wait. Her dad's this famous hotshot paleo guy and she can't dig up a bone?" Charli dissolves into cackles.

I give the empty room a flippant gesture. "Well, you know…Maybe if she spent a little more time practicing and a little less time hitting on my—"

"Your *boyfriend*." Charli singsongs the word.

"Not boyfriend. Not quite." I smile. "Not yet."

The door opens, and I clamp my mouth shut as Quinn walks in.

"Sorry," she says. "Needed my charger." She grabs her laptop cord and leaves, never meeting my eyes with hers.

"Shit," I mutter once she's gone.

"Was that her?" Charli asks.

"Yeah."

"Did she hear what you were just saying?"

"I don't know. I mean, I don't think so. She's gone now. She went back to the common room."

"She's out there with your farm boy right now?"

"Yeah."

"So get your ass back out there, lady. Remember what I told you? Don't turn around."

Quinn is back on her computer when I return to the common room. I sit down beside Chase, and his arm settles on my shoulders, pulling me a little closer.

After a few minutes, Quinn shuts her laptop and leaves.

Look of the Day:
    Cuffed denim crops (Savage Swallow)
    Mammoth Site T-shirt (altered by me!)
    Red tank top (Old Navy)
    Black-and-white polka-dot headband (made by me!)
    Pinup lipstick (Maxwell Cosmetics)
    Blue-and-white Nikes (yep, those dreaded things again)

Sorry for not posting an entry yesterday, kids—your favorite fos-silista was busy as hell in the bone bed. That's right, it was my first day of really, truly digging up mammoths. Actually, all I dug yesterday was good old Texas dirt—but hey, a paleo-girl's gotta start somewhere!

Quinn and I work in silence at the lab's screen wash station while Chase tromps back and forth with pails of dirt and gravel, handling the heavy lifting.

"God, this is so boring," I say finally, just to hear something other than the sound of water trickling in the trough.

"Yeah." Her smile is thin.

I try again. "It's way too hot to be working out here. Brendan's lucky Dr. Glass put him at the labeling station today."

"Hmm."

"Hey, how'd the rest of your training go yesterday? Any luck?"

She looks right at me, and her face takes on that unsettling blankness again, the same lack of expression I saw when Dr. Carver was helping me in the sandbox.

"I'd be happy to help you some more if you want."

"That's nice of you, but I'm fine. I just need to spend more time practicing."

My stomach knots, and I'm not sure why. "Okay. Just thought I'd offer."

Chase plunks down another bucket. "That's all of it. Finally." He picks up a screen and starts rinsing handfuls of matrix next to me at the trough, standing a little closer than necessary.

"Natalie, you know, you were right." Quinn wipes her forehead with her arm. "It's crazy-hot. I want to finish rinsing this screen, but I'm really thirsty. Do you think you could grab me a water? Please?"

I'm just about to pile more gravel on my screen, but instead, I nod and put it down. "Sure. Be right back." I'm grateful for the excuse. I'm sweating to death in this damn shaper.

Almost as soon as the air conditioning hits me, I hear Mellie call my name. She's leaving the main lab area with a box. "There's another one of these in there on the table that needs to go over to storage. Can you help me?"

I pick up the other box, and we walk together, Mellie chattering on about Eli the whole time. After we drop off the boxes, I grab a couple of waters and head outside.

The door to the screen wash station is still propped open from when Chase was carrying buckets of gravel. I hear him and Quinn before I can see them.

"Quinn, I just—"

"She doesn't have to know."

I freeze. I listen. I wait.

For a minute, they go quiet. I hear his voice, soft and rough: "God, you're so fucking hot."

When I slam the door open all the way, he has her pressed against the edge of the trough. Her hands are knotted in his hair, and he's kissing her. He's kissing her hard, and she's wrapping one long, thin leg around him, locking him against her. The sound of the door startles them—he jumps back, and she stares at me, her mouth open.

"Shit," he mutters.

My jaw tightens like a trap. The pressure makes my teeth ache. I go still. I swallow. I stare at them as something dark and horrible rises within me, humiliation wisping through my body. It's the same thing I felt when the Twinkies tumbled out of my locker, when Vic took the photo of me during the french fry contest. I want to scream, but there's no way, not when I can't even breathe.

"Natalie." Chase steps up to me.

As my vision blurs, I shove him away and run into the building. He follows, grabbing my arm to stop me.

I can't meet his eyes. "How could you do that?"

"Look, it was just...It was a mistake!"

"A mistake? What the fuck, Chase? You were all over her."

"She started it."

"Seriously? That's you're excuse? How old are you? Six?"

He exhales, nostrils flaring. "Natalie, calm the fuck down. It's not like you and I are, like...a couple or anything!"

I can't. I just can't. I wrench my arm free and keep running.

I cut through the roadkill room. It's empty. I could stay here, just me and my roadkill heart. But then a lab tech steps in and asks what I'm doing. Instead of answering, I head on to bone storage, where I choose a row that looks especially neglected. Two of the fluorescent strips overhead are out, leaving a shadowy area down near the far wall. That's the spot for me.

I sit on the floor, go silent, and listen. I stay tense and motionless, waiting for any sound. I count seconds.

The huge room is quiet. The air's as still as the dust that coats the shelves and their neglected specimens. I'm alone with the bones, and they're the crumbling witnesses to my breakdown.

I don't know how long I cry. I just pull myself into a ball and let go, shaking and bawling and gasping.

Every time I calm down a little—every time I can start to fill my lungs without fighting hiccupping sobs to do so—something flashes through my head to get me going again: Chase covered in elephant snot, the warmth of his hand around mine, that muttered "You're so fucking hot."

It's not like we're a couple. We made out once, and it was clumsy and ill-timed, and we were drunk. We held hands. He isn't mine. He never was. I let myself believe for a second that he was what he seemed, and that he and I—that *we*—might be something possible.

I know better. Didn't I learn anything from the time I spent as Fat Nat? Chase is about as decent and trustworthy as Fred Parkmore. I attract creeps. I catch the attention of assholes. As if I need further proof of that, I bring up

Dr. Carver's blog on my phone and scroll down to the entry with the photo of me. There are more comments now, including two more anonymous jerk-offs pointing out how fucking fat I am.

I find the original "who's the fat ass" comment. It has a reply now:

Cody
Left on June 20
Who's the anonymous fuckwad? Oh, it's YOU! ;P

I make a soft shuddering sound that's half giggle and half sob. I tap on my blog's app and bring up the page for a new entry, and my thumbs race over the touch screen's tiny keyboard.

Here's what I'm wondering, guys. What makes people think it's okay to judge someone—to insult someone—based on a single photo? I don't know if any of you read the comments on Dr. Carver's blog, but damn—there I am training with the most well-known paleontologist in the world, and all this one anonymous idiot can see is my weight. I mean . . . do they think they're funny? Because "who's the fat ass" isn't exactly the epitome of hilarity. Does anonymity make them feel brave? Or . . . do they think I somehow don't know? Do they assume I'm blissfully skipping through life, convinced I'm thin and fit and everything society demands of me as a female? Here's a news flash—I know I'm fat. I'm reminded of it every time my doctor tsks *at me even though my blood work is fine and my heart is strong. I'm reminded every time clothes shopping with my best friend gets awkward because the stores that carry her size never carry mine. And I'm reminded every time some anonymous commenter just can't help themselves. Douchebags gonna douche.*

I read it. Read it again. But I can't quite bring myself to post it. Instead, I save it as a draft. Maybe I'll make it public later. Maybe I won't.

Crying has left me thirsty and raw, as dry as the bones and plaster around me. I lean back against one of the shelf supports and let my eyes close halfway.

"Natalie?" The voice comes from several aisles away. It's not Chase, at least. It's female. I go still and silent again.

Quinn appears at the end of the aisle. For a moment she stands there, a lean silhouette in short denim cutoffs and a tank top that would barely fit my thigh, let alone my torso.

When she approaches, I look elsewhere, at the shelves in front of me.

"I'm sorry," she says, stopping several feet away.

"Yeah. Sure."

"It just kind of happened."

My throat chokes itself. "Fuck you, Quinn."

"I mean it. I shouldn't have…" She sits down, leans against the shelves, and starts to sob.

I don't know what to do. I want to punch her. I want to run away, but she's between me and the end of the aisle.

I wait.

Her hands cover her face, and I see that the polka-dot polish I painted on her nails the other night is already chipping. She's been working hard in the sandbox. Trying.

Finally, her sobs slow. She gasps a few times. Hiccups.

I glance at her from the corner of my eye. "Why?"

"I don't know."

"Bullshit."

Her tone trembles. "My dad reamed me out in texts again yesterday. He's coming back to finish filming. Told me to stop being an embarrassment and get my shit together." She angles her head, looking at me from under her hair.

"He's an asshole."

"Yeah."

"But...Shit, Quinn." I sniffle. "I really like Chase. Or I did."

"I know." She sobs again. "And he likes you. I'm sorry, Natalie. I was stupid."

"So was he," I mutter.

"Everyone likes you," she says, her voice catching harshly, making her struggle with each word. "Dad told me to ask you for help. He said maybe he'd just film you again instead and not even mention I'm part of the program. Just...edit me out completely. He'd rather work with you. Chase would rather be with you. And I just..."

"I'm sorry," I say, and although I kind of hate myself for saying it, for feeling sympathy after what she did, I honestly mean it. I feel sorry for her.

"All I've ever been is Dr. Carver's daughter," she mumbles into her knees. "And now I'm not even good enough at being that. I've been trying so hard with the digging. I *have* been practicing. A lot. You know that."

I cringe a little remembering my conversation with Charli from the night before. Now I know what Quinn overheard when she came in for her laptop cord.

"I've seen you in the sandbox," I say.

"It's never enough."

I rub at my puffy eyes, and my hands come away smeared with black. My eyes burn from my running mascara. When I blink to refocus, my gaze scans over the bottom shelf opposite me, and I see a yellowed identification card with "Ember Road" written on it in faded ballpoint. The paper is partially taped to a plaster jacket the size of an ottoman.

Ember Road—the road that goes right by the site.

I scoot closer.

The jacket's been there for a long time; it's coated with dust and half hidden by smaller items that have been crammed onto the shelf in front of it over the years. It wouldn't be visible at all if I hadn't been sitting right in front of it, putting it nearly at eye level. It looks like it's been there longer than the Central Texas Mammoth Site has been the Central Texas Mammoth Site.

"Quinn? Didn't Dr. Glass say all the Mammoth Site specimens had been cleaned and prepped and cataloged already?"

Her face is still buried against her knees, so her voice is muffled. "I think so."

"Then what's this?" My lips press together as I move smaller bones and bits of plaster out of the way to get to the Ember Road lump. When the way is clear, I find handholds in the plaster and tug. It's ridiculously heavy and will only slide about an inch at a time. "Help me with this."

She unfolds herself and moves closer. "What are you doing? What is it?"

"That's what I'm trying to find out."

Even together, we can only budge the lump a few inches. Finally, I wipe the dust off the identification card and squint at the rest of the faded writing.

Specimen type: Mammoth Skull (Juvenile)
Date found: 9/28/82
Date transported: 10/10/82
Grid: 28B

"A juvie?" Quinn says. "A calf?"

"I thought they were all accounted for. They're *in situ* at the site, or they've been prepped for the museum. This can't have been here since 1982."

"Dr. Glass said things used to get misplaced and overlooked back then."

"What if that's what happened with this thing?" I look at her, eyes wide. "And we just found it."

On our hands and knees, we root around for more. I crawl halfway onto the shelf so I can see around the jacketed skull. We find other plaster lumps with the same Ember Road label—a femur, a pelvis, some ribs. I can't tell if the skeleton's complete, but a good bit of it is accounted for.

A small rectangle of paper sticks out from under one of the lumps. I ease it free, and then Quinn and I stare at it together. It's a faded photograph of two men. One I recognize as Dr. Roland, the paleontologist the bone lab is named for. He wears a goofy safari hat, and he grins beneath a massive gray beard. He holds a bone fragment—looks like about a foot of tusk—in his left hand. His right is shaking the hand of another man—this one short and smiling in a denim shirt.

I flip the photo over. Scrawled on the back in barely visible ballpoint is *W. Roland, C. Flanders, 1982.*

C. Flanders? Wasn't that the name of the guy the original dig leased the land from? The guy whose kids are trying to sue for the bones now, according to Cody?

Quinn tugs on my arm. "Come on! We found a mammoth! We have to show this to someone."

I'm still in shock.

"Natalie!" she goes on, pulling harder. "Come *on.* Please." Her tone is reedy with excitement.

Together we sprint through bone storage, the roadkill room, and down the hall toward the main bone lab. On the way I realize I'm still clutching the photograph. I stick it in my back pocket to keep track of it until I can hand it over. "Dr. Glass! Mellie! Where are you guys?" I yell as I bang my way into the room.

A small crowd has amassed on the far side of the lab. At first I can't see why, but the cameras and boom mic operator give it away even before I look past them.

He's back, in all his paleo rock star glory—loosely curling blond ponytail, perfect scruff, golden tan. He's a god, even in a ratty baseball cap, faded green ringer tee, and torn jeans. He's picking away at Dr. Glass's turtle shell, demonstrating the careful craft of specimen prep. The grins and quips he tosses out for the cameras are as calculated as every move he makes with his tools on the shell.

When I holler, his producer turns and glares. "Cut!"

Dr. Carver looks at us, and his eyes bug out a little.

"Dad!" Quinn skids to a stop then bursts forward and hugs him. "I didn't think you were getting in until tomorrow."

"Got an early flight." He pulls back and holds her at arm's length, frowning at her. "How's my girl? What's the matter? You digging yet?"

She ignores the questions. "Dad, come see what I just found!"

Oh, hell no. I freeze and stare at her.

She stares back, mouth open, and quickly says, "What Natalie and I found, I mean. We both did. Dad, this is big. Come on. Bring the camera guys!"

She runs back to me. "Sorry," she mouths as we start to lead the entire group back to bone storage.

"It's okay," I whisper back. "This one belongs to both of us."

17

"Look," the producer says behind us, "I don't know what you two think you found, but if we're going to film back there, I'm going to need you to clean up a little first. You both look like—"

Mellie interrupts him. "Ladies, what do you say we powder our noses?" As we pass the restroom, she drags us inside.

When I see my reflection, I understand why Dr. Carver's eyes bugged out at the sight of us. Mascara and eyeliner smear together under my eyes, turning me into a sad panda. Clumps of dust nest in my hair and cling to my shirt. Add all that to the way I burst into the lab like a stampeding elephant, and I look more like a psych ward inmate than a dig site intern. Quinn's in a similar state.

"You've both been crying. What happened?" Mellie asks again as I lean over the sink and scrub my face with a paper towel. Her voice has a sharp tinge of alarm.

"Mellie, you won't believe it," I say between splashes. "We have to show you—"

"First you have to breathe," she says, patting my back. "Calm down and tell me everything."

I towel off and check my face again. The results of my emergency cleansing job aren't perfect—I can't get everything off without proper makeup remover, and my purse is back in Dr. Glass's office—but at least the panda effect has mostly faded. I run my hands through my hair, knocking loose the dust bunnies and brushing them from my clothes as well.

My voice shakes when I try to explain. "I was in bone storage, and then Quinn found me, and we—"

"Why were you in bone storage? You were supposed to be at the screen wash station this morning. I was looking for both of you. But then, you know, Dr. Carver showed up, and..." Her mouth twists with embarrassment. "I should have kept looking. Now please tell me what the hell's going on so I can know if I somehow screwed up again. I really need those credits."

"I..." How I do even do this? My heart is still crushed, but that's the last thing I want to think about right now. "We had a disagreement."

"About?"

"Nothing." I glance at Quinn. "We'll work it out. I was just upset." I shake my head. "It's fine. Or it will be. But we have to go!"

The group waits for us in the hall. Everyone is still gathered around Dr. Carver, like he's a flickering candle and they're all swarming moths. "Everything okay?" Dr. Glass asks when he sees us.

Beside me, Mellie nods. "A little drama. Nothing to worry about."

Dr. Carver's producer waves his hand. "Can we do this thing now?"

"Keep those things rolling," Dr. Carver tells the cameramen. The crowd follows Quinn and me into bone storage.

"Here!" Quinn says when we reach the right aisle. She and I lead the way, followed by Dr. Glass, then Dr. Carver, then the cameramen and boom mic operator, with everyone else herding behind. I drop to my knees and pat the jacketed skull, and I pull off the identification tag and hand it to Dr. Glass.

His brow furrows as he reads it. "A mammoth calf?"

"From Ember Road," I say. "This is one of our—I mean, one of the site's mammoths, isn't it?"

"I could've sworn we had them all tracked down and prepped." He crouches beside us and peers at the shelf. His glasses slip down his nose.

"But it's possible you didn't, right?" Quinn glances at her father, making sure he's paying attention.

"Things did get overlooked in storage back then," Dr. Glass says.

Dr. Carver puts a hand on Dr. Glass's shoulder. "Mind moving over, Ted? Let's see this new mammoth."

Could the day have flip-flopped any faster? Suddenly I'm scooting aside to let Thomas Fucking Carver inspect my discovery. Well, *our* discovery—Quinn's and mine.

Maybe they'll let us nickname the calf. Maybe they'll put up a plaque in the museum explaining how we found it.

This will be the beginning of my long and glorious career in paleontology.

Dr. Carver kneels next to me and runs his hands over the dusty jacket. "Well, holy hell," he says at last, after staring at the identification card for a long time. "You might just be right, kids."

"I was sure we had everything from the site taken care of," Dr. Glass stammers. "I really thought—"

Dr. Carver hushes him with a wave. "Hey, this kind of thing happens in storage. What's important is that now it's been found."

"There are other parts of the skeleton here too." I half crawl onto the shelf again, not caring how awkward I probably look on camera as I point out the other Ember Road jackets. "I mean, I assume they're from the same mammoth."

"Won't know that until everything's been prepped."

"Of course," I say quickly. "If we're right, though, this might be a near-complete specimen."

But Dr. Carver is already standing up and dusting off his knees, so I hurriedly do the same. "I assume this skeleton will be your top priority now?" he asks Dr. Glass.

Dr. Glass clears his throat. "That's not really your call, Tom—"

"Let's get that skull out of its jacket as soon as possible. I'd like to film some of the prep work."

Dr. Glass shoots him a sharp look, but he nods and pushes up his glasses.

"Fantastic." Dr. Carver brushes his hands together. "Now, if you'll all excuse me, I've got some footage to go over and a few location shots to film. Quinn?" He points at her. "Dinner later, okay? You're off at six, right? I'll call you. Good job on this, kid."

"See you later, Dad," Quinn says with a huge grin.

I wait for a similar acknowledgment, but Dr. Carver raises his hand in a goodbye salute and jogs off.

For a moment, everyone stares after him, still spellbound. Mellie puts an arm around my shoulders and squeezes. "Everyone is going to be so excited about this! A new mammoth!"

"It'll make for some nice publicity for the site," Dr. Glass says. "Especially with the museum getting ready to open." He squats again to get a better look at the jacket.

"Well, now we've completely missed our break," Mellie says. "Should we stop for a late lunch? And then maybe we can get some actual work done today?"

I don't really want to leave the mammoth calf, but I follow the others out of the storage room.

"You sure you two are okay?" Mellie asks once more, her voice hushed as we head to the cafeteria.

"Yeah," I say. Beside me, Quinn nods.

Mellie follows my gaze and nods. "Of course, I wish you'd tell me what happened this morning."

"What happened is that we found a new mammoth. Nothing else is important."

"Okay." Mellie bumps her shoulder against mine. "But if you ever do want to talk about it, I'm around. Got it?"

"Got it."

While I'm in line to pay for my lunch, Chase comes up behind me. "Hey, congrats on the find."

Without a word, I hand the cashier my food card and walk away to sit with Mellie.

I delete the rant about the anonymous commenter without posting it, and I delete another eight or nine nasty comments from my recent posts at the same time. My traffic and subscriber count are both up; my repost of the pic from Dr. Carver's blog is getting hits from paleo forums and fashion subreddits. More traffic means more trolls. I don't want to bait them by singling one out, or by giving them any attention at all.

"I bet the local news does a story about your find," Mellie says at dinner. "They'll probably interview you two and everything!"

"You think so?" The thought flutters my stomach, jostling the chicken sandwich I've just finished. Quinn is out to dinner with her father. Chase sits several seats down, silently chewing his pizza.

Mellie nods. "Definitely! It's going to be a big deal. Just watch."

Even Eli throws me a brief nod of approval.

After dinner, Chase and Brendan take over the common room television to watch baseball. I'm not in the mood for sports—or for being in the same room with Chase—so I tell

Mellie I'm going for a walk. I wander the campus sidewalks while the setting sun paints the sky a bold orange in the west.

I take out my phone. I'm not sure how public I can be about the mammoth calf yet, but sharing the news with a few people can't hurt. I've got to tell Charli, and my parents, and Aunt Judy...My fingers scroll through my contact list and land on someone else.

Even as I'm typing a text to Cody, I'm not sure why he's the one I want to tell first. We haven't spoken since he commented on my appearance yesterday...but I know he's the one who'll most appreciate the news. And then there's that reply he left on Dr. Carver's blog...

Me: *Big find today!!*

Him: *What? You weren't even digging today. ;P*

Me: *Quinn and I were in bone storage...*

Him: *Yeah, and?*

Me: *Let's just say the case of the missing mammoth has been solved!!!*

Him: *You're losing me. What missing mammoth?*

Me: *A juvie from the site. Turns out it was SO missing that no one even remembered it existed. We found it shoved on a shelf, still in its jacket.*

My phone rings. Before I can say hello, Cody's yelling in my ear. "What? A site mammoth? We've got another mammoth?"

"Jesus, Cody, watch the eardrums."

"I'm not going to apologize for getting loud, not when you've just dumped this kind of news on me. How the hell'd you find a new mammoth?"

I fill him in.

"Well, fuck," he says. "That's amazing. Too bad they'll just have to give it away."

I stop short on the sidewalk. "What?"

"Nah. Never mind. I don't want to crap all over your good mood."

"It's a little late for that. What's going on?"

He sighs. "It's just that I overheard Dr. Lauren on the phone again today."

"The lawsuit?"

"Yeah. It's not looking good."

"You're kidding."

"I wish. Without a copy of that lease . . ."

"They're not really going to give that family all the fossils, are they?"

"Everything dug up in the first three months, yeah. That's what it sounded like."

"Well . . . damn it." I count months in my head. "That includes the new calf."

"You didn't hear it from me, okay? And hey, if you find any *contracts* along with all those bones, let someone know."

"Right. I wish. All I found was an old photo of Dr. Roland and that Flanders guy." That's when I remember that the photo is still in my pocket. I'll have to remember to take it with me to the site tomorrow and hand it to Dr. Gallagher or Dr. Lauren.

"Hey, sorry. But you did ask me to let you know if I heard anything."

"No, I'm glad you told me." After we hang up, I keep

imagining the new juvie winding up in a private collection somewhere instead of in the site's museum where it belongs.

When I get back to the dorm, Chase is outside, leaning against the wall near the door. "Natalie, can we talk for a minute?"

"Nope."

"Come on."

"Still nope."

"Natalie—"

"I really don't want to hear anything you have to say."

He sidesteps in front of the door, blocking my entrance. "Look, I know I screwed up."

"Let me inside."

He shoves a hand through his hair. "She came on to me."

"Yeah, she and I have hashed that out. And how hard did you try to resist?"

"Natalie, I really like you."

I shake my head. Every inch of me grows cold, unyielding. "I liked you too, Chase. I did. And I don't do that often. That was a rare thing for me."

"So give me another chance."

"Second chances are even rarer."

"Come on."

"Shove it." I push past him and run up the stairs.

Sorry, vintage velociraptors. No LotD pic today. I'm dressed for digging, and I'm still finding cobwebs and bone dust in my hair from yesterday. Crawling around in a bone storage warehouse does NOTHING for your look.

Oh, about that. Can't give you the details just yet, which is driving me crazy. But I've got big news, kids. BIG. NEWS. I'll share that with you as soon as I can.

For now, though, I'm running late. More soon, I promise!

That morning, I uncover a small chunk of what might be a rib in the bone bed. I'm carefully digging a pedestal around it when Dr. Lauren and Quinn walk by.

"Quinn, you'll be working in G14." Dr. Lauren leads her to a square meter not too far from mine.

"Finally got cleared?" I ask when Dr. Lauren is gone.

Quinn lays out her tools. "Yeah."

"Congrats!"

Her smile is tight. "Thanks. I think my dad must've said something." She goes quiet and starts scraping.

When I drop by the welcome center for a water break, Cody waves. Except for him and me, the lobby is empty. He's at the front desk today; Brendan is on tour duty.

"Congrats again on the calf," he says when I walk over.

"Thanks. Oh, shoot! The photo." I pull it out of my pocket. "I should go give this to Dr. Gallagher while I'm up here."

He holds out a hand. "Can I see?"

"Sure." I hand it over.

"Hmm," he says after a moment. "I've seen a couple of shots from the early days of the dig, but I've never seen this one. Cool."

"I think Dr. Roland's got part of a tusk."

"Looks like it. What's Flanders holding?"

"I don't know. A paper." I hadn't even noticed it before.

"It'd be funny if it was the lease," he says, chuckling.

I don't laugh. I stare. "What if it is?"

"Don't be crazy, Natalie."

"They're shaking hands, aren't they? Like they just made a deal."

He squints at the photo. "Even if it were, you can't read a word of it."

I take the photo back and hold it close to my face, trying to make out what the paper says. "Know what we need? One of those forensics guys on TV who can enhance pictures and make them clearer."

"Quit that before you get nose prints all over it." He plucks it from my fingers and studies it again. "Look, I'm sure it's nothing. But…"

"But what?"

"Well…I mean, I guess I could scan it in. Try to blow it up and sharpen it. Wouldn't be hard."

"You know how to do that?"

"Future graphic design major, remember? I've already taken two AP classes in digital media. I know my way around Photoshop."

I grab his wrist. "Do it!"

He frowns at the photo. "I can almost make out the first line…Okay, I'll see what I can do."

"Awesome." I grin and head to the shelter.

"Don't get your hopes up," he calls after me.

As I settle back into my spot, I see Dr. Lauren frowning down at Quinn's square. "Be careful not to remove too much matrix at once, Quinn."

"I'm being careful." Quinn has her tongue out in concentration as she scrapes at the dirt. She picks at a spot, frowning when it turns out to be nothing.

At a little before twelve, Dr. Lauren suggests we break early for lunch today. "Dr. Carver was interviewed at the lab this morning, and some of that interview might show up on the noon news. I'd like to see what he says, and I thought you'd all be interested as well."

All of us—interns, seniors, and Dr. Lauren and Dr. Gallagher—gather to watch the news on the break room's small television. Even Cody sneaks back, leaving the reception desk temporarily unmanned so he can listen in from the hall.

I get my sandwich from the fridge and unwrap it as the channel's news logo appears on the screen. The logo gives way to a bright-eyed anchor with teased blonde hair, shoulder pads, and a statement necklace made up of huge rectangle-shaped beads. Perfectly painted lips stretch into a grin as she runs through her intro. Her face recomposes itself into professional somberness as she launches into a story about a string of robberies in nearby Barton Creek.

Then the smile returns. "Now, on a lighter note," she goes on, "one local prehistoric family just located a long-lost member! Here's Ana Espinosa with a report from Austin State University."

"This is it!" Mellie bounces in her seat. "Natalie? Quinn? Did they talk to you at all?"

"Nope. Haven't heard a thing." I try to sound like I don't care that I wasn't interviewed.

Across the table, Quinn also shakes her head, her brow furrowing.

Like the anchor before her, Ana Espinosa grins into the camera from amid a teased-up mane of hair. "I'm here at the bone lab that's part of the paleontology program at Austin State University," she says, gesturing to the lab buildings behind her. "The program is affiliated with Austin's Central Texas Mammoth Site, a unique Ice Age dig site that's open to the public. I spoke with world-renowned paleontologist Dr. Thomas Carver about a very exciting discovery made here at the lab yesterday."

The story cuts to a shot of Dr. Carver in bone storage. He's kneeling next to the jacketed skull, pointing out the identification card to Ana. Ana speaks in a voice-over: "Paleontology isn't a perfect science, and Dr. Thomas Carver is the first person who'd admit that. Dr. Carver established his illustrious career making historic discoveries out in the field, but it turns out such discoveries can also be made right in the lab."

The shot changes again, and now the camera focuses on Dr. Carver's face—sharp cheekbones, square jaw,

ever-perfect scruff—as Ana interviews him. "I dropped by
the lab to visit my daughter Quinn, who's interning here
and at the Mammoth Site this summer. While I was here, I
toured the storage area, where specimens from all over the
world are kept while they wait to be cleaned and prepped
in Austin State's bone lab."

"And you spotted something unusual?" Ana prompts
off-camera.

I pause in mid-chew, my mouth full of a mix of ham and
lettuce and white bread that's quickly turning to paste.

"That's right," Dr. Carver says with an easy smile. "When
a storage area like this has a lot of specimens coming in,
things can get misplaced. That's rare these days because of
computerized records, but record keeping was more lax a
few decades ago. While I was looking around, I happened
to see a jacket—that's what we call these protective plaster
casings we wrap around bones before they're transported.
Anyway, I spotted an older jacket marked 'Ember Road.'
Ember Road goes right by the Mammoth Site, so of course
I wondered if the two might be related."

I freeze and stare at the screen. The ham-and-bread
lump seems to expand on my tongue. *He* spotted the jacket?
I glance at Quinn, but she's also staring at the TV, her jaw
clenched tight.

"And when you looked closer?" Ana asks.

"It's labeled as a juvenile mammoth skull. We thought
the site had seven juveniles in all—six calves and one slightly
older male—but if this is what we think it is, that brings the
total up to eight. I'll be working with the paleontologists

here to start cleaning up this little fellow over the next few days."

Dr. Carver runs his mouth a little longer, but I stop listening. I can't ignore the end of the report, though, when he reaches down and pats the jacket. Pats the new mammoth.

Pats *our* mammoth.

Quinn and I are surrounded by awkward glances. No one wants to stare, but everyone wants a reaction. I have none to give. I have nothing left but numbness.

Quinn stands so quickly her chair topples back, slamming onto the floor behind her. She stalks out. Across the lobby, the restroom door slams shut.

The gluey mass of half-chewed sandwich creeps down my esophagus like a slug when I can finally swallow. "Well," I say at last, just to break the silence. "Guess I'll get back to work." My stomach corkscrews. I toss the rest of the sandwich in the trash on my way out.

Dr. Gallagher follows me. "Natalie?"

"Yes?" I'm surprised. Dr. Gallagher doesn't usually interact with us too much; he leaves that to Dr. Lauren while he busies himself with research and meetings and fundraising projects.

"Let's talk for a minute. My office."

My heart flip-flops unpleasantly. I follow Dr. Gallagher into his office and take a seat. He tells me to wait for him, and then he leaves. I don't know what this is about, but his expression when he spoke was grim, and I'm suddenly sure I've screwed up again somehow. While I wait, I repeatedly snap the elastic around my wrist.

He comes back a moment later with Quinn, who is red-eyed and sniffling. He directs her to the seat next to me. I sit silently and wait for the anvil to fall.

Instead, he folds his hands together on his desk and says, "I'm sorry."

I blink. "Huh?"

"I know you two are the ones who found the skull. I've heard all about it, and I wanted to tell you both how sorry I am that you're not receiving proper credit."

I feel my lungs expand for what seems like the first time in ages. "Thank you."

Quinn sniffs and mumbles something.

"Quinn, I'm sure this is especially painful for you. I wish your dad was giving you the credit you deserve."

"It's not exactly a surprise," she says softly.

"Still—" Dr. Gallagher begins.

Quinn rakes the back of one hand over her eyes. "Can I please just get back to work?"

Dr. Gallagher sighs and nods, and Quinn stalks out.

Then he turns to me. "This is such a shame. Natalie, I've seen the work you've been doing here, the effort you're putting in. Your passion for the site isn't going unnoticed. I knew as soon as I looked over your application that you were meant to be here. I wish I could say the hell with fundraising and fill the program with kids just like you. With *women* like you—God knows this field needs more women. That's not how these things work, but I wish it were."

"You're talking about the kids who get in because their parents make donations, right?"

"That beautiful dig shelter out there?" Dr. Gallagher nods to a framed photo on his wall. In it, a slightly younger, slightly thinner, grinning version of him poses in front of the shelter's doors on its first day of operation. "Dr. Carver's paleo foundation paid for half of it."

"So when he wants something..."

"We bend over," he finishes for me. "That includes accepting his daughter into the program. Quinn has talent, but she's not at your level. You didn't hear that from me, understand?"

I nod. "Is that why she's allowed to dig now too?"

Dr. Gallagher presses his fingers to his forehead. "Tom dropped by yesterday afternoon and argued very...persuasively...that his daughter should be given a chance in the shelter. Her skills aren't there yet, but we could really use the publicity we'll get if he features us on his show."

I had no idea paleontology could get so political. "But what about the skull? How can Dr. Carver just say he found it?"

Dr. Gallagher sighs again. "It happens. It's not usually quite this blatant, but credit is...*redirected*...all the time. Big shots like Carver stand on the shoulders of those who do the real work. A student or an intern makes the find, but when the paper about it gets published, it'll be under someone else's name."

"He's done this before?"

His laugh is rueful, humorless. "This tradition goes back a lot further. Are you familiar with Mary Mantell?"

I shake my head.

"But you're heard of Gideon Mantell."

"Yeah, sure. He was an early paleontologist. He discovered the *Iguanodon*, right?"

Dr. Gallagher shakes his head. "Mary was his wife. She's the one who actually discovered the first *Iguanodon* fossil. But Gideon always gets credit."

"Seriously?"

"She found it. She did the first sketches of it. But when you read about the two of them, it's always 'Gideon Mantell and his wife.' When it comes to giving credit where credit is due, science has a long way to go."

"That's kind of gross."

He puts up a hand. "Don't get me wrong, Natalie. Tom Carver has put a lot of hard work into his career. He's paid his dues, and he's made his share of very fair discoveries. But he's also cultivated a persona for himself—that of the dashing adventurer—and he does whatever it takes to keep that up. That includes taking advantage of situations like this to keep his name out there, especially right now when he's about to launch his show."

"But that's not fair!"

"No. No, it's not. There's a lot of unfairness in science."

I lean forward. "What can we do about it?"

Dr. Gallagher raises his hands in a hopeless gesture. "Not much."

"But everyone who was around that day knows who found the mammoth. Dr. Glass could—"

"Tom wields a tremendous amount of influence," Dr. Gallagher says. "Other scientists don't generally like to cross him, not when he can pull a few strings and affect things like dig funding. Besides, even if we all went to the news and explained, the most we'd get is a brief retraction that no one would notice or remember."

I flop back and run a hand through my hair, shoving my bangs to the side. "This sucks, Dr. Gallagher. I'm sorry, but it fucking sucks."

"There are two lessons you can take from this," he says. "First, understand that this kind of thing happens. It's part of the game. Anyone who's been in the field for a while knows how you feel. At least you got your first experience with it over with early. You're way ahead of your peers—and with the way word travels among paleontologists, those of us who matter will know who really found that calf."

At least it's something. "What's the second lesson?"

Dr. Gallagher gives his ample whiskers a casual stroke. "Never, ever trust a male paleontologist without a proper beard. They'll screw you over every time."

For the first time in close to an hour, I crack a smile.

That smile doesn't last. I understand what Dr. Gallagher told me—this kind of thing happens—but it still stings. Dr. Carver's been my hero for years. Of all the people who might have taken credit for the mammoth calf, why did it have to be him? I can't believe he'd steal that from me—and from his own daughter.

I don't even mind when I'm put on front desk duty in the afternoon, while Cody runs the register at the gift shop. What's the use of digging if whatever I find can just be taken away by a swaggering hotshot like Thomas Fucking Carver?

I find myself waiting for the slow moments, the lulls, because then Cody can stroll across the lobby to talk or I can duck back to help him refold T-shirts or straighten the shelves of stuffed mammoths and sabercats. Unfortunately, it's a busy day and those opportunities don't happen often.

I'm dying to vent about Dr. Carver, but we barely get to discuss him or the photograph, or the lawsuit. Instead, I sell tickets and explain the site and hand out brochures and maps, and I try not to snap my hair elastic too much. My wrist is stinging nonstop.

At closing time, I get my purse from the back and head out with the others. Cody is waiting near the front doors when we pass by. He falls into step beside me long enough to hand me a folded piece of paper. At first I wonder if he's handing me back the photo, but this is something else. I raise my brows. He just shrugs and heads out to the parking lot. I pocket the paper.

Everyone else heads to the cafeteria, but I have no appetite. Alone in the dorm common room, I finally unfold the paper. It's been torn from a notepad I recognize from the gift shop, with a tiny cartoon mammoth in one corner.

Natalie,

Sorry that asshole stole your mammoth. I feel sorry for Quinn too . . . I guess. But mostly for you. If I'm still working here when the museum opens—if the site's even still here—I'll make sure to tell my tour groups who really found that calf.

Thanks for finding a new member of the herd.

Cody

I curl up on the couch and reread the note three times. I pull out my phone. *Thanks.*

I meant it, he answers. *You okay?*

Not really. I snap my hair elastic and cringe at how badly it stings. My left wrist is covered with raised red welts.

Meanwhile, my right wrist is wrapped with the words of the hero who betrayed me. I turn the cuff so the metal plate covers my inner wrist. The quote is less visible that way.

Want to hang out? Cody texts.

Me: *Oh God yes.*

Him: *Walk around campus?*

Me: *Anything. Yes. Sure.*

Him: *I'll be there in twenty minutes. No beer this time, okay? ;P*

Me: *Maybe just one can. ;P See you in twenty.*

I check my reflection in the bathroom. My lipstick has faded and my eyeliner could use a touch-up, but I can't be bothered. The day has left me exhausted—and besides, it's just Cody. I go outside and sit on a bench near the dorm parking lot. A few minutes later, an old green pickup pulls into a spot and Cody gets out.

"Really?" I say as he walks up. "A pickup truck?"

"Welcome to Texas, darlin'," he says, exaggerating his drawl. "Just be glad I left my cowboy hat and best country line dancin' boots at the ranch."

"Funny."

"Come on. I thought that was worth a smile, at least."

"Sorry." I quirk up the edges of my mouth, but I'm sure it doesn't look smiley at all. "Not really in that kind of mood."

"Hey, I get it. That Carver guy sucks."

"Yeah." I cross my arms and look at the sidewalk. "You know, I was all ready to rant for hours. I thought that was what I wanted, but now...I'm just tired. It's like I don't have anything left."

"You just want to walk for a while?" he asks. "We don't have to talk unless you feel like it."

"That'd be really great."

We wander past the dorms, over green space and sidewalk, while the sun creeps toward the horizon and the temperature drops down to something almost bearable. Cody says nothing. He lets us be silent, and that's exactly what I need. We walk for more than half an hour before he finally speaks up.

"What are you doing?"

"What?"

"Your wrist. The hair thing."

I look down—my right hand is yanking my hair elastic almost violently. "Didn't even notice. It's a habit." I let go and wince when the elastic snaps my sore skin.

"Hold on." He stops and catches my left hand, turning it so he can see my inner wrist. "Ouch."

"Yeah." The skin there is still inflamed and striped with welts from my most recent snaps. "It's not usually this bad, but…"

His gaze goes from my wrist to my eyes, his brows slanting downward. "It looks like it really hurts."

"Yeah, it's kind of stingy."

"But you do it anyway."

"It beats the alternative," I say.

"Which is?"

"Losing my mind, probably."

"Come here." Still holding my hand, he leads me down the sidewalk to a cluster of benches not far from the amphitheater. Next to one bench is a drinking fountain.

A soft, almost sleepy kind of calm comes over me while he gently pulls the elastic off and holds my wrist under the arcing stream. The water is surprisingly cold. For a second it makes my skin throb, but then a soothed numbness sets in.

"Any better?" he asks after a minute or two.

"Yeah. Much." My thoughts travel slowly, like they're fighting a current.

"Good." He uses the bottom of his T-shirt to pat my wrist and hand dry. When he hands me back the elastic, I put it in my pocket instead of on my wrist.

"Had dinner yet?" he asks.

"Wasn't too hungry."

"Cafeteria's not far from here, right? I'm going to grab a sandwich or something. Want one?"

I point him in the right direction, but I hesitate to follow, and he notices.

"Everyone else is probably still there at dinner," I say. "I really need a break from them." Chase is still throwing me kicked-puppy looks whenever he catches my eye.

"Understood. How about the fountain at the center of campus? I'll meet you there in a few."

Relief settles in my stomach. "Yeah."

"Sandwich?"

"Sure."

"You got it." He jogs off.

Ten minutes later, we're settled on the fountain's wide concrete rim with a to-go box from the cafeteria and a couple of sodas between us.

"Cafeteria pulled pork, yum," he says between bites of his sandwich. Sarcasm twists his tone like a one-sided grin. "It leaves a lot to be desired."

"I like it."

"Sauce is all wrong. Too much vinegar. You need to try this little place outside the city. Shelby's. Best barbecue around."

"Okay, sure." I laugh a little. "Not sure when or how I'll manage, but it's on my list."

"If not this trip, then once you start going to school here."

"Yeah. If I get in."

He gives me a side-eyed look. "You kidding? You'll get in."

"If the site gets shut down, I don't even know if I'll want to go here."

"Yeah." His shoulders fall a little. "There's that."

"Would that change your plans too?"

"I'd definitely rethink things, yeah. But Austin State has a great graphic design program too, so..."

I tilt my head. "Are you that into design?"

He shrugs.

"Then why don't you want to be a paleo major instead?"

He chews thoughtfully, taking a moment to answer. "Because design's more likely to get me a decent job."

I frown.

"You know enough about paleontology to know I'm right," he says. "There are only so many digs to go around. It's hard to get funding, especially when you're up against assholes like Thomas Carver."

The comment makes me glance down at my leather cuff. "I guess."

"It's just good to have a backup plan."

I narrow my eyes. "Yeah. Which of your parents told you that?"

He scowls back for a moment then chuckles. "My dad."

I look at my bracelet again, with its engraved *Keep digging* quote. I unfasten it and toss it over my shoulder. It splashes into the fountain. I don't need any more words of encouragement from Thomas Fucking Carver.

"Wow." Cody turns and looks back at the bracelet. "Didn't see that coming. Don't expect me to go in after it—I'm not much of a swimmer."

"Cody, that water's like two feet deep."

"You've never seen me try to swim."

I can't help laughing at the vision of him flailing in the fountain. "I don't want it back."

"Did you at least make a wish?"

"Any wish associated with that thing isn't one I'd want to come true."

He leans over and bumps his shoulder against mine.

We stay out there until it gets dark. When it's time for him to go, I offer to walk out to the parking lot with him, but he insists on walking me to my dorm instead. "You going to be okay?" he asks at the door.

I nod.

"Okay. You working at the site tomorrow?"

"No, at the lab."

"Shoot. Guess I won't be able to get the picture back to you until later then."

"Oh, yeah! Let me know if that goes anywhere."

"It won't."

I frown.

"But I'll let you know," he adds. He puts his hands in his pockets. Takes one step back. Then two.

Suddenly I kind of want to kiss him.

But he says, "So anyway, good night," and walks off.

I'm taking a break for a couple of days while I work through a few things. Nothing serious, kids, so don't worry. I'll be back soon.

20

Fossilista has gained more than five hundred new subscribers since I started blogging from Texas, but after Dr. Carver's appearance on the news, there's no way I can conjure the awesome version of Natalie who posts upbeat entries and cute outfits. I also can't imagine dealing with my usual trolls right now, not when I'm already down.

I get through Thursday by keeping my head low and focusing my concentration fiercely on my work. I'm especially careful to ignore the meticulous attention Dr. Glass pays the mammoth calf skull as he saws through the plaster and removes the jacket, bit by painstaking bit. I don't want to watch. I don't want to know. It's Dr. Carver's mammoth now. He's flown back to his dig in South America, but he'll be back here as soon as the skull turns into something worth posing with.

I skip the common room after dinner and go straight to my room, which is blissfully empty. I flop on the bed with my phone. I kind of want to text Cody, but I don't know what to say. Will he think I'm bugging him if I ask about the photo? I bring up the message app and let my thumbs hover over the keyboard. Over and over, I hit a few letters then double back and delete.

The door opens, and Quinn looks in. "Can I show you something?"

I sit up, and she perches beside me with her laptop. She has a browser open, and she's pulled up her dad's website. Dr. Carver's newest blog entry, which talks about the new mammoth and includes an embedded video of the news report from yesterday, is front and center on his main page. "I don't know why either of us would want to look at that again."

"Not that." She clicks a link to log in to his blog.

"Don't you need your dad's password?"

She exhales sharply. "His password is my birthday. Want to know how I know?"

"How?"

"Sometimes he can't remember it when he needs to make an entry, so he texts me and asks. He asks when my birthday is."

"Ouch."

She types in a combination of numbers, and the blog's admin panel comes up. She brings up the latest entry and clicks edit.

"I'm sorry for the thing with Chase," she says, staring at the screen. "This won't make up for that, I know. But what my dad did was pretty screwed up, and I thought this might make us both feel a little better."

The cursor blinks at the beginning of the juvie mammoth entry. Quinn starts to type. *I DIDN'T ACTUALLY FIND ANY OF THIS MYSELF*, she taps out in bold caps. *TWO INTERNS, QUINN CARVER AND NATALIE PAGE, FOUND IT. I JUST CLAIMED IT AS MY OWN FIND BECAUSE I'M A GIANT BAG OF DICKS.*

I snort out a laugh. "Quinn and Natalie, huh? Not Natalie and Quinn?"

"You want me to switch them around? I'll switch them."

"Nah." I shake my head and wait for her to delete the additions. Instead, she hovers the cursor over the *publish* button. "Wait, are you seriously going to post that?"

"Why not?

"He'd be livid."

"Like I care."

"You *do* care, though." She's been scrambling for his approval the entire time I've known her.

"Do you realize how many years I've been trying with him? I finally do something worthwhile—something that might actually impress him—and he steals it from me. From us. I'm done." She clicks *publish*. The edited entry goes live.

"Shit. Quinn." I can't begin to guess what the fallout for her might be once Dr. Carver notices the edit. I want to grab the laptop away from her and undo the changes, but she clicks away from the edit window before I can.

"What's he going to do about it, anyway? Stop taking me along on digs? Stop making big donations to get me internships so he can turn around and criticize everything I do?" She brushes away a tear with her fingers before it can fall.

Not quite believing my own compulsion, I reach out and give her shoulders a quick squeeze.

She shakes off the sadness before it takes hold. "Hey, while I'm logged in…" She scrolls through the other entries until she finds the one with the photo of me. "I saw some of the comments on this. I'll go ahead and delete them for you."

"I don't know if it's even worth your time."

She frowns at me. "You don't want me to take them down?"

"There are always going to be assholes, Quinn. You can delete those, but there'll be others. My aunt always told me you can't hide from assholes. You just have to learn to deal."

"Yeah, but…" Her cheeks pink and she stares at the screen. "In this case, the assholes were all me." Her tone is a vocal cringe.

For a second, anger flashes hot and dark in my chest. I remember her weird blank stare that day while she watched her father help and praise me in the sandbox. The first nasty comment popped up not long after that; the rest showed up the evening Quinn overheard me on the phone. "You left those comments?"

"It was shitty of me," she says, scrolling down to the first comment.

"Yeah, it kind of was." But I catch a glimpse of Cody's reply before Quinn deletes the comment thread, and my anger fizzles out.

She goes down the list of comments and deletes hers, one by one. "I'm sorry. You're not a fat ass."

I roll my eyes. "Have you seen me lately? The tag on these jeans still says size twenty."

She falters. "Well…Yeah, but—"

I laugh a little; I can't help it. "That plants me firmly in fat territory, Quinn. I'm not putting myself down. I'm just being matter-of-fact about it."

"People shouldn't judge you just based on that, though. They don't know you."

I pause. Swallow. "Just like people shouldn't judge you based only on what you look like or who your dad is? Like I did when we first met?"

She tilts her head at me. "What did you think of me? That I'm a lucky bitch with a famous dad?"

I give her a wry, narrow-eyed smirk. "A lucky, *skinny* bitch with a famous dad, actually. I mean, what size are those jeans? Don't you dare say zero."

"Nah, they're a four." She grins at me. "But I'm bloated. These are my fat pants. I'm usually a two."

I pretend to shove her off the bed. "Shut up."

She laughs and snaps her laptop shut. "I'm going to go see what everyone's watching in the common room. Want to come?"

My phone buzzes with a new text. "In a minute. Thanks for deleting the comments."

"No problem," she says on her way out.

The text is from Cody.

Attaching a pic. YOU NEED TO SEE THIS.

He's not usually the sort to go all caps lock, so this has

to be important. I open the image. It's a scan of the photo, cropped to show just the paper in Flanders's hand. The words are much clearer, but I still have to squint at them on my phone's small screen. It doesn't help that I'm immediately interrupted by another text from him.

Have you read it??????

Calm down and give me a second! I text back. When I blow up the image as big as possible, I can make some of it out. Most of what I read is legalese, but one sentence jumps out:

THE LANDOWNER (CARL J. FLANDERS) AGREES THAT ANY MATERIALS FOUND ON THE PROPERTY DURING THE EXCAVATION PERIOD BELONG TO THE LEASEE (WARREN ROLAND ON BEHALF OF AUSTIN STATE UNIVERSITY).

At the bottom of the paper, I can just make out several signatures.

I text Cody again. *HOLY SHIT.*

Him: *I know, right?!*

Me: *It says it right there! Everything found during the dig belonged to Dr. Roland and the school!*

Him: *Tomorrow. We go to Dr. L first thing tomorrow with this.*

Me: *How can we wait that long????*

Him: *I don't know!!!!!*

I giggle at his uncharacteristic abuse of exclamation points, and I send back: *This is it! We just saved the site!*

Like anything's ever that easy.

21

The next morning, Cody is waiting for me at the welcome center doors.

I'm shaking. "Is Dr. Lauren here yet?"

"Yes. Come on!" He's holding the photo and a flash drive.

"Thanks for waiting," I say as we rush down the hall to her office.

"I knew you'd stab me with your trowel if I didn't."

"True."

We bust into Dr. Lauren's office, startling her half out of her chair. "What's wrong?" she barks.

"Nothing!" I say as Cody hands her the photo.

She slides on her reading glasses. "What is this?"

"I found it with the mammoth in bone storage," I say.

At the same time, Cody says, "It's that Flanders guy and Dr. Roland!"

"And the contract! The lease!"

"The one you can't find!"

"Flanders is holding it!"

"I...what?" Dr. Lauren squints at the photo. "How do you even know about that?"

"We've heard things." Cody is nearly breathless.

"That's not important," I add. "You need a contract, right? There's proof of a contract!"

Dr. Lauren shakes her head. "I can't read a word of it."

I paw Cody's shoulder. "Show her!"

Cody forces the flash drive into her hand. "There's a high res scan on here."

Dr. Lauren plugs the flash drive into her computer and opens the image. The contract is even clearer on her screen than it was on my phone. She stares at it for a moment, says, "Oh, my," and puts a hand to her mouth.

"I know we should've given you the photo right away," I say, "and I'm sure we overstepped some boundaries."

Cody adds, "But we figured if there was a chance we could help with the lawsuit..."

"No, no," Dr. Lauren says. Her eyes dart back and forth as she reads over the legible parts of the contract. "I'm glad you..." She pauses and looks at us, first me, then Cody. "This is real, right? You didn't edit this?"

My spine goes cold. Surely he didn't...But he did brag about his Photoshop prowess. I hold my breath, waiting for him to answer.

His brow furrows, and I see the truth in his face before he says a word. A tiny zing hits him, sharpening his gaze, causing his jaw to clench. He's hurt that she'd even think he might be making the whole thing up. *Hurt*. "It's real," he says.

Dr. Lauren and I exhale at the same time.

"This is fantastic," she says. "You two, I don't…I don't even know what to…" She punctuates her flustered words by waving her hands at us in a shooing motion. "You're both wonderful. Now get to work and let me call our lawyer. I have to find out how to get this authenticated."

"Will you keep us updated?" I ask.

"Yes. Of course. Until then, let's continue to keep the situation quiet, okay? Word's gotten out to too many people as it is, and I'm already scrambling on damage control."

We nod, and I start to follow Cody back into the hall. I pause. "Dr. Lauren?"

She's already dialing. "What?"

"You haven't given out the assignments for this morning yet."

"Oh. Oh, Christ." She rubs her forehead. "I can't even think about anything but this damn photo. What do you want to do?" She widens her eyes, prompting me to hurry, so I take a chance and bring up the one activity that might be interesting enough to distract me from wondering about the photo all morning.

"Can I prospect?"

"Yes, of course. That's fine. Just take Mellie with you." She waves again, shooing me away. She's so distracted that I probably could have asked to play a mammoth rib cage like a xylophone and she would've okayed it.

Cody high-fives me and goes off to gather his first herd of tourists.

Mellie gets us a pair of neon yellow safety vests from the storage shed, and we head out beyond the dig shelter to the riverbed.

"This is awesome," Mellie says. "I almost never get to prospect. Any idea why Dr. Lauren decided we could go out today?"

I can't say anything about the lawsuit, so I just shrug and pull on my vest. I shouldn't have bothered with a shaper today; it's going to be sweltering with so many layers. At least I used a light hand with my makeup—anticipatory trembling and precise winged eyeliner don't play well together. There's a lot less stuff on my face to melt off as we climb down toward the riverbed.

"It's good that we're having such a dry summer. I mean, it's terrible in terms of droughts and fires. But it keeps the riverbed from flooding, so . . . yay for us!" She leads the way along the gulch.

The ground here is parched. The muddy spots from last time have long since dried, since there hasn't been any more rain. The dirt is gridded with intersecting patterns of deep cracks that crumble into themselves when we step on them.

After a few minutes, we reach a thick tree trunk that lies across the riverbed, forming a low bridge from one bank to the other. "It finally fell!" Mellie says. "It's been threatening to for months. Guess it couldn't hold on anymore. Let's look here for a while. You have such a good eye for this."

"I do?"

"The pork chop?" she says, and I'm sorry I asked.

When it fell, the tree's roots lifted, tearing up a huge chunk of soil. This is an excellent place to hunt, I know; new discoveries often show up in the freshly turned earth churned by falling trees.

But we find nothing, and by the time we go back for lunch, clouds darken the western horizon.

"Oh, sure," Mellie says when thunder growls low in the distance. "*Now* the rain shows up."

The storm passes us by without hitting us, but its threat is enough for Mellie to declare all prospecting over for the day. Dr. Lauren and Dr. Gallagher are out (*meeting with the site's lawyer*, I think but can't say out loud), so Mellie hands out the assignments for the afternoon. She puts Quinn and me in the dig shelter.

"Hey," Mellie says while I'm laying out my tools, "Sunday's a free day. Got plans?"

I hadn't even thought about it. I shrug.

"Assuming I can get permission, want to head into Austin for a few hours? I'm itching to do some thrifting, and there's a great bookstore downtown."

"Do you think we'd be allowed?"

"Don't see why not. You'd have supervision." Mellie sticks out her tongue and points at herself. She looks at Quinn. "What do you say? Up for an Austin adventure this weekend?"

"I know less than nothing about thrift stores," Quinn says haltingly.

Mellie claps her hands. "Perfect! I love working with a blank slate."

"Oh, shit. You guys!" Brendan is sprawled on one of the common room couches, messing with his phone. His fingers zip over the screen as he scrolls. Whatever he's found makes him laugh almost explosively.

I'm deconstructing a T-shirt for Mellie, showing Quinn how I go about adding raw-edged vents in the knit fabric. "What?"

Quinn's eyes narrow. "I swear, Brendan, if this is another one of those fail vids with a bunch of people falling off roofs and—"

"Something happened to your dad's blog." He slides off the couch and shows us the article he's been reading.

I've been so preoccupied with the lawsuit and the photo that I forgot all about the moment of rage-induced glee Quinn and I shared the evening before. Now I remember, and my stomach clenches when I see the headline: *Carved in Falsehood: Celebrity Paleontologist Thomas Carver Steals Credit for Latest Find from Daughter?*

He stole from more than just Quinn, obviously, but I'm kind of relieved that the article plays up the father-daughter angle. Seeing the accusation featured on an online science journal I read all the time makes me nervous. The article includes a screenshot of the blog entry taken before Carver or his people had time to catch and delete the edit. Although the headline shuts me out, I'm mentioned in the article. There's no suggestion of who might be responsible for the leaked information, and the writer notes that Dr. Carver hasn't yet responded to any requests for comments.

"I just Googled it," Chase says from his seat on the far couch, and although I'm still mostly ignoring him, I can't help but listen. "*Paleo Weekly* has an article too. Even *National Geographic* has a mention on its website."

Quinn's phone vibrates with an incoming call. "Shit," she mutters when she looks at the screen, and I glance over in time to see Dr. Carver's photo before she jumps up and heads downstairs to answer in private.

"Can't say that I feel too terrible for that jackass." Mellie picks up the shirt I've been working on and examines the hemline. "I wonder who did it, though. There were more than a dozen people in bone storage when you and Quinn showed him the calf. If any of them have a grudge and know how to get into his account…"

I take the shirt from her and get back to work, wishing I could listen in on Quinn's conversation with her father. When she comes back upstairs, she heads straight for our dorm room and goes to bed.

22

"Quinn, come here."

She wanders over from where she's been half-heartedly digging through a rack of jeans. She hasn't brought up the call from Dr. Carver or anything related to his blog, and I haven't wanted to press. I've come across a few more articles about the allegation, including a Buzzfeed piece that claims to explain the entire situation using animated GIFs of Chris Pratt, but Carver himself hasn't released any sort of statement addressing the whole mess. I try not to worry, and instead I immerse myself in the hunt for hidden fashion treasure. Mellie is right—Austin has amazing thrift stores.

"I need your shoulder." With my hand on Quinn's shoulder for balance, I kick off my sneakers to try on a pair of 1960s pink Naturalizer pumps. "Look at that—they fit perfectly and they're only three bucks!"

"How do you find anything here?"

"The same way you find something at the site. You dig." I dive into the jeans, pawing past pair after pair until I find her size. "It's not often I get to look for a two, you know."

She checks the tag. "True Religion? These things would cost like a hundred and fifty at Saks."

"Here all jeans are five bucks, and this pair looks new."

"That can't be right." She turns them over in her hands, looking for a catch.

"I told you—you just have to dig." I head toward the fitting room with a vintage Leslie Fay wrap dress. By the time we're ready to call it a day, my pile of treasures has grown: an adorable 1940s elephant brooch, a two-dollar grab bag of thin headscarves (they smell like mothballs, but a vinegar soak and a good airing out will remedy that), three polka-dot bangles for a buck, and—best of all—a '50s-Hawaiian souvenir straw handbag for Aunt Judy.

Quinn gets the jeans I found her, and I also help her scout out a pink leather Ralph Lauren jacket.

Mellie buys a ridiculous fedora and just about loses her shit when she discovers a storage bin full of someone's donated yarn stash. The entire bin goes with her to the cash register.

"One more stop," Mellie says, parking downtown. "I can't bring newbies to Austin and not take them to Book People." We spend the next hour exploring the two-story indie bookstore, and I buy a gorgeous red-and-black sketchbook that'll be perfect for drawing new dress designs.

Once our retail therapy is complete, Mellie suggests we grab a late lunch. "You guys in the mood for anything specific?"

I can't remember the name of the barbecue place Cody mentioned the other evening, so I text him. *Shelby's*, he answers immediately.

"Oh, yeah!" Mellie says. "Barbecue fan, huh?"

"It was highly recommended."

"As it should be. You can't come to Texas and not have barbecue at least once," she says, "and that thing the cafeteria calls a barbecue sandwich doesn't count."

I still don't know what's wrong with the cafeteria's barbecue.

We drive through more of Austin's downtown on our way out of the city. When we pass over a bridge, Mellie says, "I wish we could stay until after dark."

"Why?" I ask.

"This is the South Congress Bridge. This is where you see the bats."

Quinn stares over the water. "I've seen bats before."

"Not like this, you haven't. The colony that lives under this bridge is insane. In the summer, they swarm out every night to feed. It's, like, a thing here. It's part of what makes Austin so awesomely weird."

Shelby's is a little out of the way, several miles down the highway. Mellie takes an exit and turns onto a dirt road that winds up a hill. There's no sign at the turn, so I wonder how anyone is supposed to find the restaurant. We take a few twists and curves, and there it is—a rustic wood cabin-style building with a painted sign that reads *Shelby's Place*. The parking lot is almost full; Shelby's hidden location is apparently not a problem.

I take one bite of my sliced pork sandwich, and I get it. Oh, I get it. The pork is wonderful—juicy and tender and rich—but the sauce really makes the sandwich. It zings on my tongue, tangy and sweet and bright, with just enough heat to make it interesting.

My phone buzzes. I have to wipe barbecue sauce from my fingers before I can take it out to read the text. It's from Cody. *Finally understand?*

YES, I answer.

"Cool," he says behind me. I jump and turn in my seat to see him walking up.

"What are you doing here?" I ask.

"I never miss an excuse to go to Shelby's." He gestures to the bench beside me. "May I?"

I scoot over, ignoring the sudden fluttering in my stomach. The restaurant is dim inside, great for hiding the worst of my sudden blush.

Mellie looks at me, then at Cody, then back at me, and her lips twitch. "Hey, Cody. How ya doing?"

"Can't complain," he says as our waitress appears to take his order. "What have y'all been up to?"

We fill him in. When Mellie mentions the South Congress Bridge, he nods. "Shame you can't stay out and see that. It's great. I'd volunteer to take a couple of the interns out to see it myself, but my truck only seats two." The glance he tosses me is so brief that I nearly miss it, but the nudge his foot gives mine under the table is unmistakable.

"Wouldn't be allowed anyway," Mellie says, licking sauce

from her finger. "There'd have to be a senior intern along, and we'd risk missing curfew. After the drinking thing..."

"Understood," Cody says easily.

I smile, but I'm surprised how much I wish Mellie had said yes.

We end up hanging out for another hour at Shelby's, lingering over slices of pecan pie. After a while, Mellie excuses herself to use the restroom. "Quinn, come with me." Mellie pulls her out of her seat. "Girls are supposed to visit the restroom in packs. Back in a few." She winks at me as she and Quinn wander off.

"So I think we were just given a little private time," Cody says, chuckling. "Which is great, since I've been dying to ask if you've heard from Dr. Lauren."

"Not a thing. You?"

"Nope."

"Damn it. I'm going to die of curiosity."

"Aww," he says, taking a swig of sweet tea. "Don't do that."

I grin. "Why not? Would you be sad?"

"Of course. No one else is half as good at covering for me on tour duty."

I reach up and give his shoulder a good shove.

He laughs again. "Will you be at the site tomorrow?"

"Lab," I say. "Another day of picking through gravel while Dr. Glass preps the mammoth calf."

"Ugh. Do you at least get to help?"

"Not qualified for bone prep."

"Well, that just sucks," he says, and he sounds so genuinely insulted on my behalf that it almost makes the situation sting a little less.

Almost.

23

The crash sounds like the time Dylan kicked his soccer ball in the living room and knocked the vase containing Mom's shell collection onto the floor. It's followed by a thud and a pained yelp. I drop my Micron pen in the middle of an identification number and run into the bone lab. I'm the only intern working inside today. Everyone else is out at the screen washing station.

An avalanche of gravel lies scattered across the industrial tile. At its center, Mellie struggles to get to her feet then gives up and falls back, wincing and wrapping a hand around her ankle.

Dr. Glass puts down the porcupine quill he's been using on the juvie mammoth skull, shuts off the overhead exhaust fan, and limps his way through the mess to help her. When he reaches out a hand, he nearly slips on stray gravel

[1][1,2][a]12

himself and has to grab one of the worktables for balance. "Careful," he says, hauling Mellie up.

"Ow, ow, fucking ow," she hisses through clenched teeth as Dr. Glass helps her to the nearest chair.

I run up, taking the long way around the room to avoid the gravel. "Are you okay? What happened?"

Mellie waves a hand toward the chaos. "I was hauling gravel. The bucket handle broke. I slipped." She looks down and tests her ankle, turning it a little. "Ow! Fuck."

Dr. Glass clasps his hands together nervously. "Do you want me to call an ambulance? Maybe it's broken."

"It's not broken," Mellie says, still grimacing. "At least, I don't think it is. Think I just twisted it. It's already swelling up."

"But still…" Dr. Glass shoves his frames up the bridge of his nose.

"The campus clinic will be fine. I'll just need some help getting there." She tries to stand.

"Wait! Hold on." Dr. Glass bows, gets an arm around her. "Okay. Now. Up."

Mellie staggers up on one foot. Her weight throws Dr. Glass off balance, and for a moment they teeter. I step up to support her other side, but Eli is there before I can manage. He swoops Mellie up in his arms and stalks toward the front doors.

"You're supposed to be supervising the interns outside," she says.

"They can supervise their own damn selves for a few minutes," he mutters.

Dr. Glass hurries after them. He grabs a cane leaning by the front door.

"Want me to clean this up?" I ask as he heads out.

"That'd be great," he says over his shoulder.

"Hope you're okay, Mellie!" I call. When they're gone, I find a broom and a dustpan in a storage closet and get to work piling the gravel in a new bucket.

Cleanup doesn't take long. I sweep up the debris and lug the new bucket out to the screen wash station.

"Special delivery." I put the bucket down by Quinn.

"Where's Eli?" Brendan asks.

I fill them in on Mellie's fall and then go back into the empty lab.

The mammoth calf skull sits on a center table, under the heavy exhaust apparatus. It's partially exposed now. It's still more than half anchored in plaster, but Dr. Glass has made a lot of progress.

It's a gorgeous specimen. Aside from a large crack down over the right cheek and some pitting on the forehead and cheekbones, I don't see much in the way of major damage. And it's so very small—at least for a mammoth. The skull can't be much larger than a basketball. It might have been the youngest baby in the herd when the flood came rushing through.

I want to work on it. Just a little. Just so I'll know I did. I glance toward the back door. Everyone else is still out at the screen wash station. No one would ever even have to know.

With a soft brush, I gently remove a little plaster dust and loosened matrix from around the nasal cavity. I use a quill to pick at a stubborn patch of dirt, gently worrying away at it until the patch of bone beneath is clean.

The process is calming. I shouldn't be doing it, but this is the only chance I'll have and I can't stop. My concentration is complete. I fixate on a square inch or so of skull, meticulously picking, gently brushing, careful, careful, careful. All that matters is that my hands stay steady, my patience strong and absolute.

I'm dusting tiny specks of matrix from the calf's cheekbone, barely touching brush to bone, when an entire two-inch chunk just…falls off. Just like that. It tumbles down and thuds onto the lab table, crumbling a bit on the way.

Oh, shit.

Oh, shit.

Not moving, not breathing, I stare down at it. A panicked roar builds in my head, a mix of my clobbering heartbeat and my careening thoughts.

"Natalie?" It's Dr. Glass's voice, but I can't look up. I'm vaguely aware of his uneven footsteps approaching from the lab door. "What the hell are you doing?"

My mouth is as dry as the fossil I've just broken. "I don't…I mean…"

"Put down the brush."

I drag my gaze to my hand, which quakes as it clutches the brush. When I don't—can't—obey, he grabs it away from me and places it on the table.

"I'm so sorry," I manage.

He's peering at the pitted cheekbone, at the little crater where the chunk used to be. "What were you thinking?"

My voice shakes as badly as my hand. "I just wanted to try."

"You're not cleared for bone prep!"

"I know!" I clamp my jaw against the tremble. "But I helped find this thing, and—"

"You haven't been trained at all. We can't have interns doing work they're not qualified for. I'm going to have to report you to Dr. Lauren."

That's when I remember that I'm already on probation. My stomach drops down to my toes.

He sighs, dismissing me with a tired wave. "Get lunch and go back to cataloging for the afternoon."

Cheeks burning, I turn to leave. That's when I see Eli and Mellie watching from the doorway. Mellie's on crutches, her injured ankle wrapped in an Ace bandage. "C'mon," she says quietly. "Lunchtime."

All afternoon, while I catalog bone fragments with Mellie and snap my elastic, I wait for the inevitable. "I'm done. Dr. Glass will talk to Dr. Lauren, and I'll be out of the program."

Mellie blows on a newly labeled fragment to dry the fresh ink. "You don't know that. Accidents happen during prep. It can be patched."

"I know. But still. I keep expecting Dr. Lauren to come marching in here to send me packing."

I'm putting away the last few specimens when I hear Quinn's voice, shrill and angry. I stick my head out into the main hall and catch a glimpse of her stalking out the front door, phone to her ear.

"Dad, I already told you! How the hell should I know who did it?" she yells as the door closes behind her.

Mellie and I glance at each other.

"Would you make sure she's okay?" Mellie puts a hand on her crutch. "I can't chase her down like this."

I head outside, where Quinn paces in the lab parking lot. Her mouth opens and closes like she can't get a word in. Even though she's on the phone, she keeps nodding her head. She sees me coming and holds up a finger for silence.

"Dad," she finally cuts in when the voice on the other end stops ranting, "if I hear anything, of course I'll tell you. But I just don't know, okay? I don't know anything about it…Yes…*Yes. Okay*. Bye."

She lowers the phone and turns to me. "I'm betting you can guess what that was about."

I nod.

Despite the late afternoon heat, she wraps her arms around herself. "He's really pissed. Did you see the article on Science Web? Now three other paleontologists are claiming he stole finds from them too."

"I saw it."

"I mean…if this stuff keeps coming out, he might get sued or something. He's built this whole empire on these discoveries, and I don't know what that would mean for my family." She looks at her phone. "He kept screaming at me about getting hacked."

"We did kind of hack his account."

She puffs out an exasperated breath. "Please. He had a

shitty password. That's not getting hacked. That's being an idiot."

I head back toward the lab and tilt my head for her to follow. "It didn't sound like he thinks you did it."

"He doesn't. He figures it has to be someone from the site, though. I guess he's ruled out his film crew, and who else would know the truth about the calf?"

"And he's hoping you'll squeal?"

"Of course."

I give her a sideways look. "Are you going to?"

"Are you kidding? Turn myself in? Like he doesn't already hate me enough?"

"But…Quinn, there were two names in that edit. If you're in the clear, doesn't that make me the prime suspect?"

She stops short. "You think I'd lie and say you did it?"

"I don't know. I'd like to think you wouldn't." But I can't stop thinking of her and Chase at the screen wash station.

She grunts and hurries ahead of me into the lab.

After dinner, I can't settle down. The common room holds too much potential for drama; Chase still looks like he's about to open his idiot mouth and let more meaningless apologies tumble out, and Quinn won't even glance in my direction.

I wander around campus before settling down on an amphitheater bench, where I text Cody. *Any contract news?*

Him: *Dr. L and Dr. G weren't in again today. More meetings. Nothing to report yet.*

Me: *Damn. Could've used some good news.*

Him: *What's up? ;P*

Me: *Nothing much. Just probably getting kicked out of the program.*

Him: *What????? Wait, I'm calling.*

"What's going on?" he demands as soon as I answer.

"Hello to you too."

"Quit it, Natalie. What the hell happened?"

I tell him about the skull. "If Dr. Lauren was out all day, maybe that means Dr. Glass didn't have a chance to tattle yet."

"If you're lucky, the whole thing will get lost in the drama."

I blink. "What drama? The contract?"

"Yeah, that and the Dr. Carver thing."

"Oh God. That."

"Yeah. He called up this afternoon, ranting about that message that got left on his blog. He thinks someone at the site hacked him. Yours truly was on phone duty."

"Ouch."

"Eh." I can hear the shrug in his tone. "It was kind of entertaining, actually. He made all kinds of threats. I kept imagining that vein in his forehead bulging and finally busting under the pressure."

I laugh a little, but the sound is humorless. "Yeah, well, that hack is the other half of my problem." I explain what Quinn and I did, and how she reacted when I spoke to her earlier.

"Well…shit. You really think she'll rat you out?"

"I honestly don't know. She acts like we're friends, but this wouldn't be the first knife in my back. And, I mean,

I get why she's worried. Neither of us expected things to snowball like this."

"So you do the ratting out then."

I rub my temple. "Things between Quinn and her dad are bad enough as it is. I can't do that to her."

"Even if it means you getting kicked out?"

"I'm hoping it doesn't come to that."

"You want me to come over and hang out for a while?"

I do, but I'm too tired to be good company. "Nah. I didn't eat much dinner, so I'm just going to grab one of those cafeteria barbecue sandwiches you're so fond of and then try to get some sleep."

"Oh, don't do that. Not the cafeteria barbecue. I can stop by Shelby's for takeout on my way. Come on."

"I . . ." I fish for an excuse, but I can't find one. "Okay."

Half an hour later, he's beside me on the bench, and the smell of Shelby's barbecue sauce is turning the amphitheater air spicy-sweet.

"Feel that?" He looks toward the horizon, where a bank of dark clouds gathers to blot out the twilight. "The air's heavy. We're in for a real Texas storm tonight."

"Dude, I'm from Florida. Rain doesn't impress me." The smell of ozone reminds me of the thunderstorms we have almost every afternoon at home.

"You'll see," he drawls around a mouthful of pork.

"I guess I will. Right now I have other things on my mind—like losing my internship."

"You don't *know* you're getting kicked out."

"No, but I'm on probation. Dr. Lauren made it pretty clear after the beer thing that we don't have room to screw up again. Even if Quinn doesn't blame the hacking on me, the damage I caused to that skull is enough."

He points at me. There's barbecue sauce on his finger. "They wouldn't even know that skull existed if you hadn't found it. That has to count for something."

"I guess, but still."

"The way I see it," he says, "you just need another moment like that. One that doesn't get stolen out from under you. You need to show them you're indispensable."

"I doubt there are more mammoths just sitting around waiting for me in storage."

"True. But…there has to be something. Wait, what about the contract?" He gestures enthusiastically, flailing his arm until a bit of pork flies out of his sandwich and lands on the next bench over. "You found the proof that might just save the whole site. That has to be worth a broken mammoth cheekbone."

I'd like to think he's right. "That's assuming the lawsuit gets straightened out while I'm still here. Legal stuff takes forever. My ass could be back in Florida before we know the site is safe."

"That doesn't mean you should give up in the meantime. You just have to keep standing out."

I shrug.

"Hold on," he says, and suddenly his fingers are under my chin while his thumb lightly brushes my nose.

I freeze as he pulls his hand away.

"Sauce on your nose," he says with a grin, licking his thumb.

"How did I manage to..."

"Must be a rare talent," he says before popping the last bite of barbecue into his mouth.

24

Cody is right about the storm. It rolls in about an hour after he walks me back to the dorm, and it's still tearing through when I go to bed. The rain doesn't fall—it slams against the windows, whipped along by the wind while thunder shakes the building. Mellie keeps checking her phone for tornado warnings.

I lie awake, listening to the storm and thinking about the dig site. The shelter protects the exposed bone, but I wonder what the weather might uncover elsewhere on the property. Tomorrow would be an ideal time to prospect, but I doubt I'll ever have that chance again now.

The next morning, Dr. Lauren and Dr. Gallagher are hurrying out the door when we arrive. "Natalie!" Dr. Lauren snaps, keeping me back while the others file inside.

I stop and wait, wide-eyed, as my entire body tenses. *Here it comes.* I don't even know if this is about the skull or the website or both.

But all she says is "When I get back from this meeting, we're having a conversation." Her tone is sharp and crisp, but at least I'm not getting reamed right here at the front entrance.

"Okay." I glance over her shoulder at Dr. Gallagher. He's already out of earshot, on his way to the parking lot, but I lower my voice anyway. "Is the meeting about the lawsuit?"

She huffs out an impatient sigh. "Yes. Today...could be big."

"Good luck," I say before following the others into the welcome center.

Cody is organizing his first tour near the back door. I catch his gaze and widen my eyes in silent question, but he just shrugs and gives his head a quick shake.

Thanks to her injury, Mellie's stuck at the reception desk today, sitting with her ankle elevated on a stool. It's a long hobble down to the dig shelter. If I let her think I'm out there digging, she'll never know if I'm actually somewhere else. Eli and the others are in the bone bed. If they don't see me, they'll assume I'm working here in the welcome center.

You just have to keep standing out. A terrible, wonderful idea detonates in my brain. I shouldn't. If I get caught, I'm done here. But what if I'm done here anyway?

Cody is waiting on a few guests who are using the restroom before the tour. "I'm going down to the riverbed,"

I tell him under my breath. "I want to do a little prospecting." I don't want to crouch in the dirt all morning, picking away at my rib bone. I want to walk and wander and ramble. If there's something to find, that's where I'll find it.

He does that furrowed-brow thing at me. It's a lot cuter than it used to be. "Prospecting's supposed to be a team thing, isn't it?"

I roll my eyes. "I'll be fine. I'll wear a vest. I have to do this. I have to keep standing out, right?" Leaving him to his tour, I grab a safety vest from the storage shed then head down the walkway and veer off toward the riverbed like I'm allowed to be there. I wait to be spotted and questioned and stopped, but that doesn't happen.

Soon I'm out of view of the welcome center, and I start picking my way down to the riverbed. Thankfully, I'm dressed for the adventure—sneakers, jeans, tank top. I've really slacked off since I stopped updating *Fossilista*. I didn't even bother with a shaper underneath.

I navigate the downward slope with care, knowing that I'm alone. If something happens, there's no one to go for help. Step by wary step, I descend.

Cody's voice calls "Wait up!" behind me. I'm startled. My shoe skids over a patch of rotting leaves. My hand shoots out, grabbing for and missing a nearby branch, but he catches my arm and steadies me.

He's wearing a safety vest.

"See?" he says. "It's supposed to be a team thing."

I narrow my eyes. "What are you doing here?"

"Coming with you."

"What about your tour?"

"Martina's covering for me for a little bit. Mellie thinks I'm taking an early break."

I shake my head. "I'm going to be out here for a while. Mellie will notice when you don't come back from break."

He shrugs.

"Cody, don't get yourself in trouble."

"I'm coming with you," he says again, his voice firm.

"Why? Because I'm a girl and I can't handle myself alone in the woods for a few hours?"

"No. Because I'd be pretty pissed at myself if you got hurt out here on your own."

"Fine." My stomach clenches and flutters again at his words, but I'm not about to let him know that, not when he's being stubborn.

"Besides, I want to prospect too. You can't hog it all for yourself, you know." He throws me a quick smirk.

"Have you done this before?"

"Nope." He grabs a thick branch, stabilizing himself for a particularly steep step down. "Not part of my job description. Maybe you can explain how this works as we go."

"Oh. Okay. Well…" I fill him in on what Dr. Lauren told us the first time we all came out here. I even tell him about the pork chop.

He makes a grumbly sound that might actually be laughter. It's so surprising that I turn to look at him.

He's grinning. "A pork chop?" he asks. "Really?"

"Hey, it's a bone! Even Dr. Lauren had to take a closer look."

"Nice."

"Shut up," I say, laughing a little. A barely there breeze weaves through the trees, warm and earthy and slightly sweetened by the scent of pine. Last night's storm left the ground saturated and the air humid, but a lot of the river-bed here is shaded, which makes the heat a lot more bear-able. It'll be a little while before my tank top gets sweaty enough to mold itself to my back. It's actually pleasant out here. I can almost ignore the multiple messes waiting for me back at the site.

I lead him to the fallen tree. "This is where we were looking the other day. Didn't find anything, though."

He puts his hands on the trunk and hoists himself over. "Let's go a little farther."

"Okay." The trunk's too high for me to scramble over with any grace, and no way am I crawling through the crud underneath, so I go to climb the muddy riverbank and cir-cle around.

But Cody leans back over the trunk and holds out his hands. "Come on."

"I'm going this way."

"Just give me your hands. I'll help."

I'd rather go my own way, but I step back to the tree anyway and reach out to take his hands. Instead, he catches my forearms in a firm grip and boosts me up and over. With his help I'm easily able to hoist myself up and push off with my feet. A second later, I'm back on the ground beside him.

"Thanks."

It's like he doesn't remember at first that he's holding my arms. "No problem. Easier than going around."

"Yeah." I glance down at his hands and back at his face.

"Oh. Sorry." He lets go, and we move on slowly, both of us keeping up a constant visual scan for anything of interest.

"Have you talked to Quinn about the hacking thing?" he says after a while.

"She wouldn't even look at me last night or this morning, so no."

"She could surprise you," he says, but the dryness in his tone isn't encouraging.

I poke his shoulder. "Stop being so optimistic. You're getting my hopes up."

"Yeah, well…Let's just say I've seen her type before. This isn't the first summer I've worked at the site."

"Last year's interns?"

He nods. "Real pack of winners. We didn't have any scholarships last year, so…"

"A whole bunch of Quinns?"

"Lots of rich parents buying their kids spots in the program. Yeah."

"She's not really that bad." The words nearly catch on my tongue. "If it weren't for all the crap with her dad, I think she'd actually be okay."

Cody makes a rough *hrmph* noise and pokes at a spot in the dirt with the toe of his shoe. "Let's just say some of last year's interns were worse."

"And that's why you gave us all such a warm welcome."

"Yeah, well, when you spend one summer watching a bunch of kids slack off in an internship you'd give your right arm to be part of, your expectations for the next summer are pretty low."

"I wish you could be in the program," I say. "I wish you could take my place if I get kicked out."

"Eh. At least I get to spend time here. I get paid to come see the mammoths every day. I can dig it…even if I can't *dig*."

I groan. "You didn't just say that."

"I did, and I'd do it again." He grins at me. "It's not an ideal situation, no…But what else can I do besides laugh about it?"

"I guess." But I'm still side-eyeing him over that terrible attempt at a pun.

"I really hope they don't throw you out," he says after a moment. "It'd be their loss."

I shrug and echo his words. "At this point, what can I do besides laugh about it?"

"Good point. You must have learned that from someone very wise."

The comment earns him a teasing shove.

I'm not paying much attention to the ground anymore, and neither is he. When we come to another fallen trunk, this one lower to the ground, I sit on it. He settles beside me. Birds call in the branches overhead. The tree cover is lighter here, and the sun breaks through the clouds just enough to dapple the riverbed with white-gold light.

"Nice out here," Cody says.

I turn my face up toward the mottled sunshine. "Yeah."

"It's good to be outside. Makes me miss camping."

"You don't camp anymore?"

"Not as much as I'd like. No time. You ever been?"

"Nope."

"Too bad. You'd like it. It's fun."

"Sleeping outside with the bugs and the humidity and no air conditioning? Sure, sounds fantastic." Strangely, though, the concept no longer seems quite as alien as it would have a few weeks ago.

After a bit, I check my phone. "It's almost eleven. We should probably head back soon."

"Yeah," he says. "Soon." But he doesn't move.

There's something perfect about being here, sitting quietly with Cody while the breeze whispers by and the clouds swallow the sun once more.

"Look," he says, pointing into the trees. It takes me a second to spot what he sees, but then I see them too—three does picking their way through the riverbed about fifty yards north. Their steps are dainty and precise. One pauses to munch a mouthful of leaves from a bush near the riverbank before cantering to catch up with the others.

They're gorgeous. It's all I can do to contain a squeal that would startle them into running. I hold it in until they're no longer visible.

"Lots of wildlife around here," Cody says. "Deer, possum, armadillo, snakes, rabbits, bats—"

"Like the ones under that bridge downtown."

"That's the biggest urban colony in the country," he says. "Probably about a million strong right now. You should really see them fly while you're here. Their numbers won't peak until August, but it's still a great show."

"You know a lot about those bats."

He gives me a half smile. "What can I say? When you

grow up in Austin, you end up writing lots of school reports about the South Congress Bridge bats."

"I bet. Kind of like all the reports I wrote about subtropical climates and the Everglades growing up in Florida."

"Exactly."

I'm about to check the time again when a nearby rustle makes me freeze. "Deer?" I mouth at Cody.

He gives his head an almost undetectable shake. "Something smaller."

I focus in the direction of the rustling, hoping to see something cool. The sound is coming from a specific spot down the riverbed, closer than where the deer had emerged. Armadillo, maybe? I'd love to see Texas's state animal in the wild. Or...

Wait, what's that?

Cody spots the source of the noise before I do. "Just a squirrel," he chuckles, pointing to the bushy-tailed animal skittering up a tree.

I'm no longer looking for an animal. I'm fixated on a patch of gray in a shallow section of riverbed about fifteen feet away, just barely peeking through the brown soil. It was probably completely buried before last night's storm. It's probably just an oddly colored bit of dirt, or a leaf, or a stone. It has to be a stone.

Or another pork chop. My stomach twists.

But...what if?

I have to know for sure, so I get up, jog over, and drop to my knees. The patch isn't much more than an inch across. It's definitely not a leaf. I run a finger over it. It's hard, but the texture isn't right for it to be rock. I brush away dirt, and the patch grows larger.

I glance at Cody. "Don't laugh." Then I lean over until my nose is just about touching the ground, and I lick the patch.

My tongue sticks.

25

"**We've got bone!**" I sit back up and start moving away dirt again. A little more, a little more...I don't even care that my mouth tastes vaguely of soil. "Is this what I think it is? Cody, look." The bone curves into an oval hollow. "I think this is an eye socket." My heart pounds all the way up into my throat. "This is a skull. I think we've got a skull. Look, see? It's lying on its side, so here's the socket, and..." I brush away more soil. "Cheekbone! See? It's kind of shattered, but it's there."

He hunkers down beside me to get a better look. "How the heck did you spot that?"

"It's my paleo superpower. I can find more than just pork chops, you know."

"Natalie...Holy shit, this is awesome!"

"Damn right, it's awesome," I mutter, pushing more dirt out of the way.

"But—"

"But?"

He catches my hands in his. "This is a major find. We can't just dig it up and lug it back and dump it on Dr. Gallagher's desk. There are procedures. We have to go back and tell someone so it can be handled the right way."

"But this is it!" It's hard to tear my eyes from the skull, but I look at him. "This thing is going to save my ass and keep me in the internship."

He cocks his head. "Natalie."

"I know, I know!" I groan and pull my hands away. "Fine. We have to get back, anyway. But just let me dig a little more first. Just a little. Let's at least try to ID this thing. It's way too small to be a mammoth, and the shape's off too. It's something else."

He nods, and together we brush away dirt with a feather-light touch.

"I just want to see a little bit of the muzzle," I say. "Some teeth." The shape of this thing looks more familiar as I brush more dirt away. I've seen it before in books and museums—the large eye socket, the strong cheekbone, the gentle felid slope from forehead to muzzle. The size is off, though. It's too big to be what I think it is, and I don't dare to hope unless I can find some proof.

And then there it is, barely in its socket and badly cracked, but still unmistakable—a curved canine tooth at least six inches long. "*Smilodon fatalis*," I murmur, barely even registering that I'm speaking out loud. "Saber-toothed cat." It's too big, though. A full-grown *Smilodon* skull would be a foot long, maybe a little more than that. I've uncovered nearly that much already, and I haven't touched the back of the skull yet.

Cody and I look at each other. We know what this means. Fossils of prey animals like mammoths are great, but predators are scarcer, more coveted. A predator find would be fantastic for the site...and judging by its size, this was more than just a regular predator. Careers are built on finds like this.

"No way are they going to expel an intern who just found something like this," Cody says.

"We have to handle this just right, though. The credit for this find belongs to us—both of us." My brain is buzzing with possibilities. "This'll keep me in the program, and you...Maybe they'll find a spot in the next session for you. Cody, you could be an intern! With a find like this, how could they say no?"

"I'll believe that when it actually happens," he says, but I see the hope sparking in his eyes.

I use my phone to track and record the exact coordinates of the skull so we can find it again, and then I camouflage the sabercat with a few handfuls of dried leaves and pine needles, just in case.

We stand—and without really meaning to, I launch myself into his arms and hug him. "A *Smilodon*! Can you even believe it?"

He's laughing. We're both high on the realization of what we've just found.

We plot as we hurry back to the site. "I want to go straight to Dr. Gallagher with this," I say, "as soon as he gets back. He talked to me after the news report about the calf, and he understood the whole credit issue really well. I think he'd make sure we're recognized, and he's not going to want someone like Dr. Carver to come along and steal the site's thunder."

"Agreed. It'll also probably get him on your side if Dr. Lauren tries to kick you out. Second thing—make sure Carver isn't anywhere nearby. I don't even want him in the same *country* as us when we reveal this thing."

"Shit. Yes." I snicker. "I'm thinking we go ahead and get Gallagher himself out here as soon as possible, and we don't let on to anyone else. No one else knows a thing until we get him on board. We'll talk to him this afternoon."

"If he and Dr. Lauren get back in time."

"Crap. Yeah. Augh!" I stomp my foot against the dirt, letting out excitement and glee and frustration all at once. "A *Smilodon*, Cody! We just found a fucking *Smilodon*!"

"I know!" Just as the dig shelter comes into view, he grabs my hand and squeezes it.

My stomach drops when I spot Mellie on the path teetering on one crutch and waving at us.

"Come on, guys." Her voice is low but sharp, and she's glaring. "Seriously? Prospecting? I can't let any of you out of my sight for five minutes." She shakes her head. "Natalie, Dr. Lauren's looking for you in the shelter. I told her you were out stretching your legs."

"Give me your vest." Cody is already shrugging his off. I do the same, handing over the fluorescent yellow garment for him to stow back in the storage shed. "Good luck," he adds before jogging off.

Mellie walks me into the shelter. "Found her!" she calls to Dr. Lauren, who is standing on the walkway near my square meter of dirt.

"Finally." Dr. Lauren shakes her head. "Natalie. My office. Now."

Her tone sends a shiver through my shoulders. "Okay."

We pass through the welcome center, where Cody leans on the reception counter. He glances over as I go by and flashes me a quick thumbs-up. I reply with a nervous shrug and hurry along after Dr. Lauren.

"I assume you know what this is about?" she asks once we've settled in her office.

It won't do any good to play dumb; I can tell that from the keenness in Dr. Lauren's eyes when she peers at me. "Dr. Glass talked to you, right?"

"Yes. He told me you overstepped some boundaries in the bone lab yesterday."

I sigh. "I didn't mean to. I just got caught up. Dr. Lauren, that mammoth—"

"I know the story," she says, "and believe me, you have my sympathy. However, I can't allow you to get away with disregarding such an important rule. You know interns aren't cleared for bone prep. Especially interns who are already on probation!"

"Yeah. I know." I stare down at my nails. They're chipped and ragged from excavating, and there's fresh riverbed dirt underneath them. I go back and forth between picking them and snapping my elastic to avoid looking Dr. Lauren in the eye. "So are you throwing me out of the program?"

"I don't know yet."

My head shoots up.

"Probably yes," she says quickly. "Don't get your hopes up. We'll need to meet with someone from the foundation, since they supplied your scholarship. I had to notify them, and they can't send a representative until Saturday. Enjoy your temporary reprieve. You're on gift shop duty today, and tomorrow you'll be put to work filing about ten years' worth of old field reports at the lab." She pauses, lacing her fingers together on the desk. "I admit that I'm conflicted about expelling the intern partially responsible for getting that lawsuit thrown out."

"What?" I stop picking my nails and grip my chair's armrests.

"Our lawyer had your and Cody's discovery confirmed by a third party, a photography expert. It's legit. We met with a judge this morning, and she accepted the photo as evidence. The Flanders family has no claim to our mammoths. It's done. Dr. Gallagher is wrapping things up in a last meeting and signing some paperwork."

"Oh my God!" I have to stop myself from jumping up and lunging at her for a hug.

"We're not in the clear yet," she says. "The suit hurt us, reputation-wise. We're having some problems with the displays we're supposed to get on loan from a couple of other museums, but I'm hoping I'll be able to smooth things over. That brings me to my second concern." Her gaze goes hard again.

My heart is still pounding from the news, so at first I don't even register what she's talking about.

"Anything you'd like to tell me about Dr. Carver's website?"

My cheeks pink. "I know it got hacked. I've read the articles about it."

"So you know about the allegation that he stole credit for the calf from you and Quinn."

"Well, he did."

"I know, but that doesn't mean I condone the hacking. Did you do it?"

"No."

"Know who did?"

I remember Quinn's anguished tone when she was on the phone with her father, and I go silent.

"Natalie?"

"You want me to lie?"

"Of course not."

Silence again.

"He's back in town, and he's furious. He's demanding we punish the guilty party and issue a statement declaring that he's the one who found the calf after all."

"Even if you did that, he has other allegations to deal with now, right?"

"True. I think he hopes that if he clears up the claim that started it all, the other accusations will stop. It might be too late for that, but he's still pushing for it."

"What happens if you don't give in?"

She sighs. "He's on the board of the museum that's lending us most of the displays for our museum. They're threatening to pull out. They're saying it's because of the lawsuit, of course, but..."

"That's bull."

"Without those displays, we won't have much of a museum. And we really need that museum."

Cody and I agreed that I'd go straight to Dr. Gallagher with the *Smilodon* news, but maybe now's the time to spill. I could tell Dr. Lauren about the skull. I could drag her out there and show her something that'll help save the museum even if Dr. Carver insists on being a dick about some borrowed displays.

Before I can get a word out, the phone on her desk rings. She answers and cringes. "Of course. Yes. Stall him for a moment if you can, and then send him back here." She hangs up and puts a hand over her eyes. "Speak of the devil."

"He's here?"

"We're done for now. Make yourself scarce, okay?" She groans and finds a bottle of aspirin in her desk drawer. "This month is going to kill me."

I don't want to run right into Dr. Carver, so I duck into the break room until I hear him thunder down the hall. Dr. Lauren's office door closes, and Carver's muffled voice starts ranting again.

I creep out and take my place at the register in the gift shop.

Cody is about to start a tour. He glances over and raises his brows.

I put out my hands in a *we-need-to-talk* gesture.

"Soon," he mouths before gathering his latest flock of tourists around him. He can't turn away quick enough to hide his smile, and I think I know why he's happy. I'm stuck at the desk…but at least I'm still here.

He's busy until after his three o'clock tour ends, and then he wanders into the gift shop. "So… ?"

"So it looks like the lawsuit is dead."

"The photo?"

I fill him in. "Dr. Gallagher is signing the final papers right now."

"That's fantastic. So you're not out of the program!"

I laugh dryly. "I didn't say that."

"They can't throw out the person who just saved the site."

"Helped save," I remind him. "You're the one who enhanced the photo. Besides, the site isn't exactly safe yet. Carver was here earlier, throwing a fit."

"Thought I saw him in the lobby before." Cody narrows his eyes and rests his elbows on the counter. "Almost didn't recognize him without his entourage and all those cameras."

"Yeah, well, he's still really pissed about his blog." I explain what Dr. Lauren said about the loaned displays. "The site needs the traffic boost from the museum. With the kind of influence Carver wields in the field…"

"So you told Dr. Lauren who hacked his site, right?"

"Cody, I couldn't. I couldn't just throw her under the bus. I wasn't exactly trying to stop her from what she was doing."

"I can't believe what I'm hearing, Natalie. Even if it means saving the site from that jackass?"

"I just want to talk to Quinn about it first," I say. "She hasn't been very chatty lately."

"I don't want to see you go home over this," he says quietly.

I drop my voice. "Hey, we still have the *Smilodon* up our sleeve. I wasn't about to tell Dr. Lauren about it while Dr. Carver was here."

He smiles a little. "Good thinking."

"It's getting late—I doubt Dr. Gallagher will be back today. Why don't you tell him yourself tomorrow?"

"Hell, no. You found the thing. You deserve to be the one who reveals it."

"I won't even be here tomorrow. It's a lab day."

"So tell him on Thursday."

"Tomorrow would be better."

He gives me a crooked smile. "That thing's probably been there for about forty thousand years, darlin'. It can wait until Thursday."

Keeping my mouth shut about the *Smilodon* makes Wednesday drag, especially once Dr. Glass shows me to the records room and puts me to work filing and digitizing a disarray of neglected field notes. Cody is right, though; I want to be the one who reveals our discovery.

By lunchtime I've lost count of my paper cuts and I'm bored and antsy. At least I'm on campus, so I can escape to the cafeteria for a break.

Mellie and I walk to lunch together. I carry her bag

while she swings herself on her crutches. "How's the screen picking going?" I ask, mostly to distract myself from the almost unbearable urge to start yelling about the *Smilodon* in the riverbed.

"Found three pieces of what I'm pretty sure are mammoth teeth this morning."

"Nice."

"So you're stuck in records, huh?"

I nod and open the cafeteria door, holding it for her. "Yeah. Scanning field notes. Honestly, I'd rather be back on gift shop duty at the site."

"Ouch."

"Yep. I'm assuming that's where they'll stick me again tomorrow."

"Don't count on it."

My heart beats in a strange, hiccupping pattern. "Did you hear something? Am I out of the program?"

"That's not what I meant. You haven't checked the weather?"

"No. What about it?" I can't get out my phone to pull up the weather app; I've got my lunch tray in one hand and hers in the other.

"We're supposed to get another storm early tomorrow morning. Sounds like it might get intense. If it's bad enough, they might not open the site at all."

The later it gets, the more it looks like Mellie might be right. By late afternoon, the weather app displays a red warning box each time I check it. We're in for severe thunderstorms overnight and through tomorrow morning, and most of the county is under a flood watch. The clouds building in the sky beyond the two small windows in the records room confirm that something nasty is heading our way.

This weather sounds more than capable of flooding the riverbed, which would be extremely bad news for the exposed sabercat. I remember how easily that chunk of bone chipped off the mammoth skull, and my stomach clenches. The force of a flash flood would decimate something that fragile.

We should tell someone, I text Cody.

Dr. G is gone for the day, he answers, *and your hero's here again.*

Carver?

He showed up with his lawyer. Been in Dr. L's office for an hour.

An insane idea threads its way through my head. *Want to show them all what kind of paleo rock stars we really are?*

He sends back a couple of question marks.

If Thomas Fucking Carver can borrow a mammoth from me, I can borrow an idea from him. *Can you come get me tonight?*

26

I sneak out just before midnight. Lightning strobes against the horizon to the left, and the sky is inky with cloud cover. The storm hasn't reached us yet, but I doubt it'll hold off until two or three in the morning as forecasted. The air is already heavy and metallic with ozone.

The headlights of a green pickup find me in the dorm parking lot.

"Got everything?" I ask when Cody pulls up.

He nods. "Get in."

Ten minutes later, we're at the site. The gates off Ember Road are closed and locked, but Cody drives past and turns onto an unpaved road about a quarter mile farther down. We bounce along over the hard-packed dirt for a ways. Thunder growls overhead as he brakes and parks. "We're pretty close," he says. "We can walk it from here."

The wind is picking up as we unload supplies from the back of his truck. He hands me a backpack and slings another over his own shoulder. There's also a high-powered flashlight for each of us, a shovel, and a nylon duffel bag—the carrying case for his tent.

"You sure about this?" he asks as a gust shoves the hair off his forehead. Lightning sparks again, closer this time. "It's getting nasty fast."

"Yeah, we've got time. Besides, I've been through hurricanes. I can handle rain." If Thomas Fucking Carver can get away with a trick like this, so can we.

"Okay." He leads the way through the forest as thunder rumbles almost nonstop in the distance. There's no clear path here. Even with the flashlight, it's not easy for me to pick my way through and find stable footing. But Cody knows the way.

"Sometimes on busy days I'll park back here and walk in," he says over his shoulder. "Saves a parking space for a paying guest."

"That's really nice of you."

"Eh. I don't mind the walk. Every little bit helps when it comes to the site."

It's not long before the forest grows sparser and a large, dark structure comes into view. The dig shelter.

"Don't go too close," Cody says. "Motion sensor lights. Security cameras."

"You didn't tell us about those the night Chase and I tried to walk to the site."

"I figured you wouldn't get close enough for it to matter." Even over the wind, I hear the smirk in his tone.

I stay close behind him as we give the shelter a wide berth and make our way down to the riverbed. Once again, he gives me a hand over the first fallen trunk. After we climb over the second, smaller trunk, I use my phone to find the location I mapped out the day before. "Should be just about…there!" I catch the pile of leaves in my flashlight's beam. Just as I locate it, my phone beeps with an emergency message, and another severe storm warning pops up on the screen. I dismiss it.

"So what exactly are we doing?" Cody asks.

"I heard about this on a podcast once." I'm not about to mention whose podcast it was. "First, we need to build a barrier. If it floods here, the water will flow downstream— that'd be in this direction, right?" I point to my left.

"Yeah."

"Okay, so we'll put the barrier here to block the skull from running water." I draw a curved line in the dirt with my foot, making a semicircle about six feet in diameter around the skull. "That's what the sandbags are for. Once that's done, we're going to tarp the skull with your tent to protect it from rain and debris."

"Then?"

"Then we run back to your truck and get somewhere safe."

"You really think this'll work?"

"I hope so. It's worth a try."

"Let's get going then."

Both backpacks are full of empty burlap sandbags. We set the flashlights on the ground, angling them to give us at least a little illumination. I hold each bag open while Cody shovels dirt. "Actual sand would be more secure," he says, "but this'll have to do." Once the first bag is two-thirds full, he hefts it over near the skull and places it over the semicircle I mapped out. We do this over and over, with Cody placing each bag as I get the next one ready to fill. The rain starts falling as we work, but for now the shower stays light and drizzly.

The wall he builds is neat and sturdy, with the bags staggered like brickwork. "You know what you're doing," I say.

"You learn this stuff when you grow up in a Texas floodplain."

"I guess so." I shove my bangs off my face. The rain's coming down harder now, and my clothes and hair are growing drenched. Thunder roars from too close by, loud and low enough to make the ground tremble beneath us. The first squall thrashes in—too strong too soon.

"Tent," he says, and I toss him the duffel bag. Due to the sandbag wall, we can't pitch the tent properly. We settle for erecting two poles near the skull then draping the tent itself over the entire structure and tacking down the ends. I cross my fingers that we're not crushing additional bones when we shove the poles into the wet dirt.

"That's as good as it's going to get," he says, squinting at the contraption through the rain.

I try to agree, but the wind whips the words from my mouth and sends them flying as a gale moves in. We grab our flashlights, but the thin beams can't cut through the downpour. "I can't see!" I say.

He grabs my hand. "I've got you," he hollers above the wind. Lightning flashes, and for a second I can see him frantically looking around. His hair is plastered to his head, and his eyes are narrowed against the driving rain. It's dark again, leaving the image of him burned into my retinas and ghosting in my vision.

"Can you find the way back?" I yell through the squall.

"The rain's got me all turned around. There's no way I can find the path back to the truck."

"Then what do we do?"

"I don't know!" His hand grips mine more tightly. "Find somewhere to ride it out?"

I remember Dr. Carver's podcast. "A tree!"

"A tree?"

"We'll climb a tree!"

"What the fuck, Natalie? You want us climbing trees during a goddamn thunderstorm?"

Doubt swirls in my head, mixing with a chilly dread... but the tree thing worked for Dr. Carver, so why shouldn't it work for us? "Lightning goes for the tallest thing in the area," I yell. "As long as we don't pick *that* tree, we'll be okay."

"You're nuts! Either way, we need to get out of the riverbed in case it floods. Come on!"

Together, we scramble up the bank. The dirt is morphing back into slick mud that sucks at our shoes. My foot gets swallowed in cold black slime. When I yank it free, my right sneaker is gone. I slip, going down on my knees before Cody hoists me back up. He gets to the top first and reaches down to help me.

We sweep our surroundings with our flashlights, trying to see through the downpour. "That one!" I say, pausing my beam on a tree that looks climbable. I've never been one for climbing trees, but I'm hoping I can manage if my life depends on it. The stronger this storm grows, the more I think it actually might.

Near the tree, I pause, training my flashlight beam over the riverbed below. The light gleams and dances, reflecting off muddy swirls of running water.

The river is flooding. It happens in seconds; what was a clear walkway moments ago is suddenly a frothing mess of brown muck. It overtakes the dry bed with all the relentless fierceness of a riptide, dragging branches and debris along with it.

I stop so quickly that Cody barrels into me, nearly knocking me off balance. I catch myself and spin around, searching with my flashlight until I find the barrier we built. Since it's on a shallower section of riverbed, the water hasn't reached it yet. It's holding well against the rain, but…"Either it holds or it doesn't." Cody grabs my arm and hauls me toward the tree. "Nothing more we can do but stay safe."

I know he's right, but I can see the water rising. Any minute now, it'll start lapping against the sandbags. What if—

"Come on!" He's waiting to give me a boost up the tree. I struggle up onto a sturdy branch, sitting on it and locking my arms around the trunk as lightning blazes directly overhead. The flash of light and the simultaneous bellow of thunder that accompanies it disorient me. When everything goes black again, I can't see a thing, even when I dare to unwrap one arm from the tree and sweep the beam of my flashlight over my surroundings.

"Cody?"

Did he climb the tree? Is he higher than me? I tilt the flashlight upward. Nothing.

"*Cody?*"

He's nowhere around the trunk either.

"CODY!"

When I twist my torso toward the river, I'm shaking too hard to hold the flashlight steady. It takes me a minute to locate Cody flailing in the muddy water. The river isn't very deep, not yet, but the current is fast and the mud is slippery. He can't get his footing or haul himself out. The river sweeps him along past our fossil, smashing him hard against the fallen trunk we'd been sitting on yesterday. He grabs the trunk, hoisting himself onto it, and for a second I can breathe.

The flash of memory is as bright as a flash of lightning. We're sitting by the campus fountain. I've just tossed my cuff bracelet in the water. *Don't expect me to go in after that thing. I'm not much of a swimmer.*

The water surges, knocking him off and carrying him farther downstream. He's coughing and sputtering and screaming my name.

I jump down from the tree and run along the bank, blinking hard against the gushing rain. Can't lose my footing. Can't fall. Not now.

"CODY!"

He's still fighting. When he wrestles his way to the bank, he slips in the mud and tumbles back into the water. Each time he makes progress, the river bogs him back down, swallows him back up.

He's barreling toward the other fallen tree, the one he helped me over yesterday. If he gets swept under it and continues downstream, I'm not sure where he'll end up.

I run ahead so that I reach the trunk first, and I crawl onto it until I'm over the swelling river. Straddling the trunk and using the flashlight to spotlight him, I yell his name and hold out a hand as the churning water speeds him closer.

He's barely keeping his head above the muck, but he hears me. He looks toward the sound of my voice, toward the beam of my flashlight.

The water sweeps him toward a tangle of exposed roots that extend into the riverbed.

"Look out!" I scream. If he can catch hold of one...But he doesn't see them. His skull connects with a knobby root as big around as my arm. Even over the rain and howling wind, I hear the impact, dull and sickening.

"*Cody!*"

Now when the water shoves him along, he doesn't fight. Doesn't move. He's too limp, too loose, too complacent. The current tugs him under my perch.

I drop my flashlight in the river as I hang down from the trunk, throwing myself as far over as I dare. My strong thighs are a vise, locking onto the fallen tree, securing me in place.

When the water carries Cody's pummeled form out from under the trunk, I stretch out farther, farther, farther, and I grab hold of the collar of his T-shirt. I inch back, trusting the strength in my legs to anchor us, dragging him along, doing everything I can to keep his head over the swirling flow. Fighting his inertia and my own exhaustion, I somehow lug him out of the river and over the mud, locking my hands under his arms and pulling, tugging, dragging, heaving until he lies safely on the bank.

"Cody!" I'm on my knees beside him, shaking his shoulders. He doesn't respond, doesn't react. The gash near his hairline seeps blood over his wet forehead, turning the side of his face dark.

I press fingers to his neck. No pulse.

No breath.

"Don't you fucking dare," I say, putting one hand over the other and starting compressions on his chest. "This is going to be something we'll laugh about!" I pinch his nostrils shut and put my mouth on his, forcing air into his lungs. "You hear me?" More compressions. "Someday we'll sit around and tell this story, and we'll say, 'Well, what can we do but laugh about it?'" Another breath. "Come on, Cody. Damn it, come on!" More compressions.

"We're going to laugh about this!"

27

He coughs in the middle of the fourth breath I give him. I pull back and turn his head to the side so he won't choke on the muddy water he's puking up. He's breathing on his own now, but he's still not coming around, and the gash on his head is still pouring blood. I yank off my T-shirt and press it in a wad against the wound. The shirt is too wet to absorb the blood, but the pressure might lesson the flow.

"Please work," I mutter, pulling my phone out of my pocket. What if it's gotten too wet? But the screen lights up when I press the home button.

I push the emergency call icon.

28

The emergency crew finds us quickly, aided by the GPS coordinates from my phone. They put Cody on a stretcher and heft him out of the forest, and they load me into the ambulance with him. Once we get to the hospital we're separated, Cody whisked off for emergency care while I'm taken to an exam room and checked out.

I'm fine—nothing but scrapes and bruises and one gash on my arm that needs two stitches. I can't remember when that injury even happened, but it's been cleaned and stitched and neatly bandaged.

I sit on a hard plastic chair in a hallway outside the IC unit. It's as close as anyone will let me get to Cody. I'm still shivering in my damp clothes. My shirt carries Cody's blood in clouded tie-dyed patterns, and I don't remember exactly how or when I put it back on. I'm missing a shoe. An orderly hands me a blanket, which I wrap tight around my shoulders. My breathing is fast and shallow—and I can't control it.

I'm caught in a whirlwind; nothing in my head wants to focus. When Dr. Gallagher and Dr. Lauren rush in, I can't even explain what we were doing on-site. I just keep asking about Cody.

Mellie's here too. She's brought me a change of clothes—fresh jeans, my Savage Swallow tee. I change in the restroom, disposing of my muddy pants and shirt in the trash can on my way out because I can't deal with them right now. When I get back to my chair, Mellie has another blanket waiting.

A nurse comes by to check on me. She says something about shock and shines a penlight into my eyes. She wants to speak with my parents on the phone. I barely notice her taking my cell from me so she can access my contacts.

My parents are frantic, especially since I haven't been able to explain much to them either. I've called them and let them know I'm all right, but I can't go into detail beyond that. Not yet. I've also heard from Aunt Judy. Even Charli somehow knows something's happened. I'm trying to communicate, I'm trying, but it's just too much and I can't deal. I can't. I can't.

A man and woman rush by with a nurse. She shows them into the IC unit. Cody's parents. I know instantly. His father is an older version of him, tall and dark haired with the same light olive skin.

The nurse comes by again and hands me a drink of water and a pill cup containing two tiny capsules. "It'll calm you down," she says. I swallow them without asking what they are.

Dr. Gallagher stalks off to track down a doctor and demand an update.

The medication enters my system, and the spinning in my mind finally starts to slow. I slump forward a little, suddenly more exhausted than I've ever been in my life.

"Natalie?"

I look over. Mellie is poised to catch me if I fall out of my chair. I sit up straighter. "I'm okay."

"What happened?" It's at least the sixth time she's asked, but it's the first time I feel capable of answering.

"Cody and I found something in the woods. We were trying to protect it."

When I can finally string the words together, I tell Mellie and Dr. Lauren everything.

"We wanted to tell someone about the skull right away, but with Dr. Carver always being around...After what happened with the mammoth calf, I mean..." I'm breathing hard. The words almost choke me. It all seems so beyond ridiculous now, the idea that we could handle the skull and the storm ourselves and end up site heroes.

Mellie pats my shoulder and murmurs for me to calm down.

"I can't stand not knowing," I say. "What if he's...He has to be okay. If he's not, it's my fault, and I can't...He has to be okay."

"He's going to be fine." Dr. Gallagher's voice startles me half out of my chair.

Mellie asks the question I can't articulate. "Can we see him?"

The doctor beside Dr. Gallagher shakes her head. "Not until this afternoon. He's stabilized and resting." She points at me. "You could use some rest too."

This afternoon? I have no idea what time it is, but the hazy morning sun shocks me when Mellie and Dr. Lauren lead me out of the hospital. The storm is over.

I'm still thinking about Cody and the stunt we pulled. My mind won't let it go. "Do you think it held?" I ask, staring dully at the parking lot.

Dr. Lauren is rubbing her forehead. "What?"

"The barrier we put around the skull. Do you think the *Smilodon* made it?"

She shakes her head. "I don't know. We'll find out soon enough, I guess. Dr. Gallagher will check as soon as the water recedes."

Mellie takes me back to the dorm, where I collapse onto my bed. She says something, but I'm already drifting off, and I can't make it out.

I wake up disoriented around two o'clock. For a second I wonder why I'm asleep in the dorm room in the middle of the afternoon. It all flows back, like debris in a swollen river. The memories make me sway with confused vertigo.

Afternoon. I have to get back to the hospital.

I stumble into the bathroom. The shower brings me back to myself. I toss on the first clothes I can grab, pull my wet hair back in a clip. I don't bother with makeup.

I have to find Mellie.

She's in the common room. "How are you doing?" she asks when she sees me.

"Hospital," I say.

She takes hold of my shoulders. "Are you up to going back? Maybe you should rest more."

"I'm fine. Please, Mellie. I need to see him."

"Everyone's wondering about you," she says in the car. "We're trying to keep things business as usual, so Eli and the other interns are at the site, but they all keep texting me to find out how you are. Especially Quinn."

I stare out the window. "Seriously?"

"They've all been really worried."

"Yeah, well…Tell them Cody and I survived some wild Texas weather."

Mellie clucks her tongue. "This is Texas, Natalie. You handled a thunderstorm and a flood, yeah—but around here, any day without a tornado is a good day."

29

"We laughing yet?"

Cody says this with a pained half smile, and the meds he's on make him slur his words a little, but his stare is clear and focused. He sits up in his hospital bed, one arm in a sling. A series of butterfly bandages shuts the gash on his forehead. The skin around it is angry and purple, a mottled bruise that stretches down and blends into a black eye. His lip is busted. His cheek is scraped and raw. His parents have stepped out for something to eat. They're angry as hell with me, so Mellie and I waited until now to slip in and visit.

I'm a lot calmer now that I can see he'll be okay, but seeing his injuries still makes me shaky. Tears prick behind my eyes, but I don't let them fall. "You heard that?"

"Yeah, I kind of heard it. Felt like I was dreaming, but now I'm guessing I wasn't."

"And you remember?"

"Like I'd forget? You were giving me mouth-to-mouth at the time."

"Jeez. Cody." I'm blushing. I hope the scratches on my face are enough to camouflage the extra redness. He gives me a teasing smirk. It amazes me that he can joke around in his condition.

Then his expression sobers. "You okay? You look okay."

I manage a smirk of my own. "Just okay?"

"You look beautiful," he amends. "Just like always. But are you okay?"

"I'm fine. Just some bumps and bruises."

"So...the skull? Did it make it?"

"I don't know yet."

"Hey, Natalie?" Mellie holds out her phone to show me a text. It's from Dr. Gallagher. *Show Natalie*, it says below a photo of our barrier. The tent is blown partway off, and the ground around it is muddy and partially washed out, but the sandbags appear to have held. "I know right where that is," Mellie says, squinting at the photo. "I've walked by that section of riverbed a hundred times, and I never spotted anything."

"It's just because that storm the other night uncovered a little of the skull," I say.

"No." She gives me a pointed look. "It's because you're a damn good prospector. Women can't afford to be humble in this field, Natalie."

While I'm holding the phone, another photo comes through. This one shows our *Smilodon* skull in the mud. Its empty eye socket stares at me. Its toothy mouth grins.

It's okay.

It's okay.

Another text comes through. *Tell the kids this one belongs to them.*

Without a word, I hand the phone to Cody. I sink into a chair beside his bed.

"We did it," he says, staring at the photos.

"We did. Hey, Cody?"

He looks at me. "Yeah?"

"Now we're laughing."

"Not yet," he says, grinning and wincing at the same time. "Let me heal first. Laughing is hell on bruised ribs."

My parents fly into Austin that evening, which surprises me.

"Of course we came, honey," Mom says after crushing me in a fierce hug at the dorm. "We got on the earliest flight we could catch. We had to make sure you were all right."

"But doesn't Dylan have a soccer game tonight? It's the regional finals, isn't it? You never miss those."

Mom looks at me with wide, tired eyes. "Natalie, you are so much more important than a soccer game."

"You freaked us out, kid," Dad says. "And hey, someone else came with us too."

I squeak in shock when I see Aunt Judy rushing in behind him, a whirl of cherry-print fabric and tattoos and piercings.

"My favorite niece!" She catches me in a hug even tighter than Mom's. "What the hell have you been up to out here?"

"You came too?" I say when she lets go and I can finally breathe again.

"You kidding, babe?" She catches my chin in her black-manicured fingers and angles my face to inspect a scratch on my cheek. "I was scared to death about you. Had to see for myself that you were okay. I just about had a stroke. Didn't I, Jeannie?" She steps back and swings an arm around my mom's shoulders, giving her a squeeze.

It's a strange thing, seeing the two of them together like that. Especially since Mom isn't scowling at Aunt Judy for once.

30

Usually, my armor makes me feel invulnerable—or like I look invulnerable, at least. Not this morning, though. I don't even bother with a shaper underneath my navy, bone-print dress. Fear clenches at me far more tightly than any shaper or corset ever could. Trembling hands force me to keep my makeup light—tinted lip gloss, neutral shadow, a touch of mascara that I apply purely out of habit. Instead of straightening my hair, I leave it wavy and pull it back in a ponytail. It'll frizz if the weather is humid...but does that really matter so much?

Dr. Gallagher ushers me into the ASU conference room for the meeting with the foundation representative. My parents flank me at the table, Mom to my left and Dad to my right, as I stare down the people who will decide my fate.

Along with Dr. Gallagher, Dr. Lauren and Dr. Glass are present. Cody's parents glare at me from the far end of the conference table. Next to them is an older woman in a tailored suit and pearls. Dr. Gallagher introduces her as Mrs. Keller, the foundation rep.

The final two people at the table surprise me—Dr. Carver and Quinn. He crosses his arms when he sees me, his jaw tightening under his scruff. She won't meet my eyes.

Dr. Gallagher folds his hands together, resting them on the conference table. "You've placed us in a difficult position, Natalie."

"I know. I'm sorry."

"We originally scheduled this meeting to deal with your unauthorized actions in the lab—actions that led to the damaging of a site specimen. Since then, the matter of Dr. Carver's website hacking has also come to light. Now we have your stunt from the other night to deal with as well. *And* you're already on probation for drinking. Frankly, I don't even know where to start."

I want to snap my hair elastic, but Mom has her hand clasped around mine.

"Sounds like more than three strikes to me," Mrs. Keller says. "The foundation recommends immediate expulsion."

"I understand that," Dr. Gallagher says. "But it's important that we consider all sides of Natalie's time as an intern. Some of her accomplishments here have been nothing short of exceptional."

Dr. Lauren nods. "She provided us with information that got the lawsuit against the site dismissed."

"And yes," Dr. Glass cuts in, "she damaged a fossil. A fossil we wouldn't even know about if she and Quinn hadn't found it buried in storage."

Dr. Carver clears his throat.

Dr. Glass sighs and shoves his glasses up on his nose. "Give it a rest, Tom."

"In addition," Dr. Lauren says quickly, "Natalie and Cody made an incredible discovery while they were out prospecting. Granted, they shouldn't have been out there in the first place."

"But sometimes the greatest finds require the greatest risks." Dr. Gallagher distributes photos of the skull around the table. "We're pretty sure that the cat they uncovered is a *Smilodon populator*, not a *Smilodon fatalis* like I originally thought."

I stare. "Wait, it's a *populator*? I didn't think those even lived around here."

"Neither did we. There's never been one found any-where in North America before. It'll be a major draw for our museum. It redefines part of our focus at the site. Hell, it redefines a lot of what we know about this region during the Ice Age. This is huge—and it's all because of Natalie's prospecting talent and the actions she and Cody took to protect the skull."

"What about the fact that she put our son in danger?" Cody's father breaks in. "Cody's in the hospital because of this girl." He has the same eyes as Cody, only his are rimmed with dark circles. He and Cody's mother look exhausted.

"She didn't exactly drag your kid out there against his will," Mom snaps.

"I did ask him to go, though," I say quickly. "It's my fault he was out there during the storm. I'm sorry. It was stupid of us. I realize that. But we didn't want the sabercat to get washed away."

"Cody's life is worth more than a pile of bones." Cody's mother's eyes narrow as she looks at me, and her tone is thin and brittle.

"Of course it is!" I say. "But he didn't want that skull to be lost or damaged any more than I did. This—all of this, the site and the fossils and the science behind them—this is his passion. Just like it's my passion. We couldn't leave the skull to chance, especially not when we knew how much it would mean to the site."

"That doesn't excuse your recklessness," the representative says.

"I'd make different choices if I could do everything over. But if it came down to taking a risk or losing the skull, I'd still take the risk. Maybe I wouldn't ask Cody to go along, but I'd do anything I had to do to save that fossil."

"Enough of this." Cody's father frowns. "I want to get back to my son." He looks at Dr. Gallagher. "Are you sending her home, or do we need to talk to our lawyer this afternoon?"

Dr. Gallagher's eyes harden, and his tone is careful and measured. "Let me remind you that your son was trespassing on site property. He isn't blameless in this. You and he are lucky we haven't pressed charges. That may change if you start throwing around legal threats."

"Cody will be facing consequences, just like Natalie," Dr. Lauren adds. "At the very least, he's looking at suspension or termination. Do you want to press the matter?"

Cody's parents glance at each other, and his mother shakes her head. My chest clenches at the thought of Cody losing his job because of something I convinced him to do.

Lips pursed, Mrs. Keller straightens the papers in front of her. "Let's get back to Natalie. If you don't expel her, the foundation is prepared to pull the rest of her scholarship."

"Then you're making the decision for us," Dr. Lauren says. "I still don't feel like you're considering all the good she's done here."

"What about my website?" Dr. Carver cuts in, his voice curt. "This kid's antics made me look like an idiot!"

Beside him, Quinn cringes slightly.

"We're getting there." Dr. Gallagher shuts his eyes for a second and takes a breath.

"No, we'll get to it now," Dr. Carver says, his voice getting louder. "That hack hurt my credibility. It damaged my image. I want to know what the site is going to do about the deplorable behavior of one of its interns! Because I guarantee you, if you want those museum displays—"

I can't take it anymore. "Hey, guys? Everyone?" I stand, smoothing my hands over the skirt of my dress. "Look, I understand why you want to throw me out. I broke a lot of rules. I admit that. But the things I did? Prepping the calf, prospecting, protecting the *Smilodon*? I did all that because this is my thing." I look at Cody's parents. "It's Cody's thing too. I'm sorry he got hurt. I'm so sorry my bad decisions landed him in the hospital. But he wanted to

be part of the *Smilodon* discovery, every step of the way."
I turn back toward Dr. Gallagher and Dr. Lauren. "Hell,
I hoped you guys would be so impressed by our find that
you'd let him dig sometimes. Instead you're talking about
firing him. Please don't do that. The site means so much
to him. Don't take that away from him because I came up
with a bad plan."

I pause for a breath. "I love the site. I love paleontology.
This is me, and I'm not going to apologize for it. *I'm done
apologizing for being myself.* My experience here so far has
been amazing, and I hope you let me stay. I want to be part
of the site. But I also want to be true to myself, and you
know what? I'm a paleo nerd, and sometimes paleo nerds
are going to take risks for the sake of some dusty old bones.
So if you're going to expel me, do it. I'll walk out of here
with my head high."

I have one more thing to say. This time I turn to
Dr. Carver. "As for you—I didn't mess with your website,
but I was in the room when it happened. Your blog got
edited for accuracy. That's it."

He frowns, his eyes bone-hard. "Bullshit. You hacked my
site. That alone should be enough to get you thrown out."

I straighten my spine. "Prove it."

Dr. Carver gestures toward Quinn. "Tell everyone what
you told me."

Quinn opens her mouth slightly then freezes when her
eyes lock with mine.

"Tell them," Dr. Carver prompts. "Tell them how
Natalie borrowed your laptop. You said you checked the
browser history and realized she'd logged into my site."

A chill roots itself in the pit of my stomach. I stare her down. "Yes, Quinn. Tell us."

Her eyes go misty, and then she stands and glares at Dr. Carver. "I did it."

His eyes widen, and anger tightens his voice even more. "Excuse me?"

"I did it. Okay, Dad? I edited the post. I logged into your site, and I wrote those things."

"You told me—"

"I lied. Natalie was there, but I did it. And you know what? Everything I wrote was true. *Everything*."

Dr. Carver's nostrils flare. His face flushes. "We're done here," he mutters, standing up.

"No, we're not!" Quinn blocks his way. "Do you ever even think about how you act? Did you wonder, even for a second, how it made me feel when you'd get mad at me for not being allowed to dig? When you'd tell me to work harder and stop making you look bad?"

"Quinn, cut it out," he snaps. "We'll talk about this later."

Quinn's voice grows shriller. "And when you went on the news and claimed you found the calf—what kind of father does that? I finally do something right, and you take credit for it? What the hell, Dad?"

"Quinn—"

"And now you think you can come in here and get whatever you want. You thought Natalie was great as long as she was worshipping you. Now you're willing to threaten the whole dig site just to get her sent home. What is *wrong* with you? Could you maybe stop being a bully and try being human for once?"

Dr. Carver takes her by the arm and leads her out of the room. I hear her start yelling again in the hall before the heavy door closes behind them.

For a moment, we all stare at each other across the table.

Finally, Mrs. Keller speaks. "Well then…Dr. Gallagher, what's your final take on Natalie's situation?

"Does it matter?" he asks. "If you pull her scholarship, she's out either way."

"We're still interested in your reasoning."

"This hasn't been an easy decision." Dr. Gallagher rubs a hand over his bearded chin. "I've never met an intern with as much passion and potential as Natalie. Her contributions to the future of the site have been incredible, and I don't want to lose her for the sake of setting an example. However…"

Above his beard, Dr. Glass's cheeks turn a mottled, angry purple. "Vince."

Dr. Gallagher holds up a hand for him to be quiet. "However, I can't ignore the trespassing, the underage drinking, or the ease with which she chose to put her own life, as well as Cody's, in danger."

My heart sinks all the way down to my vintage pumps.

"I'm very sorry, Natalie," he says, "but I have no choice but to expel you from the intern program."

His voice seems to echo in my ears, and whiteness creeps in around the edges of my vision. I breathe deeply and slowly so I won't pass out.

Dr. Glass slams his palm against the conference table, jarring me back into the moment. He stands and stalks out. Cody's parents follow him.

There's more to the meeting—when I have to be out of

my dorm room, what paperwork has to be filled out—but I rely on my parents to listen. I can't tune in anymore. Not to this. I just can't.

I keep it together until we finally leave the conference room. Aunt Judy has been waiting for us in the hall. Immediately, she's by my side, hands clasped together over her red dotted blouse. "What did they say?" Before I can answer, she gets a clear look at my pale face, my desperately blank expression. "Oh no."

Her face falls, and that's what finally breaks me. I crumble and start sobbing. The nerve I had earlier—the fierceness that let me promise to leave with no apologies and my head held high—has died away. "I'm so sorry." The words come out as gasps. My lungs are hungry for oxygen I can't seem to deliver. "I screwed up. I let everyone down."

"Babe!" Aunt Judy's arms are around me. "Don't you ever say that."

"You haven't let anyone down." My mom hugs us both. My dad is there as well. They surround me and let me cry. I'm getting mascara all over Aunt Judy's blouse, but she won't let me wiggle free.

They don't let me go until I calm down enough to stop gasping for air. When I can finally pull away, Mom hands me the travel pack of tissues she always has in her purse. I scrub at my eyes, not really caring if I've turned into a smudged raccoon. Still, I'd like to clean up a little, so I duck into a nearby restroom.

At the sink, I rummage through the arsenal in my purse until I find my packet of cleanser wipes. I swipe until I've removed every trace of smeared mascara and my face is clean. My hands move automatically, digging the basics from my makeup bag and lining them up on the counter—powder, concealer, mascara.

When I find my tube of Pinup, I pause, staring at the shiny black cylinder. It reminds me of another time I'd had red eyes and blotchy skin from crying. It was the first day of summer after eighth grade, and I'd been sitting at the vintage vanity in Aunt Judy's bedroom. Fred Parkmore had somehow gotten the number for my brand-new phone, and he and his friends spent the morning texting me memes. It was all trash like *Good news: fat people are harder to kidnap!* and *Round is a shape, so congrats, you're in shape!* When I confessed this to Aunt Judy, she muttered a lot of colorful phrases. After helping me figure out how to block their numbers, she sat down with me at the vanity and did my makeup for the first time. When she was done, I liked what I saw in the mirror—but I felt like I was looking at someone else. It was a mask to help me hide from people like Fred. It was part of what would become my armor.

I don't think I want to hide anymore.

I uncap the tube and twist up the lipstick. I still love the color, but from now on, if I'm going to wear it, it'll be because I want to. The same goes for the perfect eyeliner, the dresses, the shapewear, the shoes—all of it. If I'm feeling it, I'll wear it. If not...well, the world can deal. I'm doing this for me, not for anyone else. There's no more Fat Nat, no more Awesome Natalie, no more fake-it-till-you-make-it. There's just me.

My phone buzzes in my pocket. It's Cody. *Any news?*

Me: *I'm out.*

Him: *Fuuuuuuuucckkkkk.*

Me: *Pretty much, yeah.*

Him: *They're all idiots, and I hope mammoths step on them.*

I chuckle. *Nah... Well, maybe Carver.*

Him: *Funny you should say that. Made you something.* It's a Photoshopped image of an enormous mammoth foot with a blond ponytail and part of a green shirtsleeve sticking out from underneath.

I laugh so loudly that I'm pretty sure my parents can hear me from the hall. *Too bad that's waaaaay out of proportion,* I reply, adding his favorite tongue-sticking-out emoji.

Made these too. He texts a link to a post he made on a paleontology forum. It's a couple of memes. The first is a screenshot of Dr. Carver on the local news, smiling and pointing at the jacketed skull: "When You're a Famous Scientist but You're Credit-Stealing Garbage" is superimposed on the image in bold text. The next one's a Photoshopped pic of Dr. Carver running away with a mammoth calf skull tucked under his arm like a large, lumpy football. This one reads: "Next He'll Steal This Meme." The post already has several replies, and they're all just as scathing as I could ever hope for. Other people are already making and posting memes of their own.

Me: *You just made me snort-laugh.*

Him: *Good.*

When our conversation's over, I apply the lipstick and skip the rest of my makeup. Before I leave the bathroom, I flash my reflection a grin that feels surprisingly real.

"Lunch," my mom says as soon as I reappear. I don't feel like I have much of an appetite, but half an hour later, when the waitress at a barbecue restaurant near campus places a plateful of baby back ribs in front of me, my stomach gurgles.

"Too much vinegar in the sauce," I say after my first taste. "Still really good, though."

Mom shoots me a weird look, her brows arching upward.

I shrug. "Spend enough time in Texas and you learn these things."

For a few minutes, we eat in near silence. The meeting replays in my head, and suddenly I realize it never occurred to me to silently guess Mrs. Keller's weight. I didn't guess our server's either. In fact, I can't remember the last time the digital display in my brain lit up. It used to be so automatic.

"Okay," Dad says finally, as our plates are cleared. "Let's figure this out. First thing's first, Natalie—your flight. I'll call the airline and see if we can switch your ticket so you can fly home tomorrow with us."

"Wait." Aunt Judy waves a manicured hand. "Aren't we going to fight this? Natalie, babe, we'll figure out a way to get you back into the program."

I shake my head. I heard the resignation in Dr. Gallagher's tone when he gave his decision. Even if he were to change his mind, my scholarship is gone. "Tomorrow's fine," I tell Dad, and numbness sets in. I don't want to leave Texas. I don't want to leave the site.

I don't want to leave Cody.

But Aunt Judy isn't giving up, and the wink she tosses

me tells me she's got something besides the internship on her mind. "My flight back isn't for a couple of days. What if Natalie stays in Austin with me? Might be easier to get her ticket switched with a little more notice."

Dad's mouth purses as he considers. "That might work. Natalie, you okay with that?"

I don't have much to add beyond another nod.

"Good," Aunt Judy says. "I was hoping to do a little thrifting while I was out here. Now my favorite niece can show me the best shops."

Searching for thrifted treasure is the last thing I want to do, but I can't find the energy to say so. I just sip my soda.

It's not until a little later, when Dad goes off to call the airline on his cell and Mom goes with him, that Aunt Judy lets me in on her real plan. "After all you've gone through with this Cody boy, I thought you might want a chance at a little more time with him before you head home."

For the first time, a little flutter of . . . something . . . breaks through the numbness. I feel my cheeks grow warmer. "He's still in the hospital, though. And his parents aren't exactly my biggest fans. I doubt they're going to want me hanging out with him."

"We'll figure it out." She gives my arm a squeeze.

I want to tell Cody everything that's going on. When I pull out my phone, a text from Dr. Glass appears on its screen.

We need to talk before you leave Austin. Coffee on campus?

I reply with a suggested time for this afternoon. He confirms immediately.

31

Dr. Glass and I find a small table in an empty corner of the student lounge. We sit, and I wait for him to say whatever he needs to say. I hope it's not a scolding; I got enough of that this morning.

"Okay," he says after a sip of coffee. "First off, I don't want you to think I'm excusing anything you did. You made some pretty terrible decisions."

Great. "Yeah, I know." I stare down at my iced coffee, concentrating on the swirls of blending milk that ribbon between the ice cubes as I slowly stir.

"That being said, I think Vince's decision was bullshit."

That makes me look up.

"You were going home either way, unfortunately," he goes on. "The foundation wasn't going to let you keep your scholarship. But Vince shouldn't have bowed like that."

"He was right. I screwed up. A lot."

"Yeah? Guess what? There isn't a paleontologist alive—a *good* paleontologist, anyway—who can't say the same thing. All the best ones are mavericks and rule breakers."

I frown.

His glasses slip, and he shoves them back up his nose. "The thing is, Natalie—there's a line."

"A line?"

"Yeah." He draws his hand across the table, tracing an imaginary barrier. "There are calculated risks, and then there are risks that are just damn stupid. You don't seem to know the difference yet. Your ambition worries me. Don't get me wrong—ambition is great, and I admire it. I'm glad you have it. You need it, and we need more ambitious women in this field. But you can't use it as an excuse for recklessness."

"I didn't mean to. I just couldn't bear the idea of the skull getting destroyed."

"No, you couldn't bear the idea of someone else stealing your find. Otherwise you would've told Dr. Gallagher or Dr. Lauren and let them deal with it the right way."

I can't deny his words, so I stay quiet.

He goes on. "I've met only one other person who's as driven as you."

"Who?" As the word leaves my lips, I realize I already know.

"Tom Carver."

I can't accept it. I shake my head.

"Where'd you get the idea to save the skull from the flood?"

I swallow. "Dr. Carver's podcast."

He leans back and crosses his arms. "Yep. Knew it. That's one of his favorite stories. Want to hear how it really happened?"

"Not that I doubt he'd lie at this point, but how would you know?"

"I was there. Remember when I told Quinn I'd worked with her dad? He and I were on some of the same digs back in the day."

I think of the way they addressed each other by first name in the bone lab, and of the way Dr. Glass sometimes reacted when Carver's name came up in conversation. "You're not his biggest fan. I'm guessing the work you did together has something to do with that."

"That jackass and I dug together for more than two years, all in all."

"So what really happened?"

"Well, we did have to protect that *Apatosaurus* skull from a flood. That much was true. We piled up some sandbags and covered the whole thing with a tarp, just like he said. Then we got the hell out of there before the storm came through. We hoped for the best, drove into town, and waited out the mess in a Denny's."

"You didn't climb trees?"

"In a thunderstorm? Of course not! And Tom was the first one in the van when the lightning started flashing. We had to finish piling the sandbags without him."

My throat clenches and I gulp to loosen it. "I knew it was a risk, but since he'd done it—"

"The way he tells the story these days is fucking ridiculous, and I'm going to call him later and give him hell about it. That's the kind of thing I'm talking about. Taking risks is part of being a scientist. It's how discoveries are made. But there's risk, and then there's—"

"Insanity."

"Recklessness. I don't want to see you go in that direction." He reaches down and hitches up the leg of his jeans. It's his right leg, the one that he favors when he limps, and now I finally see why. His calf and foot are artificial. "Want to know how this happened?"

"Was it during the flood?" I think of Cody suddenly, and my stomach sours.

"No, during the flood I was scarfing down mediocre pancakes with fake maple syrup and burned coffee. This was a year later, on a cave dig near San Antonio. Tom wanted to do a little off-the-books prospecting in a part of the cave that hadn't been inspected or approved for digging yet. I went with him because . . ." He pauses.

I fill in the blank. "Because solo prospecting is dangerous."

"Exactly. And when the cave-in happened, I'm the one who got my foot smashed into hamburger meat."

I don't realize I'm holding my breath as I listen. My stomach keeps twisting. I put down my coffee and swipe a napkin across my mouth.

"You've probably heard him tell the cave-in story by now too. In his version, he rescues three people and no one ends up with more than cuts and bruises."

I nod. Dr. Carver once featured the story on *Carved in Bone*.

"Yeah, well…To his credit, he did pull me out of the rubble. Left a decent chunk of my lower leg behind, but it wasn't good for anything by then, anyway. That was my last dig."

"I'm sorry," I say softly, because I don't know what else to offer.

He waves my words away. "I don't need an apology. You didn't do this. Hell, Tom didn't do this. I made the decision to go with him. I took the risk. But if he'd been just a little less ambitious, if he hadn't needed to be the one making the biggest discoveries…" He shrugs. "Ancient history. But I thought you should know."

"Yeah, I think I needed that." I nod, still absorbing the gravity of his admission. "Thank you."

"I hope you'll keep it in mind when you're in the field."

I snort. "No worries there. I think this morning pretty much sealed my fate."

He tilts his head at me. The action makes his glasses slip again.

"I'm done," I clarify. "I've just been tossed out of a really prestigious internship by a respected paleontologist. It's backup plan time." *Not that I have one, not yet.*

But he shakes his head. "Look, I'm not saying it won't be hard. Paleontology is a small world, and you've got a fight ahead of you. Some digs and some scientists won't want anything to do with you, at least not right away. The fact that you've made an enemy of Tom Carver isn't going to help either. You need another chance to prove yourself."

"Yeah? And who's going to give me that?"

He thrusts a thumb at his chest.

"You don't dig anymore."

He finishes his coffee and puts his cup down just a little too hard. "Maybe I'm going to change that."

"What?"

"After the cave-in, it took a while to get back on my feet, figuratively speaking. And literally too, I suppose. The idea of going back out in the field terrified me. The lab was safe—no floods, no cave-ins, no risk. Just a lot of cleaning up other people's discoveries.

"I have my limits now," he goes on, leaning to pat his leg, "but I get around well enough on this thing. No reason I can't still go on digs. At this point, I should be leading them."

"And if you were, you'd take me on? Even after everything I did?"

"I can't make any promises, but I've got some feelers out. If I can get the right support in place, if I can get the funding...yeah. I'd want you interning as part of my team. Your drive scares the hell out of me, but it also reminds me of what it's like to be out there, hoping you're the one who makes the big find. Paleontology needs people like you— and people like you need the right guidance. You in?"

I nod. "Of course!"

"Good. I doubt anything'll happen before next summer, but I'll see what I can set up in terms of an internship and will be in touch. In the meantime, I'm going to make sure you and Cody get proper credit for finding that sabercat." He stands to go, giving his glasses a final shove. "I'm not letting you give up on the bones, Natalie."

—

Mellie sniffles at her desk while I pack my things, puzzling out how to fit my vintage finds into my suitcase along with all the clothes and shoes that came with me from Florida. My parents will be picking me up in about an hour.

"I can't believe they threw you out," she says, winding a scrap of green bamboo yarn around her fingers. She's already declared herself too depressed to knit, but she still can't keep her hands off her stash.

"I can. I screwed up."

"Still wish they'd been a little nicer about it."

I shrug. I'm not happy, of course, but the initial sting has faded. My talk with Dr. Glass left me sober and clearheaded.

Mellie opens a desk drawer and pulls out a thin strip of off-white crocheted fiber. "I wasn't going to give this to you until the end of the program next week, but…plans change, right?" She hands it to me. "It's a headband. I noticed you wear headbands and scarves a lot, so…"

"Mellie, thank you. It's beautiful." The yarn is thin and dainty, the crochet intricate. To show her how much I like it, I slip it over my head and arrange my hair around it. "How's it look?"

She manages a smile. "Really nice."

I shove at my suitcase, compressing the contents enough for the zipper to close.

"I think everyone's in the common room if you want to come out and say your goodbyes."

"Give me about fifteen minutes. Then I will."

Mellie nods and leaves me alone.

I prop up my phone on the desk and start the video app. I can see myself on-screen as I step back. I changed out of the bone-print dress as soon as I got back from the meeting. I'm in cuffed jeans and a Mammoth Site shirt, the one I resized with extra panels. I'm still makeup-free aside from a fresh coat of Pinup, and my hair is definitely showing some frizz.

That's okay, I realize.

"So guys…Hi. It's me, your favorite fossilista." For once I don't paste on a fake grin. My smile is smaller than usual, but it's real. "I've got a lot of catching up to do, I know. I haven't talked about it here yet, but those of you who keep up with paleo news might've heard about a little…drama involving a certain rock-star paleontologist, and I'll talk about that really soon.

"In the meantime, I wanted to let you know that I'm going to change things up a little. Don't worry—I'm still going to talk vintage finds, and I'll still show you how to wing your eyeliner or deconstruct a T-shirt, and I'll still squeal about paleo news, and I'll still post look-of-the-day pics. Just…maybe not every day.

"Here's the thing—sometimes I'm just not in the mood for any of that. Sometimes I don't want to worry about what I'm going to wear and what I'm going to put on my face. Sometimes I just want to sit and talk to you guys about whatever's on my mind. I've held my tongue for a long time so that I could stick to giving you what you want, what you subscribed to *Fossilista* for, but…I think it's time to expand.

It's time to get a little more, well, mammoth.

"I'm not even sure what all this means yet, but I hope you guys will stick around while I figure it out. Maybe we can figure it out together."

I take a deep breath, and then I upload the video to my blog. An "Upload Complete" notification pops up on-screen, triggering cold dread and fluttering exhilaration. I want to sit and refresh the blog's dashboard, waiting for the first comments to roll in. They won't all be positive. As long as I maintain *Fossilista*, I'll have to keep dealing with negative feedback. Maybe that'll be a little easier now that I'm not putting so much effort into maintaining a facade. As long as I needed armor, I worried about it being pierced. Letting that go somehow makes me feel less vulnerable, not more.

Still, I'll drive myself nuts if I keep staring at *Fossilista*'s dashboard. To distract myself, I reread the texts Cody and I exchanged this afternoon.

Him: *Getting released tomorrow. Gotta see you before you go home. We'll figure something out. Miss you, darlin'.*

Me: *I reckon that's a sure bet, Tex. You miss me even more than you miss your pickup truck and your trusty hound dog, pardner?*

Him: *;P*

I stare at the messages until my heart stops hammering. Right. Common room.

Before I can leave, the door opens. Quinn peeks in. "Got a second?"

"Yeah." We haven't really spoken since the meeting.

She leans against the desk, arms crossed. "So my dad's letting the hacking thing go. He's working on a statement right now. He's giving us credit for the calf."

"He realized how stupid the whole mess was?"

"No, his publicity people finally convinced him that withholding exhibits and basically acting like a dick about the whole thing was murdering his reputation. It's all damage control. He's already lost two sponsors, and it looks like his show might get canceled before it even airs."

"Are you going to be okay? Your family, I mean?"

She shrugs. "I guess. I think so."

"Well…that's good." I double-check that my suitcase is zipped.

"Natalie, I'm sorry."

I finally look at her. "Did you really tell him I hacked his blog?"

She breathes in, shoulders trembling. "He was so angry. He was sure I knew something, so…I told him what he wanted to hear."

"And I was already in trouble anyway," I say evenly, "so you figured you might as well throw me under the bus."

"I tried to make it right," she says.

"They're not sending me home because of his blog, so I guess it doesn't matter."

"It does, though," she says quickly. "I messed up. I'm just so used to doing whatever it takes to…to make him happy. To make him give a shit about me." She swipes the back of her hand over her eyes.

"Has it ever worked?"

She laughs a little, ruefully. "Not for long. You know, I'm not even sure I'm that into all this paleo stuff. I thought I was, but maybe I've been doing it all for him."

I drag my suitcase over by the door. "I guess that's something you'll have to figure out."

"Yeah. Natalie?"

I look at her.

"I want us to be friends. Can we do that?"

I think of each betrayal, and I weigh them against the waver in her voice and the tears she's once more wiping away. I consider whether I can imagine myself ever trusting her enough to consider her a friend.

Finally, I nod. "Yeah. We can try."

My parents are downstairs, so my goodbyes go quickly. Brendan clasps my hand and says, "I don't care what they think—that flood business was badass." Eli gives me a stalwart nod and puts an arm around Mellie, who is crying again.

Chase tries for a hug, which I deftly sidestep. He settles for a handshake instead. "Take care," he says, and I tell him the same.

The hug Quinn gives me is strong and warm and real enough to make me think we could actually be friends someday. Maybe.

32.

"**Aren't your parents going** to kill you when they realize you're not home?" It's Tuesday evening. Aunt Judy and I will fly home tomorrow, but right now I'm heading downtown in her rental car. I've just picked up Cody half an hour before his parents are due home from work.

He shrugs and grins. "What are they going to do? Break my arm?"

"That's not funny."

"They'll get over it, Natalie. I couldn't let you leave, not without seeing you again."

His fractured arm is still in its cast and sling, but the bruising on his face has yellowed and faded. The split on his lip is closed, and the puffiness around his right eye is gone. The gash at his temple is still held shut with a butterfly bandage, but it's healing as well. His movements are careful and deliberate, thanks to his bruised ribs, but he's already miles better than he was when I saw him in the hospital. He's not up to driving yet, so Aunt Judy offered me the use of her rental car for the evening.

"Turn here," he says, and I do. "Any news on Smiley?"

"Dr. Glass texted. He said they started the excavation today."

"Wish we could be there."

"Me too."

"Turn in up there and park. See the sign? Amy's Ice Creams?" He points. "Still pisses me off that you got thrown out and all I got was a two-week vacation." Cody's unpaid suspension will give him time to rest and heal before he goes back to work.

"I'm just glad I didn't get you fired or arrested."

He gives my comment a dismissive wave. "I'd gladly go to jail for you, darlin'."

The ice cream shop is decorated with murals of psychedelic cows and paintings and prints by local artists. Cody knows the guy behind the counter.

"What the hell happened to you?" the guy asks, boggling at Cody's injuries.

"Fell hard for an amazing girl."

My breath catches.

The guy looks from Cody to me, his eyes widening.

"Long story, man," Cody says. "Two bowls of the regular, okay?"

"Extra chocolate?" the guy asks.

"Of course."

I grab the bowls while Cody pays, and we take over a small circular table near the back of the shop.

"Mexican vanilla with dark chocolate hot fudge," he says, digging in. "Tell me this isn't the best damn ice cream you've ever tasted."

I scoop up a bite of melty ice cream and steamy chocolate goo and spoon the mix into my mouth. "Oh. Oh my God. Why is everything so much better in Austin?"

"I know, right? I worked here for about six months before I got the mammoth job. I gained like ten pounds."

"Oh, gee. Ten pounds. How'd you bear it? I'd gain about three tons if I worked around this stuff."

Cody answers me with a wry, narrow-eyed grin. "And you'd still be gorgeous."

I lick my spoon. "You're not the only guy who calls me that, you know."

"Is that right? Who's my competition?"

"There's this one boy, Fred Parkmore, who asked me out every week of sophomore year."

Cody squares his shoulders. "When you start school again, tell him you're spoken for."

"Believe me, I'm looking forward to doing just that." Charli and I have discussed it on the phone. She's already anticipating the potential fallout with wicked glee. "You don't have to worry about him, though," I tell Cody. "He doesn't matter."

"Damn right, he doesn't," Cody laughs.

Tonight I'm wearing jeans, mint-green vintage ballet flats Aunt Judy bought me, and a matching green tank top with no shaper underneath. The crochet headband from Mellie keeps my hair off my face. I'm wearing almost no makeup and only two pieces of jewelry—a delicate stud in my new cartilage piercing (Aunt Judy's treat—Mom is going to strangle her when she sees) and a new leather cuff Aunt Judy had her jeweler friend overnight to our hotel to replace the one with Dr. Carver's quote. This one is engraved with a drawing of a mammoth skull. Inside, the leather is stamped with the words "Risk it."

It's a more casual outfit than I would have worn on a date a year ago—but Cody's dating *me*, not my wardrobe.

I don't need my armor. Not tonight. Not with him.

My phone vibrates with a text. "It's from Quinn." I press my lips together. "She says we should check her dad's blog. Should we bother?"

"Sure, why not?"

There's a new video on the main page—just Carver staring into the camera in what looks like a hotel room. His eyes are harsh and sunken with exhaustion. The scruff I used to find so appealing just looks messy and unkempt now. He launches into a gruff apology, reading the whole thing from a paper in his hand.

"His retraction," I say.

"Bastard doesn't look too sorry."

Carver throws around a lot of well-rehearsed phrases like "deep regret" and "unfortunate misunderstanding," things his publicist probably outlined for him to say. At least he finally names Quinn and me as the true finders of the mammoth calf. "Credit is everything in this field, and I got caught up in the pursuit of that. There's no justification for the choice I made, or for the fact that I attempted to further my career at my daughter's expense."

He clears his throat and puts the paper aside, rubbing a hand over his fuzzy cheek. "Finally, it has come to my attention that some of the information in my podcast may be...misleading to my listeners. Look, guys..." He pauses, clasping his hands on the table in front of him, and he goes off script. "I like a good story, all right? Sometimes I might...embellish...certain elements for the sake of storytelling. That would be a fine thing if I were a creative writer, but I'm a scientist, and scientists are supposed to value the truth. I've pulled all episodes of *Carved in Bone* until I can go through them and add corrections where necessary. Any stories you've heard me tell...I'm not advocating you actually do the things I've claimed to have done. Okay?" He points at the camera. "That goes double for you, Natalie Page. Although I have to admit, from what I've heard..." His face stretches into a tired smile. "That was a pretty hard-core stunt you pulled, kid. Nice find."

I put my phone back in my pocket.

A few minutes later, Cody scrapes the bottom of his ice cream bowl with his pink plastic spoon. "We should probably get going if we're going to grab a good spot."

I'm done too, so I toss my bowl in the trash and follow him out.

He directs me to the South Congress Bridge, and we find a space in a nearby carpet store's parking lot. "Here's to not getting towed," he says, taking my hand as we set out toward the bridge.

The walkway lining the bridge is already growing crowded, but we manage to grab a space at the railing, facing south.

"Perfect timing," Cody says, nodding to the setting sun. "Won't be too long now."

I look at him in the golden, predusk light. I look at the faded bruises, the bandage at his temple. He'll probably have a scar there for the rest of his life, and it'll be there because of me. I'm not sure I'll ever entirely forgive myself for putting him in that much danger.

But it's done.

"So," he says after a moment, "I'd really like to kiss you."

I turn toward him, my heart flipping and hammering and soaring all at once. "Your lip's still healing. I don't want to hurt you."

"You won't," he says.

"Okay then."

He presses his lips to mine. His mouth is warm and minty, and he keeps the kiss soft and easy. His good arm wraps around my waist, nestling me closer but not locking me in place.

Now this? No question. This I like.

When the kiss breaks, I press my forehead to his.

"You know this is going to suck, right?" he asks.

"What?"

"The long-distance thing. If that's what we're doing."

"Oh, yeah. That's what we're doing."

"Won't be easy."

"It'll just give us more to laugh about." I inch closer and wrap my arm around his. He leans over and kisses the top of my head, and I press my cheek to his shoulder.

The bats begin to fly.

At first they emerge a few at a time, gliding out from under the bridge and heading south in a swirling formation. More follow, until they seem to form a solid black swarm that spirals like a dancing pillar of smoke. The crowd around us buzzes with hushed exclamations of wonder and surprise at the sight. Dozens of people hold up phones and cameras, taking photos and video as the bats go out to feed.

I don't need photographic proof of this moment. I'll remember it always; it's that kind of perfect.

"Damn," Cody murmurs close to my ear. "Lost count."

"I'm at 800,573," I joke. "And they're still coming, so stop distracting me."

He chuckles against my hair and puts his good arm around me. "My darlin' is such a speedy counter. She's so awesome."

I can't help but grin. *He thinks I'm awesome.* For a long time, I wouldn't have agreed with him. Now, though...Aunt Judy's philosophy got me through a lot, but I no longer need it, any more than I need my armor. I don't have to try to be awesome.

Cody's right. I just *am*.

ACKNOWLEDGMENTS

Thank you, Mom and Dad, for taking me to the Museum of Natural History when I was six, and for always believing in this book and its author. Dad, I wish you were here to see your newest book grandbaby in print, but you saw the process begin and I'm so grateful for that. You knew this would happen. And thank you, Jesse, for being the best little bro and Mario Kart rival I could ask for.

Thank you, Dava Butler, forever the Egon to my Ray. You are an amazing friend, and this book exists because you coordinated so many extraordinary opportunities for me to research and learn. (Remember when we met elephants? And then we smelled like elephants??) Thank you for answering so many paleo questions, for supplying the screen-picking gravel that almost got confiscated by airport security, and for always threatening to send a bag of you-know-whats to you-know-who.

Thank you to Eric Smith of P.S. Literary for being the MOST AMAZING AGENT and stopping my heart with a single tweet. Thank you for your relentless enthusiasm. Thank you for your support and dedication. Thank you for doing that Reddit AMA. Thank you thank you THANK YOUUUU.

Thank you, #TeamRocks, for welcoming me into such a supportive and awesome family! Y'all are the best.

Thank you to my fantastic team at Turner Publishing—Stephanie, Todd, Heather, Maddie, Leslie, Stephen, Lindsey—for believing so completely in Natalie's story, and for wanting to introduce her to the world. Missy and Kathy, thank you for catching the details I didn't!

Thank you, Rhonda Jones, for always listening to my writing-related gripes, for calling me out when I tried to start this story in the wrong place, and for asking the question that cemented my willingness to fight for Natalie's authenticity.

Thank you, Susan Edgington, for getting me to California and putting up with me while I ran around La Brea pointing at mammoths. That afternoon reminded me how much I love this story.

Thank you to every one of you who read *Mammoth* at one stage or another. Thank you for your enthusiasm and your honesty. <3

Thank you to Eva, Raegan, Jeremy, Matt, and everyone I met at the Waco Mammoth National Monument. Y'all are the heart of Natalie's dig site.

Thank you, Don Esker, for explaining so much about the Waco mammoths and sharing your dig site stories.

You inspired some of Natalie's shenanigans, and you're proof that Dr. Gallagher's comment about beards is totally inaccurate.

Thank you to Anita at Baylor's Mayborn Museum for letting me tour the fossil collection and sharing so much of your knowledge.

Thank you to Amanda and Margaret at Cameron Park Zoo for letting me meet your elephants. And thank you to Tembo and Tanya for being so amazing and delightful!

Thank you to Matt Brown and Chris Sagebiel for making it possible for me to visit the Jackson School of Geosciences Vertebrate Paleontology Lab. Chris, so many scenes exist because you took the time to show me around.

Thank you to Metro in downtown Augusta, Georgia for putting up with me camping out in one of your booths for hours and hours and hours while I drafted this book. I miss your coffee.

And thank you to Paul Feig, Katie Dippold, Leslie Jones, Kristen Wiig, Melissa McCarthy, and Kate McKinnon for gifting me with a team of wonderfully odd, brilliant, oh-so-capable women fighting to be taken seriously. I needed that boost of science-geek inspiration on so many levels, and I'll always answer the call.